THE
BORGIA
BLADE

THE BORGIA BLADE

Florence Ryerson
and
Colin Clements

COACHWHIP PUBLICATIONS
Greenville, Ohio

For Edgar Allan Woolf and Pico

The Borgia Blade, by Florence Ryerson and Colin Clements
© 2023 Coachwhip Publications edition

First published 1937
Florence Ryerson, 1892-1965
Colin Clements, 1894-1948
CoachwhipBooks.com

ISBN 1-61646-555-7
ISBN-13 978-1-61646-555-1

1

Q. Silver said the letters would do.

I said: "I hope the hell they will!"

"Why?" Q. kidded. "Didn't you like Auburn?"

"Not so much I want to go back. Anyway," I said, "shut up! It ain't healthy to talk with hot stuff around."

He saw I was right and put the letters into his pocket. It wasn't really necessary. They wouldn't have got us into trouble, even if the names I'd signed were phony, because they hadn't been presented to anybody—yet.

They were all letters introducing H. Findley Bleigh of New York, London and Paris, to Vincent Welch, Esquire.

One was from Gabriele d'Annunzio.

One was from the Curator of the British Museum.

One was from a big collector in Paris.

The other didn't matter. It was just from a screwy little wop in Italy who knew a lot about the Borgias. Q. had heard him lecture somewhere, and threw him in to make good measure.

That's the way Q. is. Details never get away from him. I've known him to phone clear from 'Frisco to Warsaw to get a guy's name right, when ninety-nine times out of a hundred nobody this side of the Atlantic would know the difference. It's the hundredth time, Q. says, that fills the Big House.

Which is why I'm a two-time loser while Q. has never seen the inside of a pen—except once, when he came as a lecturer. He met the chaplain somewhere and got invited down to talk to the boys, while I was taking a rap for some paper-hanging.

He gave us a swell talk, too. Helpful and encouraging. All about taking our punishment in the right spirit and growing into better men. He urged us to come to him when we got out of stir and let him lend us a hand . . . . all that with me and Bill Mowbrick, who had pulled off the Tiffany job with him, grinning like apes in the front row.

I couldn't take him up on the invitation, because when I finished my rap he was across the pond raising hell all up and down the Riviera. But next year he came back—with a lot of bright ideas. This business of the Borgia Blade was the brightest of the lot.

I don't know where he got the Blade, Or how.

"Maybe I found it in a hock shop," he told me.

"Or a hook shop," I said.

"Then again, maybe I won it in a crap game. *Quien sabe?*"

From which I guessed he'd lifted the thing somewhere. Probably from one of the palaces he was always getting invited to visit.

The Blade was in his suit-case now. He'd brought it out of the hotel safe along with a roll of bills he didn't want to use unless he had to, because they were some of Bill Mowbrick's phonies.

Our things were packed. The car was waiting below, as they say in swell books, ready to take us out to Welch's place. The bus was hot, too, but it was safe enough. The guy who owned it was shooting grouse somewheres in Scotland. Q. had met him in Sussex, at the country place of Lady This-and-that. They'd played bridge, and Q. hadn't cashed his last check. He'd figured on using the signature to better advantage.

That's how we came to have a swell suite of rooms at the Ritz and the use of a Rolls.

Q. said to me, "Why not? He can't sleep on both sides of the Atlantic at the same time. He ought to thank us for airing the beds."

We planned on using the car for a quick getaway when the Welch job was done. It would take us to the flying field where Q. had Bill Mowbrick waiting with a plane. That way we could be over the border before they found out the letters were phony, or Welch showed the Blade to any one at the Metropolitan.

Q. thought the experts wouldn't spot it even then. The Blade was old, all right. Old enough to be passed as an antique by the customs.

"Maybe Cesare Borgia *did* own it." Q. grinned. "Fellow I got it from said so. Who am I—or you—to call him a liar?"

I said: "But Old What's-his-name at the British Museum didn't say so, did he? Nor that fellow in Paris. What if Welch gets in touch with them over the phone?"

"On Saturday night?" Q. wanted to know. "It's not likely. To-morrow we'll be on our way—with what I'm after."

"And a couple of bullets in your tail."

But I didn't mean that. Q. always manages to pull things off without getting into any shooting scrapes. He doesn't even carry a rod, which is a swell idea, if you've got the guts to get away with it.

It's the fellow with the artillery that gets jerked. If anything slips up, Q. always looks as kosher as your Aunt Het. When they frisk him all they find is a ticket to the symphony and a receipt for a donation to the Community Chest.

The Welch place was a good two hours drive from town. Along the river mostly. But the last half-hour we went through woods that seemed to cover half the county. Q. told me it was all part of Sant' Angelo.

I asked: "Why Sant' Angelo?"

"Because that's where one of the Borgias lived. Casa Sant' Angelo. Welch is a nut on the Renaissance. He's shipped a lot of stuff over from Italy and uses it in his house. Some of it is more than five hundred years old."

"And I'll bet all the maids are the same," I said, discouraged, "with me headed for the servants' quarters! Can't you let me be your secretary instead of your valet?"

"Spelling the way you do?"

I shut up, remembering how I'd switched i's and e's in the letter that was supposed to have come from the British Museum guy and how Q.'d caught it.

He said: "You lay off women."

"Why should I?"

"We're here on business, that's why. And not monkey business, either!"

"Maybe if you tell me what we *are* here for it'll help."

But Q. wouldn't. He's like that when he's on a job. An oyster is gabby by comparison. All I'm supposed to do is stand by and obey orders. Sometimes I don't know what's up until it's all over. And sometimes not then. I just take my cut of what Q. pulls out of the hat and keep my trap shut.

Of course on the Sant' Angelo business, I had a vague idea. There was the Blade. What I'd written about its being a "rare example of cinquecento craftsmanship," and "an authentic Borgia relic," told a lot. I knew, too, that Q. hadn't made up his mind until a few days before who he was going to try it on.

There'd been three different marks to choose from: Vincent Welch, Porter Creel, Mrs. Arabella Statts. All rotten rich. All interested in antiques.

Creel went in for clocks and weapons.

The Statts woman for old jewelry.

Welch was bugs over anything that was fifteenth- or sixteenth-century Italian.

After a lot of buzzing around, Q. found they'd all been bidding against each other for years at auctions and private sales, and hated each other's guts, Welch was the richest, and the farthest out of town. So I fixed up the letters and we got in touch with him by telephone. He invited us up to Sant' Angelo for the week-end. It looked like it was going to be a pushover.

That's what Q. said.

Me, Joe Lynch, I wasn't so sure.

A butler met us at the door. Working with Q.—who never touches anything that isn't high class—I've met up with plenty of butlers, but this one faded them all.

He looked like a cross between an undertaker and the minister who says the last kind words over the deceased.

The way he told us "Good afternoon" was the same as if he was saying, "Ashes to ashes and dust to dust."

So far as I was concerned, when the front door closed behind us we might just as well have been hearing the dirt fall on the coffin lid.

The minute I came into that place I knew it was bad medicine. Not that anything looked wrong. It looked fine. Sweller than any place I'd been in yet. But there was something about it . . . maybe it was a kind of musty smell, or the way the hall was like a big stone church, or maybe it was just the way the trees hung over it and the shadows crawled across the windows. Something made the hair on the back of my neck rise up and the palms of my hands go sweaty.

Q. said: "You may tell Mr. Welch that Mr. Bleigh is here."

The butler said: "Yes, sir. Very good, sir. Mr. Welch is expecting you."

There wasn't anything for him to be suspicious about. When Q. turns high class he does a swell job.

Silver isn't his real name, any more than H. Findley Bleigh. It's just a moniker he made up. Because he liked

the sound of it, I guess. Quenton Silver. Q. Silver. Sometimes they call him Quicksilver. And it's a good name.
He's like that. Quicksilver, I mean. Quick, and bright, and
hard to catch hold of.

I've never met any one that knew where he came from,
but he works just as well on either side of the big pond.

Wherever he is he puts it over because he seems to
have been everywhere and done everything, and when I
say everywhere and everything I mean everywhere and
everything.

Once in Shanghai we met a guy who said he'd known
Q. when he was studying art in Paris. At Lisbon a South
American fell on his neck and talked about when he was
running a bank in Rio, and in a coffee-house in Stamboul
a waiter claimed he'd stoked coal in the next furnace on a
Liverpool to Sargon run in a freighter. None of 'em looked
like they were lying, either.

So now the butler looked solemn and said:

"Mr. Welch is expecting you, sir. But he's not here at
the moment. He's driven to the village. Would you care to
go to your rooms?"

A funny-looking footman was already bringing our bags
from the car.

We climbed the marble stairs, which looked like they'd
been swiped from the Grand Central Station. We went
down a hall filled with carved-up furniture, even sweller
than you'd see in the Roxy lounge. We reached a suit of
rooms, which the butler said were in the Medici wing.

The first thing I noticed was that they were like the hall
downstairs, high and dark, and about as cozy as a skating
rink. The next thing I saw was that all the windows looked
down a hundred feet of cliff to the river.

2

"I wish to God we were out of this joint," I said, when the butler—his name was Frazier—had cleared out and Q. and I were alone.

He laughed and called me an old woman.

"You're always yelling 'wolf.'"

"Just the same—"

"Things look fine."

"Yeah?"

"If Welch hadn't accepted us, he'd never have let us in."

"Maybe."

"No 'maybe' about it. This place is as full of treasure as the Tower of London. He keeps it guarded like a mint. Did you notice the high walls when we came in? With two men at the gate?"

"You bet I noticed 'em."

"They say Welch brags that a thief couldn't get in unless he dropped from a plane—and then he'd be shot before he landed. And here we are all safe inside."

"That's what I'm kicking about. You don't seem to figure it works both ways."

"What do you mean?"

"If you can't get in, you can't get out."

"We'll get out when we want to."

I had to let it go at that, because Frazier was back with some drinks Welch had ordered in case Q. was done up by the exhausting drive of almost two hours.

I was about to sing out "Three fingers," when Q. gave me a look, and I remembered I wasn't supposed to be drinking with him just then.

Later, Q. sent me down to the servants' quarters to see what I could learn.

Frazier was in the pantry with a cute little blonde. I saw right there I'd been wrong about thinking all the maids would be antiques. When the butler's back was turned, she gave me the eye.

I began to think the place wasn't going to be so bad, after all. Then Frazier took a drink with me and opened up. What I learned from him gave me the pip again.

"We aren't the only pebbles on the beach," I told Q. when I got back to his room.

"Meaning what?"

"Meaning that we've dropped into the middle of an Atlantic City convention. New York, Boston and Philadelphia are spending the week-end."

"Well," Q. said, "with a place this size you can't expect the old boy to keep it all to himself. There are over twenty bedrooms."

"Is that all?"

He nodded. "Just cozy and homelike."

"Then they'll have to put up cots in the halls. The accommodations are going to be crowded."

Q. frowned at that. He didn't want too many people around while he was settling his business with Welch.

"Not so good," he said slowly, and it looked to me like he might be persuaded to scram. So I moved in on him.

"Wait until you hear the line-up," I said. "You'll go into a nose dive."

"I'll risk it. Who's to be here?"

"Creel. Also Mrs. Starts."

"What?" He goggled at me.

"'S a fact. Welch asked 'em both."

"You're crazy. Welch and Creel aren't on speaking terms."

That's one of the things he'd found out while we were looking them up. They'd had a row over something Welch had bid in at a Christie auction.

"Just the same I'm telling you—"

"And the Statts woman is suing Creel over the Queen of Scots crucifix."

"Figure it how you like, they're both coming."

"Who says so?"

"Frazier. He's the butler. I've been talking to him."

"Is he a blond? Curly-headed?"

"No. Why?"

"I just wondered." He reached out and picked a hair off my sleeve.

"That's a maid," I told him. "She says they're coming, too. She's been making up the beds."

Q. grunted.

"Who's here now?"

"Who isn't? There's a doctor. Rubin Jaffee, his name is. And a Miss Laurette Duchene. She's engaged to Roger Storey."

"Welch's nephew?"

"Yeah. She's been here for a week. The kid brought her down to get acquainted with his uncle."

"Where's she from?"

"Frazier didn't say. She has her mother and a maid with her. That makes, if I can count, seven besides Welch and God-knows-how-many servants in this nice, quiet spot you picked to pull whatever it is you're pulling."

"Sounds like plenty."

"What you going to do?"

"Take a shower. And, oh, yes, Lynch, you may lay out my dinner togs."

"Well, I'll be—"

"It'll keep you from thinking."

That's all I got out of him, but I knew he was worried, by the way he burned up cigarettes and didn't whistle in the shower. Usually he's tuneful, *Old Man River* being his favorite, with *Holy Night* holding second place.

"I can understand Dr. Rubin Jaffee," he said, coming out of the bathroom.

"What about him?"

"He's an old friend of Welch's. Lives here most of the time. But there's something screwy about the other two. Creel and that Statts woman. They've got me guessing."

"Maybe Welch smelled a rat and got them down here to advise him about buying the Blade."

Q. looked thoughtful, then shook his head.

"Not possible."

"Why not?"

"Too early. I haven't said anything about wanting to sell. Just told him I had it with me, and that his friends at the British Museum had suggested he'd like a look at it because it was his period."

"Say, listen—"

He was working something out and didn't seem to hear me.

"As it stands, I'm doing him a favor."

"I don't get you."

He scowled at me, then he said:

"One collector to another."

"Yeah, this is a pretty place, and all that, but we didn't come down here just to look at the scenery."

He got sore at that. I could tell by the way the lobes of his ears turned red.

"If," he said to the top of the bed post and not to me, "he makes an offer for the Blade I shall be as insulted as hell."

"Yes, you will!"

"I mean it."

There was a knock at the door. A polite tap, tap.

Frazier came in and told us Mr. Welch was back. If convenient, he would like to see Mr. Bleigh in the library.

Q. put on his coat and straightened his tie.

Frazier stood in the doorway making funny noises through his nose. He said:

"Mr. Welch would you like to see your man, too."

"My man?" Q. was smoothing his hair, which is straight, and black, and thick. "You mean Lynch?"

"Yes, sir."

You could see Frazier didn't like it. He coughed and looked away.

"That's what he said, sir. That you were to bring your man."

Q. stared at him. I know he was trying to figure things out. Finally he gave it up.

"Very well." He took the Borgia Blade out of his bag. It was wrapped in a piece of faded-red silk and tied with a tarnished-gold cord. "You may bring this," he said, and handed it over.

I took it under my arm.

We followed Frazier.

"The library is off the conservatory," he told us. "Mr. Welch wishes us to use the private stairs."

I didn't understand what he meant at first, but I saw soon enough. We didn't go down the main stairs. Instead, we went along the hall and through two carved doors. On the other side of them was an upper hall that had open arches. Q. said it was called a loggia. Anyway, it looked down into a conservatory that was two stories high and as big as Radio City.

The place had whole trees in it. Rubber. And banyan. And mango. It had banana plants. Tree ferns. And vines that climbed like snakes. There were flowers, too. Big, splashy hibiscus. Yellow, spotted orchids. And blood-red bougainvillea.

In the middle was a pool and furniture. Mostly marble.

"Magnificent!" Q. said.

"Yes, sir. It has been much admired." Frazier didn't sound like he was crazy about it. "Mr. Welch has brought flora and fauna from all parts of the globe—but they do keep stopping the drain. The roots, if you know what I mean, sir."

He went on. We followed.

There was a door at one side of the loggia. Frazier pushed it open and we went down some circular stairs. They didn't come out into a hall, like I'd expected, but ended in a room with books and a fireplace.

A man was sitting in a big carved chair behind a big carved desk. He was smoking a big cigar. He was a big man, as tall as Q. and a lot heavier. His hair was gray, and he had deep lines in his face, especially around the mouth. But he didn't look old. He looked strong and full of fight. You could see at a glance that he knew what he wanted and would raise hell till he got it.

Frazier said: "Mr. Welch."

Welch came around the desk and shook hands with Q. He offered him a whiskey and soda. Q. took it and passed over the letters of introduction.

While Welch read them, Q. strolled around the room with his glass in his hand.

The walls were hung with pictures. There was a lot of stuff on shelves. Statues. Silverware. Bas-relief plaques.

Heavy furniture, old, moth-eaten, and full of worm holes, was scattered around.

Q. looked them all over and said things about the Renaissance. Florentine work. And a guy named Cellini.

Welch said "Yes," and "No," and they argued about a crazy wooden image Q. said was a primitive.

They made me think of two wrestlers pussyfooting around each other and watching for a hold.

Welch didn't say anything about the letters, but pretty soon he looked at what I was carrying.

"Is that the Borgia Blade?"

I said: "Yes, sir."

Q. took it, unrolled the silk, and handed it to Welch.

I saw the old boy's eyes light up. I can't say I blamed him. Even forgetting it was old, it was a swell-looking piece. Q. said the experts had called it "a blade," because it wasn't either a dagger or a sword but something halfway between.

It was about fourteen inches long and as sharp as a razor. Its cutting edge was steel inlaid with gold. The hilt was gold, too, with jewels set in an enamel design of flowers and fruit.

It didn't make it hard to hold, either, like most fancy knives. The design was planned to help the grip. The blade-part fitted into a scabbard that was made of thin gold, like the hilt, and had the same design as the handle, with the jewels growing smaller and smaller toward the point. There was a ring with a chain on it, so it could be hung on a belt.

In the middle of the scabbard, and again on the hilt, was a flat place in the gold with a bull's head and the letter B worked out in silver and enamel.

Welch looked at it thoughtfully while Q. pointed out details which proved, according to him, that it was late

fifteenth century and made for one of the Borgias, probably Cesare.

The old man looked like he took all Q.'s line with a
grain of salt, but I could see he hated to put the Blade
down. His hands sort of patted it, even after it was on the
desk.

All he said was: "Very interesting. Did you pick it up
in Italy?"

"In Florence," Q. told him. "In a junk shop. The dealer
didn't know what he had, of course."

Welch took the cigar out of his mouth and studied the
end of it thoughtfully.

"H'm, Florence, you say? That's odd. The last time I
saw this piece it was in Ravenna."

Q.'s eyes went blank.

He asked: "Ravenna?"

"Ravenna. Yes. In Count Salvatori's collection." Welch
laughed.

The laugh was a sort of a growl deep down in his throat.

I didn't like it, I didn't like it at all.

"I heard later his palace had been robbed. Did you happen to know the Count, *Mr. Silver?*"

3

"Mr. Silver," Welch repeated, and looked at Q.

I looked at him, too. I wasn't surprised that Welch had seen through the bluff of H. Findley Bleigh. You could tell he was too smart to put anything over on. But to recognize Q. as Silver, *that* was bad. A damned sight worse than anything we'd foreseen.

Q. sat up. His hand went to his pocket. I got ready to do a nose dive through a window, found they were all barred, and changed my mind.

Welch grinned like he was enjoying himself.

"I happen to know you never carry a gun, Mr. Silver."

Q. brought out a cigarette case and helped himself to a smoke.

"You seem to know a lot about me."

Welch didn't answer that. Not directly. Just said:

"Last year I spent a week-end with the Prefect of the Paris police."

"You did?"

"I did. That was in August."

Now it was Q.'s turn to grin.

"Oh. *August?*"

"Yes. He seemed to have you on his mind. Cigar?" Welch opened a box and pushed it across the desk.

Q. shook his head, and lighted his cigarette.

Welch closed the lid of the cigar box.

"I don't suppose you have anything left from that loan exhibit at the Louvre?"

"What makes you think I ever had anything from the Louvre?"

"It was the Prefect who thought so—not I."

"Yes?"

"Yes."

"Your friend, the Prefect, could be wrong."

"He could. But there were several things I'd have liked in that collection." Welch studied Q.'s face. "Several things."

Q. leaned far back in his chair and stretched out his legs. He didn't seem worried. Just amused.

He said: "Sorry. I can't help you."

Welch sighed.

"That's that . . . but I *would* have liked those da Vinci flagons."

"They weren't really," Q. told him.

"Fakes?"

"Um."

Welch brightened up like Q. had lighted something inside him.

"Are you sure?"

Q. said: "Dead sure. Somebody put over a fast one."

That seemed to please Welch, the same as it pleases a kid to be given a stick of candy. He asked a lot more questions, quick and sharp, about something he called "The Cardinal's Ring" and something else he called "A Corregio."

Q. answered him "Yes," and "No," and said he'd no idea where they were.

I could tell by his voice he was lying.

After a while Welch asked would he like to see his collection, the part that was too valuable to leave out in the room.

Q. said he would, and Welch went over to a sort of alcove at one side. It was about four feet wide and the same
in depth, with red curtains at the far end. Welch pulled
a cord and the curtains went back against the wall. They
covered a steel door—thick, like the door of a safe. It
wasn't locked and Welch swung it open. The space beyond
was dark. He reached out and switched on a light, then
went down three steps.

Q. and I followed.

The room wasn't very large, about ten by ten. No windows, just safety vault boxes on one side, with drawers and
shelves around the other three. Welch said it was walled with
steel, like a bank vault, and beyond the steel was cement.

The shelves held all sorts of things. Jewels, flagons
and crucifixes, queer-looking watches and clocks, funny-
shaped weapons, and cups with little figures holding them.

Everything—Q. told me later—was Italian, and most of
it the real thing in antiques. There was a big fortune, he
said, in that one little room.

Welch didn't seem to mind letting us see his things. He
took out one after another and showed them off, bragging
about how he'd come by them. Lots of the ways were the
kind most men don't mention, let alone brag about.

I got the idea, he was so big, so strong, and had been
rich for so long, he thought laws didn't apply to him, that
when he wanted a thing he was entitled to it just because
he was able to grab it.

Later on Q. said I was right. He said he believed it
was the reason Welch went in for collecting stuff from
the Renaissance period. The big men in those days were
all murderers and thieves. The Borgias. The Medicis. The
Orsinis. They ruled the roost, so long as they were able to
stay on top. The minute they weakened they flopped.

I got tired of looking long before Welch got tired of
showing his things. But finally a clock chimed seven. It

seemed to surprise him, because he put down the silver statue he was holding and said:

"Some of the guests will be arriving soon. We'd better talk business."

We went back into the library. He didn't sit down, and neither did we.

Q. said: "What business?"

I knew he'd been wondering for the last half-hour what the old boy's game was.

It was clear enough he respected Q.'s judgment about his things, but he wasn't showing his collection just to brag. There was more to it than that. Now he was going to lay down his hand.

"I've a little job for you," he said slowly.

Q. told him: "But I'm on a vacation."

"If you were, you wouldn't be here." Welch picked up the Borgia Blade. "You didn't come to sell this. What you'd get would be chicken feed, for you. You planned to use it to get into Sant' Angelo and then take a shot at the stuff in there." He nodded toward the strong room.

Q. didn't say "Yes," or "No," but I knew Welch had hit it. That's what had been in Q.'s mind, all right. There was a kit of tools in the lining of his bag upstairs that proved it.

Welch said: "Never mind that now," like he meant it. "The Prefect told me he expected you to break for America, because he was making it too hot for you on the other side. That letter you sent made me think H. Findley Bleigh might be Q. Silver, so I told you to come down, on the chance. I've something in mind—" he stopped and glanced at me.

"He's safe," Q. said.

"I knew he was, or you wouldn't have had him with you. I wanted a look at him, too. I judge people by their faces."

Q. grinned.

"Well, don't judge Lynch by his!"

"About that little job," Welch went on, "I want something out of Creel's safe."

"Porter Creel?"

"Yes. It's nothing very valuable."

"If it weren't valuable you wouldn't be getting me to do the job."

"All right. If you like, it *is* valuable. But it's nothing very large. Just a button."

"One of the Medici buttons?"

"How did you know?"

"I've heard things. There were three, weren't there?"

"Yes, three. I have one. Creel has one, and Mrs. Arabella Statts has the third."

Q. whistled.

"How'd they get separated? The three were together last time I saw them."

"Where was that?"

Q. looked at him a minute, then:

"Le Coq had them," he said.

I knew Le Coq. One of the smartest crooks in France.

Welch grunted, sort of disgusted and mad.

"It was Le Coq who brought them to America," he said. "He got the three of us to bid against each other. Creel, Mrs. Statts, and myself."

Q. said: "I'll bet you upped the price."

"You're right. It hit the sky! Then he sold 'em to all three of us."

"How?"

"Each of us got an original—and two fakes."

Q. whistled again.

"Pretty smart."

Welch's jaw set.

"One isn't worth a damn. It's the three together that count." He looked at me for the first time. "They were made for Lorenzo the Magnificent—a wedding present to his bride."

"You don't say," I said, and "Well, well!"

Q. explained: "They're not ordinary buttons, Lynch. They're as big as saucers, encrusted with jewels, and worth—" He looked at Welch.

Welch said: "Three thousand apiece . . . if you get both of them."

Q. just laughed.

Welch argued: "You don't have to do it all on your own. I'm helping."

"How?"

"I'm keeping Creel and Mrs. Statts here to-night, so you can do the job."

"How about the servants?"

"They've been taken care of. Creel lives about an hour away. Mrs. Statts has an apartment in New York. You can clean up the whole business to-night."

"For twenty thousand . . ."

"They're not worth it!"

"Sure they're not, but it isn't the buttons you care about. It's the satisfaction you'll get out of putting it over on those two."

Welch didn't say any thing.

"They'll be damned sure you took them." Q. was reading him like a book. "But they won't be able to do anything about it, because the buttons are hot goods in the first place. They'll just have to beef—and you'll know they're beefing. You'll get a kick out of it that's worth twenty grand."

Welch sat smoking his cigar. He seemed to be weighing things in his mind.

"It might be worth fifteen," he admitted.

Q. said: "Done. What's your plan?"

There was a knock on the door. It opened. A young chap came in. He was short and slim, with longish brown hair and eyes as big as a girl's. He had a stutter when he was excited, and his mouth kept twitching, even when he wasn't talking. I guessed he was Roger Storey, the old man's nephew that Frazier'd told me about. I guessed right.

"Uncle," he began, then stopped when he saw Q. and me. "I'm s-s-sorry. I d-d-didn't know there was any one here."

"Mr. Bleigh," Welch said. "My nephew."

"G-g-good evening," the boy said, and to Welch:

"They've j-j-just come. They want to s-see you right away."

"Bring them in."

Roger Storey left the room with quick, jerky steps, like he was scared.

Welch said to me: "You may go. Frazier will take care of you." Then to Q., "I'll tell you my plans later. I want you to meet Mrs. Statts and Creel now. You'll have dinner with us, and then come back to breakfast in the morning. It'll look better that way."

I started up the stairs, but before I reached the top Roger came in with Creel and the Statts woman.

Creel was short, with a thin, mean face and a fish mouth. His eyes were gray-green, and the lids hung down over them as if to keep you from seeing what he was thinking.

Mrs. Statts was big and horsey. She had hair that was black when it should have been gray. She was dressed in a suit, but she was wearing diamonds that hit you like headlights. When she talked she bellowed. She didn't waste time saying "Hello," or "How are you?" Just stood in front of Welch and roared:

"Well, what is it you want of us?"

Welch smiled at her, all sweetness and light.

"I want you to meet Mr. Bleigh," he said, "Mr. H. Findley Bleigh, the collector."

Neither of them said anything. They just turned and looked at Q. The Statts woman's nose twitched like she smelled something. Creel's eyelids dropped down until he was looking out of Chinaman slits.

"He's brought one of his treasures for me to see," Welch went on. "A weapon credited to Cellini—made by him for one of the Borgias. I thought you would enjoy looking at it, so I invited you down. . . ."

He was still talking, quick, oily, and pleasant, when I reached the head of the stairs and came out into the loggia. That was at seven.

By eight o'clock I'd met Margot Pierre.

By ten we were in quarantine for smallpox.

At twelve-thirty Q. came upstairs and told me somebody'd bumped off Welch.

4

I was alone in the bedroom when Q. came in. Margot had left me by then. Margot was the Duchene girl's French maid. I'd met her at dinner in the servants' quarters. She was an eyeful. Had a figure that was slim, and round, in all the right places. She had black hair, jet black, and red lips that looked like they wanted to kiss somebody right away quick.

When she rolled her big black eyes at me and said, *"Bon soir,* Monsieur," she damn near wiped out the little blonde, but not quite. The blonde had nifty eyes, too. Sea blue, with green in 'em. She had a way of fluttering her lashes, and a sort of cooing in her voice.

That's neither here nor there. What I want to say is, this Margot girl was hot stuff. When I say hot, I mean *hot*.

She seemed to fall for me right off. After dinner we hung around for awhile in the servants' sitting-room, just for the looks of the thing, then went off on our own.

Margot pretended like she wanted to show me the place, she'd been there several days before we arrived, but we didn't go far. Just to a seat in the back hall. It was dark, and quiet, and looked out on a corner of the conservatory. It was a swell place for getting acquainted. I'll say it was. And for other things.

But that comes later. Anyway, I stayed with the Margot girl until eleven o'clock, when she had to go put her mistress to bed, because she had a headache.

I went up to Q.'s bedroom to wait. Believe it or not, I read a book while I waited. Maybe Welch had put it on the table in the room for a joke. Anyway, it was called *The New Criminology*. It was all about glands, and how guys who steal and murder aren't really bad at heart, just nice boys whose endocrines won't behave. It handed me a laugh.

I was marking some choice bits for Q. to enjoy, when he opened the door and came into the room.

First minute I laid eyes on him I saw something had gone sour.

His face was white as the front of his shirt, which wasn't so white at that. It was all spotted and streaked with blood. He was holding his coat across it, but the minute he got inside the room he started to shuck it off.

"What the hell?" I asked.

"Hold your tongue," he snapped. "Poke up that fire."

We burned the shirt in the fireplace, and a handkerchief that was sopping with blood. We watched every scrap. Not a thread got away from us.

We didn't dare burn the coat. Nobody'd miss a shirt. But a dinner coat was different.

I took the stains out of it as best I could with water. Then I hung it in front of the fire to dry. An expert could have found the places quick enough, but they didn't show unless you looked close.

All this time Q. didn't say anything. Just worked, swift and sure, way he does when we're in a tough spot.

Like always, I kept my mouth shut and waited for him to make the first move. But when everything was straightened out and he still didn't come through I couldn't stand the strain.

"Who was it?" I asked him. "Is he dead?"

Q. nodded.

"Welch. I'll say he's dead. Throat cut from ear to ear."

"'Throat cut'!"

That was the craziest thing I'd heard yet. In a pinch, I could figure Q. shooting. But throat cutting . . . it wasn't in the picture.

I didn't stop to argue, just picked up the bags and tossed them on the bed. There was a pair of shoes on a chair. I dumped them in and reached for the brushes on the bureau.

Q. stopped me.

"We're not lighting out," he said.

"With a murder—"

"We're standing pat."

"You're going to sit here and wait for the police to nab you?"

"Maybe I didn't do it."

"You had blood enough on you!"

"If I'd done it there wouldn't have been any blood," he said irritably, like I'd accused him of being clumsy.

"Then how the hell did you get your shirt—"

"I got it when I fell over him in the strong room."

I sat down on the edge of the bed and said:

"You'd better begin at the beginning and tell me what it's all about. I can't go it blind this way."

He saw I was right and loosened up. While he talked, he stalked up and down the room.

Q. is tall and thin, and walks like an Indian. His face is like an Indian's, too. Straight features. Brown skin. He told me once his great grandfather was a Cherokee. I believed him, because you never can tell what he's thinking. Not even when you watch his eyes. You just have to guess, and then, nine times out of ten, you're wrong.

He said he hadn't killed Vincent Welch. Maybe he hadn't. Then again, maybe he had. I didn't know. I was waiting to hear his story. He gave it to me straight, and quick.

"I went to the library to see Welch. He'd told me to come back after every one was in bed. Said he'd tell me what he had planned about those De' Medici buttons. When I went in—"

"How'd you go?"

"Through the conservatory. I knocked on the door first. When he didn't answer I let myself in. I couldn't see him anywhere, so I went toward the strong room. The door was open. I thought he might be in there."

"And then, maybe you thought you could pick up something."

Q. shrugged.

"Yes, there was that. It was dark, but I figured on using my lighter. I jumped down inside."

"What do you mean 'jumped'? There're steps, aren't there?"

"The steps were shoved to one side. They're made of wood, and are movable. They probably got shifted in the struggle."

I was getting so swelled up with questions I nearly busted.

"What was Welch doing down there in the dark?"

"You tell *me*. You haven't heard the worst of it yet."

"I've heard bad enough."

"Oh yeah? Listen to this—the knife he was killed with is lying right by the body. It's the Borgia Blade."

I did a back flip on that one.

"The Blade! Why th' hell didn't you bring it away with you?"

"And risk getting caught with the bloody thing in my hand?"

"You're going to stick around here and let them hang it on you?"

"What is this, a game of questions and answers? They can't hang anything on me. I didn't have the Blade. Welch had it."

"A swell chance you'll have of proving it. You say you didn't kill him. I'm trying to believe you. But the police won't. You brought the Blade down here. They'll find out who you are. . . ."

"They'll find that out anyway."

Q. wasn't walking now. He was standing in front of the fire, looking down at the flames. He had put on pajamas and a dark blue dressing gown. Rotten clothes for making a get-a-way.

"If I clear out now," he said, "they'll figure I'm guilty. Couldn't figure anything else."

"But you could get away."

"Maybe. And spend the rest of my life dodging dicks on a murder charge—while the guy who did it got off free. Not me! I'm going to stay right here until the thing is cleared up."

"They'll pin it on you like a rose."

"Not if I sit tight. I haven't any record in America. They haven't even my prints in the files."

That was right enough. But the same didn't go for me. Q. saw what I was thinking.

"Got an alibi?" he asked.

"Kind of a one. That Margot girl—"

"Who's she?"

"Miss Duchene's maid."

"The blonde?"

"No, brunette."

"My God, you work fast! How long were you together?"

"Almost all evening. There's a sort of hall off the servants' quarters. We were up there."

"Doing what?"

"None of your damned business."

He grinned at me.

"Nasty man! Do you think she'll give you an alibi?"

"Sure she will. She'll need one herself, won't she?"

He looked thoughtful.

"Yes," he said. "Every one in the house will need one."

I asked: "Did anybody see you come upstairs from Welch's study?"

"I don't believe so. I came up by the servants' stairs. Every one was in bed."

"Every one except the killer."

"That's what I mean."

"Who do you think killed him?"

"How the hell should I know? I'm not clairvoyant. There are his nephew and five guests in the house, and God knows how many servants. Any one of them may have done it. Any two, for that matter."

"Or it may have been an outside job."

"There's that, too," he admitted. "Though it's not likely. What with the wall, and the guards. They're keeping extra close watch because of the quarantine."

I'd forgotten the quarantine, though it had seemed pretty bad at the time. It happened about ten o'clock, when I was with Margot in the hall. Frazier had come along. He was wringing his hands and making noises again through his long nose.

One of the boys in the kitchen had been sick all day. He'd collapsed about nine, and a doctor had been sent from the village. He'd said "smallpox" and had ordered the whole place into quarantine until the next morning, when he could come out and vaccinate the lot of us.

Q. said, still looking at the fire:

"Funny thing about that quarantine. I mean the way they all took it. Creel nearly foamed at the mouth."

"Scared?"

"Not scared. Mad. I gathered he hadn't intended to stay all night."

"Welch was expecting him to stay."

"Yes, but Creel refused. Said he had to be in town in the morning. Mrs. Statts said the same."

"Then you think—"

"Hanged if I know. But it seems pretty screwy to me— the quarantine coming like that, right when he wanted 'em kept in the house."

"Welch looked like a cagey old bastard."

Q. nodded.

"Who do you think killed him?" I asked again.

"Damn it, don't keep asking me that!"

I could see Q. was a whole lot more nervy than he let on. Sitting and waiting for somebody to discover what he already knew was getting him down.

"Why don't you find out about that smallpox business?" I asked him. "You can phone to the village. It'll give you something to do."

He said: "Good idea," and picked up the telephone. He rattled the hook a couple of times, then swore under his breath. "I forgot . . . I cut the wire!"

"Why in hell did you do that?"

"So it would take longer to get the police. Give us more time to investigate."

"And when do you intend to start?"

"As soon as somebody finds the body." Q. started to put down the telephone. He froze.

There was a shot in the garden. Two more followed. Then a scream.

5

It was Creel who was shot. Porter Creel, the skinny man with the mean-looking mouth, I'd seen in Welch's library.

The way his mouth looked wasn't any lie, I guess. They said in the servants' quarters he'd made his money out of shipping. Got his start when he was a skipper by ramming another ship in the fog, then towing it in and claiming salvage.

Later, he bought boats that were ready to junk, fixed them up with fresh paint and sent them out with insured cargoes. If some of the crew went down with the boat, it was just too bad.

That's the kind of a guy he was. Even without looking at his mouth, you could have told by his eyes he was a rum lot. They were so near together they would have met if they hadn't been split apart by the thin, sharp bridge of his nose.

When we got downstairs we found he wasn't dead. Just winged in the left shoulder. One of the guards had taken two shots at him while he was trying to climb over the wall.

The shots and scream had routed every one out, and they all, guests and servants, came piling downstairs. They were in bath robes, negligées, and what-have-you. The noise they made, jabbering and screeching, was fit to raise the dead.

I was feeling pretty good by then. I figured they'd find Welch's body, and here was Creel caught trying to make a get-a-way.

It looked like the whole case would be folded up and put in your pocket before morning. Q. and I could slide out with one or two choice bits from the collection downstairs. With Welch dead maybe they wouldn't even be missed.

Frazier brought some towels and a basin of hot water. Q. and Mrs. Statts helped the Doctor work on Creel.

"It's an outrage!" Mrs. Statts roared. "It's a damned outrage!"

She wasn't in a negligée, I noticed. She wasn't in a dinner dress, either. She was in a dark suit, the one she was wearing in Welch's library when I first saw her. I wondered why she had it on at this hour.

"That fellow ought to be jailed," she went on, and glared at the guard. He was a big Greek by the name of Politos. "He ought to be pumped full of lead!"

The bunch around her made sympathetic noises.

The Duchene dame said, "And I'd like to do it! I bet you could sue him. Anyway, you could sue Mr. Welch for hiring him."

Creel didn't say anything.

I thought, He knows Welch is dead. He ought to. He bumped him off.

"Maybe you could collect as much as ten thousand if you worked it right," Mrs. Duchene went on.

She looked like the kind that would think what you could collect. She was big, and blonde, and had round blue eyes, a round nose, a little round, red mouth set in the middle of a round, white face that looked like it was made of soft custard.

"Hush, mother!" Laurette Duchene said. She was the daughter, the one Margot worked for. She was blonde, too. But not platinum, like the other. A red-gold blonde, with pansy-brown eyes and a swell figure—which she didn't mind showing. She was wearing a kind of a thin green-blue thing with big sleeves. You could see a lacy nightgown under it, and her hair was all which-a-way, as though she had been in bed when she heard the shots.

"Hush, mother!" she said again. "Mr. Creel needs quiet. Isn't that right, Roger?"

Roger told her she was right. You could see he'd agree with her if she said black was white. He never took his eyes off her, then or later. He was like a bird looking at a snake.

But she wasn't a snake. Just good-looking. Vivid, and determined. That's the reason he was so crazy about her, I guess, because he was weak and uncertain himself.

His stutter proved that. He said:

"Yes. Mr. C-C-Creel ought to be q-q-quiet," and turned to Dr. Jaffee. "Can't we c-c-carry him up to his room?"

"Not until he stops bleeding. We'd better send to town for some tetanus serum."

"But the quarantine, sir . . ." Frazier put in.

The Doctor said: "Nonsense," impatiently. "Of course we'll have to send some one. Where's Welch?"

That was the first time any one, except Q. and I, had noticed Welch wasn't there.

Frazier said he'd try to find him.

He went first to the old man's bedroom, and then to the library. While he was gone, I watched the library door like a cat watches a mousehole, wondering if Frazier'd be knocked out by what he found, or if he'd be calm about it.

He was calm. He came back, and just as if he was announcing dinner, spoke softly to Dr. Jaffee.

"Mr. Welch is dead, sir."

Nobody got it for a minute. That is, nobody but Q. and me. The Doctor didn't even stop working on Creel's arm, just looked up impatiently.

He asked: "What's that?"

"I said, sir, Mr. Welch is dead."

"Dead?"

"Yes, sir."

Creel sang out, "Where?"

Roger sputtered, "H-h-how?"

Q. asked: "Are you sure?"

"Quite sure, sir. He is lying in the strong room with his throat cut."

Then Mrs. Duchene threw a fit, and one of the servants, a fat dame with red hair, began to scream like a siren.

The Statts woman let out a few bad words. "I knew he'd get it sooner or later," she said. "The dirty double-crossing skunk! I knew it!"

Laurette Duchene was the only one who kept her mouth shut. Her mother was flopping around like a chicken with its head off, but she didn't seem to notice. Just stood staring at the library door.

Margot had come in with the other servants. She took charge of Mrs. Duchene.

Q. was the first to do anything.

"Come on!" he said, and started, hot foot, for the library.

Dr. Jaffee went with him. I followed. Frazier came last, like he wasn't crazy about going back into the room.

The place was the same as when we'd seen it earlier, except that only one light was on. The lamp by the desk. The strong room was open and the curtains on either side were pulled back.

Frazier lifted the desk lamp and held it over his head. A little light fell on the floor inside.

Dr. Jaffee said: "Good God!" but not like he was swearing, more like he was praying. "Vincent!" He started to go down into the room.

Q. held him back.

"Wait," he said. "You'd better turn on the light. There's a switch somewhere, isn't there, Frazier?"

"Yes, sir. It's here. But it isn't working." He touched a switch near the door. It snapped twice. The room stayed dark.

Q. said: "That's damned funny."

"The globe must be burned out, sir," Frazier told him. "It wouldn't go on when I was in here before." He turned toward the Doctor. "Be careful," he said, "the steps have been pushed out of place."

The Doctor was already down in the vault.

Q. snapped on his cigarette lighter and handed it to him. It sputtered a bit, but it lighted up the whole place. You could see the shelves on the sides and the safety boxes, Welch was lying on his belly in the middle of the room. His head was twisted sidewise, so that the face was turned away. That was all right with me. I never did like the sight of blood, and the place was full of it.

Q. said: "Better not move him any more than you can help."

The Doctor lifted the body and looked at the throat. The cigarette lighter dropped out of his hand.

It went out, and he had to grope for it. He came back toward the door. His voice was like nothing I'd ever heard.

"His head has been half cut off," he whispered.

I thought he was going to keel over.

Q. reached down and grabbed him by the shoulder. "Hold on," Q. said, "we'll help you up."

Frazier disappeared, then came back with some whiskey.

The Doctor drank it, his teeth chattering against the glass.

I suddenly realized the dead guy down there was his friend. He didn't mean anything to me. I'd seen him only twice. But it was hard on the Doctor.

"Poor Vincent," he kept mumbling. "Poor, poor fellow."

Q. snapped out quickly:

"We must send for the police!"

Frazier repeated like an echo:

"'The police.'"

We went back to the library. Frazier picked up the telephone. It was dead, of course, just like Q. planned it should be.

Frazier clicked the receiver up and down, then looked solemn and cross-eyed at the mouthpiece.

"It seems to be out of order, sir."

Q. took it from him and listened.

"Wire's been cut!" He looked fiercely at Frazier. "What the hell's the meaning of this?"

"I don't know, sir. Unless the murderer cut it—or perhaps Mr. Welch himself."

"Why Welch?"

"Because he didn't want Mr. Creel or Mrs. Statts to use the telephone."

Q. looked at him hard. I could see he was wondering how much Frazier knew.

Was he, maybe, listening through the keyhole when Welch made his proposition to us? Or was he in on something else, something we didn't know about?

Like he always does, Q. took command.

"Go back of that," he said.

"I don't know what you mean, sir."

"Yes, you do. Was that smallpox quarantine phony?"

Frazier stared at the floor, then he nodded. His face was stretched out long.

"Yes, sir. That is, the man really was broken out, but it was chickenpox. Not smallpox."

"Then why did the health officer . . . ?"

"I can't exactly say, sir. But after he'd said 'chicken-pox,' Mr. Welch had a talk with him and he changed it to 'smallpox.' I believe it was because Mr. Welch wanted to keep Mr. Creel and Mrs. Statts overnight. He'd planned on their staying, but it seems there was a sale at Silo's in the morning. They both wanted to be there. They refused to stay, and Mr. Welch was very much upset."

"Why?" Q. was watching the butler like a hawk to see if he'd show how much he knew.

He didn't show anything except the whites of his eyes.

"I really couldn't say, sir. Unless it was because Mr. Welch was a gentleman who always liked to have his own way. He couldn't bear to be crossed in anything. It made him, as you might say, quite wild with anger."

"Is that true, Dr. Jaffee?" Q. asked.

The Doctor seemed to come out of a trance. He didn't look like he'd heard anything that had happened.

"I'm—I'm sorry," he muttered. "I'm afraid I wasn't following."

Q. didn't give Frazier a chance to repeat. Instead he asked:

"Why didn't you treat that man in the kitchen?"

"I did!" The Doctor seemed surprised. "I saw him earlier in the evening."

"Did you believe it was smallpox?"

"No, I diagnosed chickenpox, but Vincent insisted on sending for Dr. Ascher, the health officer from the village. He felt he owed it to his guests. Ascher said 'smallpox,' and I couldn't very well argue, since I'm no longer in practice."

"All right," Q. interrupted. "We have that straight. He wanted to keep Creel and Mrs. Statts here for the night, so he bribed the health officer to clamp down a quarantine. Now where do we go from there?"

"The police?" Frazier suggested, and Q. nodded.

"Is there some one you can send?"

"There's Politos," Frazier told him.

"Who's he?"

"One of the guards."

"You can trust him?"

"Yes, sir. He has been with us for years."

Politos—and, believe it or not, his first name was Narcisse—was the guy who had winged Creel.

He was a big, black, bull-necked Greek. And yet he was good-looking, too, in a kind of a gorilla way. Anyway, some of the women seemed to think so.

Q. sent me out to see that he got off safely. I knew what that meant.

While he was getting his coat, I plugged a hole in his gas tank. I figured that would leave him sitting high and not so pretty about half-way to town, and Q. would have an extra hour or two before the dicks landed on us.

I hoped to persuade Q. to clear out, but when I got back to the house he had everybody lined up like they were school kids. He was looking at their hands.

I knew the guy who'd cut that throat must have got himself damn well smeared up. If he didn't know much about blood, he might wash his hands without noticing he'd left stains under the finger nails. Q. knew it too. He was looking for just that.

He didn't get anywhere. Creel was stained from the wound in his shoulder. Dr. Jaffee had handled both Creel and Welch. The same went for the butler, while Q. and Mrs. Statts had helped dress Creel's shoulder. The rest of the crowd were clean—which didn't mean anything, really, because they might have been smart enough to scrub thoroughly.

I could see Q. hadn't really hoped to find anything. He'd just lined them up on the chance. For another reason, too. The guy who jumps in and takes charge in an emergency, while every one else is running around in circles, is top man from then on.

Q. had sense enough to know that. He had lined them all up just to show he was boss, and the meek way they obeyed gave him a hold over them, a hold he never lost, even after the dicks took charge.

While he was looking them over, they talked plenty.

"It's terrible, perfectly terrible!"

"Oh, *do* you think you can find out who did it?"

The Duchene woman whimpered like a puppy left out in the rain.

"I wonder who'll get his collections?" Mrs. Statts talked like a battle-ax, chopping away in dry, hard hacks.

"Probably the nephew," Creel said, and they both looked at Roger as though they hated his guts.

Roger wasn't looking at them. He never looked at anybody except the Duchene girl if she was in the room.

"You're sure you're warm enough, d-d-darling," he kept asking her every two minutes. "You're sure? Don't you want me to get you s-something to drink? Aren't you getting t-t-tired?"

Every time he asked her a question she shook her head.

"No, Roger. No!" She didn't even turn her face, just sort of lifted her hand like he was a fly buzzing around.

Mostly she watched Q. When he'd finished looking them over and said they could sit down, she asked:

"Is there anything we can do to clear this up before the police arrive?"

Q. grinned at her. It wasn't the first time they'd talked. They'd had a long chin together right after dinner. That was when I was sitting with Margot in the little hall off the conservatory.

It was dark up there, and the conservatory was light. It was easy to see everything that went on. We could hear, too. Which made it fine for me.

Q. came out of the drawing-room with the Duchene girl. She was wearing something slinky and white. Her hair was bound tight to her head like a gold cap, and there was a band of green stones holding it. They weren't phony stones, either.

As she walked along she was singing the song the radio was playing inside. Singing it a lot better than you'd expect from an amateur.

They strolled among the trees and vines for a minute, not saying anything. Then Q. picked her a flower. The girl took it and put it in a loop of ribbon at her waist.

Q. said: "Not there. *There.*"

He took a diamond pin that was shaped like an arrow from her shoulder and pinned the flower on the front of her dress. He took some time to it, but she didn't draw away. Just stood smiling up at him.

When he was through, he said:

"So you're going to marry Roger Storey?"

"I may."

"It won't work."

"Why not?"

"He's neurotic. Maybe even epileptic. He'll go bad on you."

She stopped and looked at him, not angry. Curious. "Why should you bother to tell me this?"

"I thought maybe you didn't know . . . and some one ought to tell you."

"I don't see why it should be *you.*"

"I'm just a kibitzer at heart. I don't like to see you wasted."

She didn't say anything for a minute. I couldn't see Q.'s face, but I knew he was laughing down at her in the kind of way he has with women.

I remembered what he'd said about our not being there for monkey business and had to put Margot's hand over my mouth to keep from laughing out loud.

"You'd do better to take the old man," Q. told her. "Perhaps you've thought of that, Lottie Dukes."

She gave a gasp, and Margot echoed it.

I did a little gasping myself, because, of course, I knew who Lottie Dukes was—the smartest con woman in the game.

I'd never seen her. She'd been working in Europe ever since the Blackmore case. There was nothing the dicks could lay their hands on in that, but they made it so hot for her she had to beat it out of this country.

We used to hear about her, now and then, pulling high-class stuff on the other side. Some of the hauls they told about would make you green with envy.

She had a way with her, that gal.

"Mon Dieu!" Margot said. *"Mon Dieu!* He knows her!"

I said: "Shut your face." I wanted to hear what they were saying.

Lottie didn't try to deny anything, just looked at Q. with her brown eyes wide open.

"You knew all the time?"

"You hair is different, of course," Q. told her. "It was darker when I met you in Cannes. You're a little thinner."

"Five pounds!" she snapped.

"And you've done something to your eyebrows. I never forget a face. Nor a figure." He ran his eyes down to her slippers in a way that made her wriggle.

"What are you going to do about it, *Mister* Silver?" she asked.

I saw then that she had known all along who he was, and I know Q.'d guessed she was on to him and had fired the first gun.

"What are you going to do?" she repeated.

"Nothing."

"I don't believe it!"

"Why not?"

"Because you must be here for some reason."

"Perhaps I want to sell Welch the Borgia Blade. You saw it at dinner."

She looked at him some more, then shook her head.

"Not big enough. You wouldn't take the risk for that."

"Maybe you're right," Q. agreed. "Do you like Gertrude Stein?"

"I find her a trifle obscure."

"Do you really? I enjoyed *Four Saints,* especially the music."

I gathered some one was coming into the conservatory. I was right. It was Welch.

That was the second time I saw him that night.

The third time was when he was lying dead on the floor in the strong room.

6

Right then I began to wonder if I hadn't been a little too sure of Margot. Not that she wasn't crazy about me, but she was the Duchene girl's maid, and if Laurette Duchene was Lottie Dukes it was a pretty good bet Margot wasn't any wilting violet.

I began to see why she'd suggested that place to sit. Maybe she wanted to hold hands in the dark, and again, maybe she wanted to pick up some dope on the side. For that, the place was swell. It was like looking down on a stage, without any of the actors knowing they had an audience.

She could have gone there alone, of course, but if any one had seen her they might have figured she was there to get an earful. With me along, it merely looked as though we had found a quiet spot for a little necking.

At that, she was a pretty hot number and I couldn't get sore, because I wasn't above picking up a bit of information myself. I just took a new grip on her and listened to what Welch had to say.

Like I mentioned before, he was a fine-looking old boy. Big. Broad. But a little too heavy around the jowls from over-eating. Just to see him you could tell he liked wine and women, and was willing to pay top price for both.

He seemed surprised to find Q. with the Duchene girl. I guessed she'd given him a sort of come-hither at dinner that had made him expect to find her alone.

She looked at Q. half laughing, half pleading, like she was urging him to clear out and give her a chance. But Q. wouldn't see it.

"What did *you* think of *Four Saints?*" he asked Welch.

"Virgil Thomson's music's not bad, but that Stein woman," he made a face, "ought to be in a straight jacket. Creel wants another look at the Blade," he told Q. and took the Dukes girl's arm. "I've something to show you. That new orchid is blooming."

Q. had to take the hint and scram.

Welch was showing the orchid to the girl last I saw.

If I'd known that inside of four hours I'd be looking down on him, sprawled out on the floor, in the spot marked X, I'd have paid more attention to his talk. But I didn't. So far as I was concerned, he was just an old boy on the make for a dame, and I didn't care whether he got what he was after or whether Roger Storey got it.

I preferred to see how far I could go with Margot without getting my face slapped.

I found out. She didn't slap, she used a pin. But I didn't mind, I'd had my fun.

By that time Welch and the girl had come around to our side of the conservatory again. They were talking a mixture of botany and small talk. Not so small, either, when you figured what was back of it.

He said: "That's a philodendron. It's one of the earliest plant forms . . . practically unchanged since the Pleistocene period. That damn fool boy's just told me he wants to marry you."

"It's a queer-looking plant, isn't it? With all those tentacle things sticking out like an octopus. So he tells me, too."

"Those are roots. It uses them for holding on to the tree. What are you planning to do?"

She said: "Just the same, I wouldn't like it to get in my hair. I'm considering his proposal."

"I wouldn't. Not seriously."

"What are those greeny-yellow things with red spots up there?"

"Another variety of orchid." He told her the name, which I can't remember. "Marrying Rod wouldn't pay—his father didn't leave much, and he has a mother . . . in a sanitarium for mental cases."

"Have you any lavender orchids? The kind the florists carry?"

"No. And you won't have any, either, my girl. Carnations will be about your style . . . with asparagus ferns."

"You think money is what I want, don't you?"

"Money's what you've got to have if you wear dresses like that one. It's Chanel, isn't it?"

"No, Robert Piquet. You seem to know something about women's clothes."

"I should. I've paid for enough of them."

It was about here that I found Q. was listening in. He was beyond us, just a shadow at the end of our hall. I didn't know how long he'd been there.

"I like that climbing vine," the Dukes-Duchene girl said. "The one with the red flowers."

"It's a begonia. Semi-tropical. Not very rare. Do you like Paris?"

"Well enough. I like the south of France better. And there's a place in North Africa—"

"We might go there."

"You take a lot for granted, don't you?"

"And it's usually granted."

"Yes?"

"Yes. We could go in my yacht."

"Without Roger?"

"Without Roger. It would pay you better, even for a short time."

"You—" She began to laugh, first quietly, then with little gasps. "You . . . sound like . . . something out . . . of an old melodrama! You really should have . . . a purple-black mustache, and twirl the ends."

He got sore. I could tell by his voice, and the way his neck sort of swelled.

"There's no use trying to pull that stuff with me," he said. "I know too much about you."

She said: "Personally, I don't like the spotted ones. They smell too strong and they look like snakes. Do they grow in dirt?"

"In moss. They have to be kept warm and moist. They're from Bolivia."

I surmised some one was coming in the door. I was right. It was Roger Storey.

I shifted Margot over to the other knee. The left one was asleep. Q. was gone, or, anyway, was out of sight.

Roger seemed pleased about something. It was plain he'd had a few drinks. It made him cheerful. It also made him God's own fool.

"How do you l-l-like my girl?" he asked, putting his arm around the place where the waist of her dress would have been if it had had any waist.

Welch said: "She prefers orchids. And she wears Piquet dresses."

"And sometimes Worth, and LeLong," the Dukes-Duchene girl said. "Your uncle is going to give me my trousseau for a wedding present."

That was cheeky enough for any one.

"I knew you'd l-l-like her," Roger stuttered, pleased and excited. "I knew everything would be all r-r-right."

"And Uncle Vincent has offered us his yacht for our honeymoon," Lottie Dukes went on. She looked sweet, and cool, and innocent. She put her hand on Welch's arm and patted it. "For a trip to North Africa. Isn't he an old darling?"

Welch didn't say anything, just reached up and picked a spray of the spotted orchid, the one she'd said looked like a snake. He pulled out the flower Q. had pinned on the front of her dress and put the orchid in its place.

He said: "For a wedding bouquet," and grinned at her.

Margot slipped off my knee and moved over to the end of the couch. She began to smooth down her dress.

She needn't have bothered. Frazier came into the hall where we were, but he was in too much of a hurry to notice us. He went through to the conservatory, and told Welch about the servant coming down with smallpox, and about how the health officer had quarantined the place.

7

That brought Creel, the Duchene girl's mother, and Mrs. Statts into the mess. They had been in another wing of the house, playing bridge with the Doctor. Like a radio on two stations at the same time, they were all talking at once.

Creel said: "I can't stay. It's out of the question! Have to attend an auction in the morning."

"Me, too," the Statts woman snapped. "They can't hold me. I've been vaccinated!"

"But it doesn't always take. My cousin broke out in red spots *all* over. They said it was chickenpox, but it was smallpox just as sure as anything." This from Mrs. Duchene. "My God, forty on her face alone—and you simply couldn't count the rest of her!"

Then everybody began to jabber. The women said they wouldn't . . . and there was no reason . . . and why *should* they . . . and it was outrageous, and displayed their vaccination marks. Was my face red!

Frazier, trying to look in seven different directions at the same time, said:

"The health officer was quite firm about it, sir."

He told us they'd taken the sick man to town and left two guards. Every one would have to stay until the doctor came back and vaccinated us in the morning.

After that there was just a lot of noise and beefing
around.

Creel was snappy and sore. Mrs. Statts roared like a cow
that had lost her calf. The Dukes-Duchene woman whimpered, but the girl seemed calm enough. She didn't mind
staying cooped up in that house, Lottie Dukes didn't. It
would give her time to get in a few more cracks at Welch
and the boy. Either way, I figured, she stood to win.

What happened among them all I didn't learn until
later. So far as I was concerned, the evening stopped when
Frazier came in with the news of the quarantine and Margot moved to the other end of the sofa. After that, we went
out to the kitchen for a cold snack and a bit of beer with
the rest of the servants, then Lottie Dukes rang for Margot
and we went on upstairs.

It was about an hour later that Q. came hurrying in
with blood on the front of his shirt.

Knowing all this made the group in the hall, after the
murder, a lot more interesting. When I saw the Duchene
girl looking snooty and aristocratic in her green-blue negligée, I knew it was only Lottie Dukes putting on an act.
And her mother, with her fainting and her hysterics, was
just old Pearl Dukes, of Dukes-and-Dukes, the vaudeville
team that used to close the show in the five-a-days, before
the old man drank himself to death and Lottie turned out
so smart.

After seeing Politos off to get the police, I went back to
the house. I felt pretty pleased about puncturing his gas tank
and wanted to tell Q., but Margot grabbed me in the hall.

"What kin' of man eet is you work for, eh?" she asked.
"He make trouble and more trouble." She finished with a
lot of French words I didn't know, but I could guess by the
looks of her face pretty much what they were.

I gathered Q. had ordered all the women into the drawing-room. Guests, maids, and cooks. The lot of them. They

were to stay put until he got back. They were sore as hell, but they obeyed.

Like I said, he'd got the jump on the whole shebang by taking charge at the beginning.

He left Creel with the women and the Doctor, who was re-dressing his shoulder. Roger and me he took with him to the library, while Frazier lined up the men servants in the dining-room.

I knew what Q. was after in the library. He wanted to find who'd killed Welch, before the police arrived.

If he could figure that out it might save our necks. But, even more he wanted to make sure there wasn't anything he'd overlooked the first time he was there, and to make fresh finger-prints all over the place, so if any showed up he would have witnesses who'd testify he'd made them after the murder. You don't pal with Q. as long as I have without knowing the way his mind works.

When we got to the library we found Lottie Dukes was with us.

Q. told her: "I said all the women were to stay in the drawing-room."

"I heard you," she said.

"Well?"

"I'm here."

"I'd rather you went back."

"I don't doubt it." She looked at him in a funny way. "I'm pretty good at noticing things."

"Perhaps you noticed some flowers," Q. said, so politely I knew he was burning up.

I looked around and saw a spray of yellow orchids with red splotches lying on the desk. It had been crushed by the corner of a big book that was lying across it. You could smell the sickly, sweetish odor from where we stood.

"Those orchids are mine," Roger said quickly. "I picked them in the conservatory and brought them in."

"Yeah?" Q. walked over, closed the book and showed the stem of the orchid. There was a diamond pin, like an arrow, stuck through it. "When did you leave it?" he asked Lottie Dukes.

"About eleven."

"You're sure?"

"It might have been later—perhaps twenty past."

Roger said: "But, d-d-darling, you went to bed at eleven. Don't you remember? Your head ached. I walked upstairs with you."

"Yes, but I came down again. I found I couldn't sleep. I was nervous about that smallpox business. So I came downstairs to get a book."

Q. asked: "What stairs?"

"The circular ones that come down here." She pointed toward the side of the library. "Mr. Welch had promised me a book on old jewelry. I thought I could read myself to sleep."

"I'd have brought it to you," Roger told her. "All you had to do was call."

"I know, dear." She put a hand on his arm. You could see it was like an electric shock to the poor goof every time she touched him. "I know."

Q. grinned at her.

"That being settled, what were you after beside the book?"

Lottie looked like she wanted to bite him, but instead she smiled.

"There *was* something else."

"A necklace?"

"Yes. How did you know?"

"This." Q. picked up a flat box from the desk, near the flowers. It was empty, but the satin inside had a curved line around it where something had been.

Roger stared from the box to Q., and then at the girl.

"What is it?" he asked. "What are you t-t-talking about?"

Lottie said: "A little present your uncle gave me." She hadn't intended saying anything about it, you could see that. Now she had to, and she was sore as hell. "When I got down here he was in the vault. But he called to me and said he'd be right out."

"The light was on?" Q. asked.

She nodded.

"Yes; the light was on. I could see it from here. When he came out he was carrying that box." She looked sidewise at Roger. "He said it was an engagement present."

"What was it?"

"A necklace of diamonds and sapphires. Antique."

Roger said: "That was to prove he was g-g-glad Laurette was marrying into the family. Before he m-m-met her he kicked up an awful row. But in the f-f-four days she's been here she won him over."

"Fast work," Q. said under his breath. "Very."

She didn't look at him gratefully, but like he was a rattlesnake and she was waiting for him to strike.

Q. asked: "Was any one else in this room while you were here with Welch?"

"Nobody. I stayed just a little while, then I went back upstairs."

"Wearing the necklace, I suppose?"

"Yes. That's why I took off the flowers. They got in the way when he—I mean I—was putting it on. I forgot and left them there on the desk."

Q. swung around to Roger.

"And when were you in here?"

"How d-d-did you know I was here?"

"I didn't. But I do now! What time was it?"

"About eleven-thirty, I t-t-think." You could see he was talking wild, saying one thing and thinking another.

"Maybe a quarter to twelve. I d-d-don't know. I just dropped in to say g-g-goodnight to my uncle."

"It wasn't eleven-thirty. It was a whole lot earlier."

"How d-d-do you know?"

"Because you're a damned poor liar. You're so anxious to swear you saw your uncle after she went upstairs that it sticks out like a sore thumb. If you'd been here *after* she was, you'd have noticed those flowers. Bound to. Their smell alone would have made you notice them. And you wouldn't have looked so goggle-eyed when you saw them just now."

The boy didn't even try to argue.

"It was after I came downstairs from seeing her to her room," he admitted. "About eleven. I wasn't here long."

"Just long enough to get into a row, eh?"

"Yes . . . no. We d-d-didn't row."

"Somebody did."

"What makes you think so?"

"That book on the table. It was smashed down hard enough to practically pulp the flowers."

"We were over there." He pointed toward the opposite end of the room. "Besides, I don't pound things when I'm mad."

"So you were mad?"

"No!"—he looked like he was thinking of something else—"everything was pleasant."

"He didn't talk about a will?"

"No. Why should he?"

I wondered, too; but Q. didn't go into the question any farther, because the Duchene girl butted in with:

"There was some one came in after I did."

Q. asked: "Who was it?"

"Frazier."

"What for?"

"He wanted Mr. Welch to take a look at the conservatory. Something was wrong with the pipes, he said. He was afraid it might cool off too much in the night."

"Maybe so, and maybe it was just a gag to get him out. We'll check on that later. I'd like to take a look at the vault in there. Want to go with me?" he asked Roger.

The boy shook his head. He turned a kind of light green.

"No," he said. "D-don't ask me! I c-c-couldn't!"

"*I* can," Lottie Dukes said.

Q. told her: "Not you. It's no place for a woman!"

"I can stand it. You're not going in alone."

They looked at each other. Clear as day, I saw the whole thing. Even if they didn't think each other guilty, she was sure Q. was up to something. And Q. wouldn't have trusted her with a plugged nickel. It was a swell situation for a play, but not so hot in real life.

I asked myself: What if the girl decides to squeal when the police arrive?

I made up my mind right there and then to put in some heavy work on Margot and see what I could find out.

Q. was going into the vault. He took a paper and pencil with him, and told me to hold a light so he could make a sketch.

While he drew, he talked over his shoulder, like he was trying to memorize how things were.

He said: "Welch is lying half on his face, half on his left side. About two feet to the left of the door. The steps are pushed aside as though there was a struggle." He reached out and pushed at the steps. "Yes, that's possible. They're easy to move."

"They were made that way especially," Lottie Dukes explained. "Mr. Welch told me he used them for reaching the top shelves and safety boxes."

"What's all that rubbish on the floor?" I asked.

"Looks like a clock." Q. looked closer. "It is. An old clock, badly smashed and there's"—he broke off and spoke very low—"there's the knife that killed him. It . . ." You would have sworn he was seeing it for the first time and the shock was almost bowling him over. "My God, Lynch, it's the Borgia Blade!"

I said quickly: "Look, there's a paper, lying on the floor beside his hand!"

Q. picked it up.

"It's a printed form, a will and testament."

So that was why Q. had asked about the will! He'd seen it on his first trip down. The time he discovered the old boy lying dead.

Roger, behind me, gave a funny choking sound.

"You're s-s-sure it's a will?" he asked.

"Yes. Know anything about it?"

"N-n-no."

From the way he was stuttering I guessed he was lying.

Q. must have come to the same conclusion. Quick as a wink he asked:

"How much do you get?"

"W-w-what d-d-do you mean?"

"How much of the old man's money comes to you?"

"I d-d-don't know. Honestly, I d-d-don't. Sometimes he used to say one thing, and s-s-sometimes another. Depending on whether he was m-m-mad or not."

"But you'll get some of it?"

"I s'pose so."

Any other relatives?"

The boy shook his head.

"Just my mother and me. He didn't get along with my mother."

"I'll take a look at it," Q. said.

"I wouldn't," Lottie Dukes told him. "The police mightn't like it."

Q. decided he wouldn't. Trying to do anything with her there was just about as pleasant as trying to operate with a lighted stick of dynamite in the room.

"Maybe you're right," he admitted. "No use making the police sore. I'll leave things alone. But I'm going to take a look at that book."

"What book?"

"On the desk. The one that mashed your flowers." He was out of the vault by now. He went over to the desk and picked up the book.

"*Old Clocks & Watches*," he read. "'By F. J. Britten.' Who cares about old clocks here?"

"My uncle did," Roger told him. "And Dr. Jaffee is writing a book on them." Roger wasn't stuttering now. He seemed eager to give information. "Mr. Creel is nutty about old clocks, too. He has a collection. He nearly had apoplexy when my uncle got Henry VIII's clock away from him."

"What's that?"

"Henry VIII's clock."

"Is it here?"

"Yes. Over there in the corner."

Sure enough, there it was. I didn't think much of it, myself. Although there was a lot of gilt-work, fleurs-de-lis, lions, and whatnots stuck all over, it looked like something out of a pawn shop. Maybe it was, at that. Q. looked at it. Seemed interested.

"Does it go?" he asked.

"It did," Roger told him. "But they took out the works. My uncle, and Creel, and Dr. Jaffee."

"What for?"

"They had an argument before dinner about whether the works dated back to Henry, or whether they were put in later. So they opened it up in the shop."

"Where's the shop?"

He pointed. "In there."

We went through a low door at the left of the desk.

The shop wasn't very big, but it was complete, with work-benches and everything you could think of in the way of lathes and tools.

Roger said: "My uncle had experts come out to fix up the stuff he bought. Furniture. Clocks. Even jewelry. He wouldn't let anything go out of his hands. He made 'em come to the house. Lots of times he and the Doctor fixed things themselves."

Q. swung around to the Dukes girl and pointed to a bunch of junk in the middle of the room.

"Was that stuff there when you came in this evening?" he asked her.

It didn't work. She shrugged, then took out a cigarette. Roger lighted it for her.

She asked: "How should I know? I wasn't in here."

"You're sure?"

Roger went off like a fire-cracker. "D-don't you speak to her l-l-like that!" he yelled. "I w-w-won't have her b-b-bullied . . . d-d-do you h-h-hear?"

Q. didn't bother to answer. Just moved across the room and looked in a closet, then tried a door which led, Roger said, into the conservatory. It was locked.

"Who has the key to it?"

"I think Frazier has one."

Q. said to me: "Cut along and find the butler."

I cut. Not through the main hall but out a side way that went by the back stairs toward the butler's pantry.

This took me down the hall that led past the conservatory. It was almost dark except for dim light that came in from the side. Some one was there. I could tell by the sounds.

I stopped, and went back to look through the window near where Margot and I had been sitting earlier.

It was Mrs. Statts and Creel. They were having a hell of a row.

8

Mrs. Statts said Creel had double-crossed her earlier in the evening when he tried to get away without her.

Creel said she was lucky not to have been along. Said the big Greek might have potted her, too.

She said that was neither here nor there. He'd promised to meet her. She'd stood around half an hour in the cold waiting for him. He was a dirty sneak and worse.

I thought: That explains the suit she was wearing—when all the other women were in wrappers and negligée. She and Creel had been planning to light out together, and, at the last minute, he'd left her flat.

It wasn't his fault he hadn't got away with it. She could thank Politos, the Greek.

"Why the hell *should* I take you?" he shouted.

"Why the hell shouldn't you?" She came right back at him. She was a great big camel of a woman taller than he was, and twice as mean.

"Well—"

"Maybe you had some reason," she said, and squinted her eyes. "Where were you that hour between twelve and one? Why didn't you come to the terrace when you said you would?"

"I was delayed."

"Where?"

"It doesn't matter—I had business to attend to."

"Business with Welch?"

"No, you—! Don't you try to hang anything on me! I wasn't near Welch!"

"Can you prove where you were that hour?"

"Sure I can!" (He sounded shifty to me.) "I can prove it by the butler."

"You can if you get to him first, you mean."

What he had called her was right. She was just that. There didn't seem to be any reason for her to accuse him of the murder. She couldn't have been that mad, just because he'd stood her up. It didn't make sense. But she went right on, tooth and toenail, digging into him.

"That's the reason you didn't come for me! Because you'd cut his throat and had to get away quick."

Creel screamed at her, "That's a lie!" Then he seemed to think better of it. He quieted down. "You're just trying to kid me," he said. "Where were *you* when it happened? Under the library windows?"

"No. About twenty feet beyond. Anyway, they were locked."

"How do you know?"

"Why—" She gave a sort of gurgle and stepped back. "I—I—heard some one say so."

"You didn't! You tried them! Maybe they were locked . . . maybe they weren't! Maybe you went inside—"

"Why should *I* want to kill him?"

"Why should *I* want to?"

"Oh, are you talking about killing again?" It was Mrs. Duchene. Pearl Dukes, that was. I knew her by her voice, which was all up and down, in the wrong places. She was trooping in from the next room, eager as a wet pup to be friendly, and about as welcome.

"I can give you reasons," Mrs. Statts grunted, then said to Pearl: "We were talking about Welch."

Creel interrupted: "What reasons?"

"It's terrible," Pearl wailed. "Simply ter-r-rible. I had a brother who was murdered. *Almost,* that is. They rescued him just in time. Wasn't that *for-r-tunate?*"

The Statts woman said: "Very fortunate," in a tone like she meant "Take her away and drown her." Then, to Creel: "I'm saving my reasons to tell the police."

"Police?" Pearl squealed. "Don't say *police!* They give me the jitters. Not that I've ever had anything to do with them," she added quickly.

I guess Mrs. Statts and Creel saw there wasn't any chance to have a quiet talk. They got out of the room as soon as they could, and went in opposite directions.

Pearl Dukes looked after them, first one way, then the other. When she saw they were gone she gave a quick glance over her shoulder and hurried to the pool in the middle of the conservatory.

It was a big pool, with a lot of pond lilies and fish. Gold fish, blue fish, and red snails that crawled up the edges.

Pearl got down on her knees, grunting a little. She pulled up her sleeve, made a face, and plunged her fat arm down into the water. It looked as if she was hiding something. She got up, wiped her arm on the hem of the nightgown under her wrapper, and hurried out of the room.

I made the pool in twenty seconds flat. I stripped off my coat, rolled up my sleeve, and reached down into the water.

I groped around and fished up a handful of gravel.

I got two snails and a lily bulb and a piece of broken shell.

Then my hand struck something that was buried in the mud.

I pulled and it came up.

It was a rubber hot-water bottle. Inside was a diamond and sapphire necklace, and something else wrapped in paper. I pulled it out, and found it was a long, thin knife.

9

It took me a little while to find Frazier. He wasn't in the dining-room, where the men servants were shooting craps. He wasn't in the hall or the drawing-room, which were full of maids and other females, all gabbing. I found him out in a side hall, talking to Creel.

I marked up the Statts woman one for that, because if Creel wasn't handing him over some money I'm an Eskimo.

Frazier was saying: "Yes, sir. I understand perfectly. Thank you, sir. I shall remember."

Creel said: "Shut up," and walked off.

I told Frazier Mr. Bleigh wanted him in the library. I almost said "Silver," but caught myself in time.

At that, I lied. By the time we got back, Q. wasn't in the library but in the hall. When he found out the women had disobeyed him and had roamed all over the place, he was plenty burned up. Which showed he didn't know as much about women as he thought he did. Tell 'em to stay put and they're bound to go gallivanting. Tell 'em to go gallivanting and they'll huddle together like sheep.

Q. rounded every one up again.

"Do you want to get this murder cleared up before the police arrive, or don't you?" he asked. He sounded like a school-marm.

They said they wanted it cleared up before the police arrived, and at least four of them meant it, you bet. They were: Statts, the two Dukes-Duchene women, and Margot, who was looking pretty well sunk.

The other servants didn't count. You could see at a glance they didn't have anything to do with it. One was fat—the cook. One was skinny—the housekeeper. The half-dozen others were just nit-wits, maids, footmen and kitchen helpers.

I gave them the once-over and wiped them from my mind.

Q. did the same. I could tell by the way he ran his eyes over them and asked them, all in a lump, if they had seen anything. If they'd heard anything. If they knew anything.

The answer was: "No, sir," and "No, sir," and "No, sir," right down the line, until he got to a kitchen girl, a stupid-looking hunk, who'd been downstairs in the hall back of the pantry a little after midnight.

She said she'd gone to get some soda for a stomachache. Maybe she had. She blattered about seeing the ghost of a man without a head. It was carrying its head under its arm, she said, and it went up the backstairs.

"A tall, skinny ghost," she whispered. "I knew it was a spook because it didn't make airy a sound. No sound at all!"

Q. didn't ask any more. He knew, and I knew, what she had seen was Q. himself going up the back stairs with his kit of tools under his arm.

He told the servants they could go to their rooms and stay there until the police arrived.

Clucking like a lot of chickens, they scurried off in all directions.

Margot was leaving with them, but he called her back. She gave me a dirty look.

I edged her over in a corner and said:

"Look here, sugar. You don't need to worry. You couldn't have bumped him off. You were with me all evening."

She looked up at me, her eyes getting bigger and blacker. *"Comment?"*

"Sure you were. Don't you remember? We stayed right there in that hall, close together" (and how!) "until that quarantine business. After you got through putting Duchene to bed, you came downstairs and joined me in that spot off the conservatory. We were there when we heard the shooting outside."

She waited a minute, considering. Then she nodded and smiled. Her teeth flashed between her lips, which were plenty red.

"Zat is true!" she said. *"Absolutement!* 'Ow could I forget? We are in ze hall togezzer, you and I . . ."

I winked.

"Sure we were. And if somebody asks did we notice anybody in the conservatory, we didn't. We were too busy, see?"

"Mooch too busy." She winked back. "Jésus-Marie, I weel say we were!"

So that was O.K. Margot wasn't sore, and I had an alibi. Both of us had alibis. Maybe not so hot, but they'd do in a pinch.

Q. was finishing with the women when I got back. He wasn't much on detective stuff, the kind you read in books, but he did jot down on a piece of paper what each of them claimed they were doing between ten and one o'clock.

The Doctor fixed Welch's death somewhere around midnight.

Q. put it later. About twelve-fifteen, because it was twelve-thirty when he walked in on the body. The wound was still bleeding, the kind of blood you only get right after death.

The Statts woman said she'd played bridge until almost twelve, then gone up to bed. Said she couldn't sleep, so dressed in her tweeds to take a little walk around the grounds. That explained her outfit, of course. But it was a lie. I knew because of what I'd heard when she was jawing Creel in the conservatory.

The Duchene girl repeated what she'd already told—how she'd gone upstairs at eleven, let Margot help her into a negligée, then gone downstairs for a book. She'd seen Welch in his library, she said, stayed long enough to get the necklace, then gone back upstairs again.

Her mother looked sick. I knew what was bothering the old girl. She was thinking she needn't have hidden that necklace in the bottom of the pool, since Lottie was telling about it anyway.

"Me?" she said when Q. turned to her. She acted surprised—like she wasn't the next in line. "You mean what did *I* do?"

Q. said: "That's just what I mean. You're closing the show."

She got red at that, because it's what she did in her old vaudeville days. She didn't know Q. was onto who she was. There hadn't been time for Lottie to tell her, so she stood with her mouth open, gasping like a fish out of water.

Q. waited, humming, absent-minded like, "Don't Splash Me"—the song she used to sing in bathing tights back in the days when a bathing suit that didn't have bloomers and a skirt was considered scandalous.

Then she knew the worst, and it didn't help her nerves any.

Q. said: "Don't hurry on my account. Take time enough to make it a good story."

That brought it all out with a rush.

"After we stopped playing bridge—around midnight—I went to bed," she told Q.

"In the same room with your daughter?"

"No. The next room. I'd been drinking some highballs, and I went right to sleep. I didn't wake up until those shots were fired and everybody began running downstairs. If you don't believe it—"

"Why shouldn't I believe it? Isn't it true?"

"Sure it's true!"

"Then it wasn't you who sent Frazier to call Welch out into the conservatory?"

"No!" she snapped. "Whoever says it was is a liar!"

That interested me. Did Q. know something? Or was he guessing? Either way, he was boring in on Pearl Dukes like he was a District Attorney cross-examining her.

He asked: "You're sure you didn't see Welch after he left the drawing-room and went to the library?"

"No! No!" She was screeching like a parrot. "How many times have I got to say it? And what business is it of yours, anyway? Who gave you the right to question us?"

"That's just what I was going to ask," Lottie Dukes said, not like she wanted to defend her mother but more as if she wanted to be nasty. "I can't see that you've any more right to ask questions than *I* have. Maybe not as much. For instance, where were *you* between eleven o'clock and one?"

Q. said: "I'm saving that for the police," and she shut up like a clam.

She remembered, I guess, that neither of them were in any too good shape for meeting the dicks. Her record was worse than Q.'s.

Q. didn't waste any time. He turned to Margot.

"What's *your* story?" he asked.

She gave it, like we'd worked it out. Told him she was with me until her mistress called, then put her to bed and came back to me again. Told him we'd sat in the hall at the side of the conservatory until almost one o'clock. We were there, she said, when we heard Politos shoot and Creel yell.

It was screwy, of course, but there was nobody to check on it. Anyway, it was as good an alibi as either of us could think up offhand.

Margot wasn't hardly through spilling it when Q. got into another fight with Lottie Dukes. It seemed as though they couldn't keep out of each other's hair, those two. If one thing didn't set 'em off another thing did—and usually it was both.

Q.'d ordered all the women upstairs to their rooms, and Lottie swore she wouldn't go. She was exactly like a kid that won't be sent to bed.

She said: "I intend to stay right here until the police arrive. I'm going to hear what you tell them."

"Well, I'm not!" her mother yawned. "The rest of you can do what you like but *I'm* going to find me a drink and go to bed. If the police want to see me they can come up to my room—one at a time."

"If the —s want to talk to me they can wait until morning," snapped the Statts woman.

Margot muttered something in French that meant the same thing, only more so.

They all left, except Lottie.

Pearl Dukes led the way, waddling along in her red kimono. She went toward the pantry, looking for a drink.

I waited a minute, until Q. gave me the eye. I guessed he wanted a chin with Lottie, so I lit out after Margot.

I found her in the butler's pantry with Pearl, who was encouraging Frazier to bring out some Three-Star Hennessy which he was cherishing like it was melted diamonds.

Most of the men were in the dining-room. I could hear Porter Creel's voice. He was talking, shrill and excited, to the Doctor.

Frazier seemed anxious to get in to them with the bottle, but Pearl hung on to him. At first I thought it was the Three-Star she was after, but I was wrong.

"Look here," she said, "I never sent you in to Welch to-night to get him out of the conservatory, *did* I?"

"No, madam," Frazier said, and blinked.

I couldn't tell whether he was lying or not.

"You know it wasn't me."

"No, madam."

"Well, you've got to tell 'em so."

"I beg pardon?"

"Listen, you've got to tell 'em who it was sent you."

He didn't say anything to that, just stood there with his frozen-butler face.

I took a hand.

"You might as well come across," I said. "We know the pipes weren't busted. Somebody told you to use that gag for an excuse to get Welch out of the library. Am I right?"

He blinked again. It looked as though he wasn't going to answer, but after awhile, he nodded.

"Yes," he said. "You are right."

"Who was it sent you?"

He wasn't in any hurry about answering that either. I remembered the greenbacks I'd seen pressed into his hand. I guessed they were holding him back.

I said: "Listen, you don't need to tell us. We know it was Creel."

Just then two sirens began screaming way off in the woods. Coming in the night like that, they sounded creepy, even though we knew it was just the police.

Frazier decided to come clean. He had his money and Creel couldn't get it away from him. I could fairly see him figure it out.

"Yes," he said. "It was Mr. Creel sent me. He paid me to get Mr. Welch out of the library. Then he gave me some more to keep still about it."

I didn't wait to hear the rest, just beat it back to Q. on the run. I wanted to get the information to him before the dicks landed on us. But I didn't get a chance, because I found him up to his neck in a row with Roger Storey.

Q. wasn't taking it very seriously.

Lottie Dukes was sitting, cold and scornful, on the arm of a chair, watching what was going on.

Young Storey was jumping up and down like a turkey cock. He was calling Q. names he could have been shot for. I gathered he thought Q. had been insulting his fiancée.

He said: "You talked to her like a bu-bu-blackguard! You —!" He told Q. that Miss Duchene was a "l-l-lady," which must have been news to Q. and to Lottie, too.

All this time the police sirens were coming nearer and nearer.

Lottie was getting whiter and whiter around the gills, while Q. grinned at her like a hyena.

The cars reached the house. We heard the slam of the doors as the dicks piled out.

"I know she's a lady," Q. said to Roger Storey. "You don't need to tell *me*. You'd better save that line for the police."

"What do you mean?"

Q. winked at him.

"They're the babies who may need convincing."

"You dirty son of a—" Lottie started, then rang off, like she'd suddenly remembered she was a lady and had better stick to it.

Somebody began pounding on the front door with the metal knocker.

We all started for the hall, where Frazier was admitting the dicks. Q. was ahead of us. Before Lottie could get in a word he had welcomed them grandly, like he was master of the place.

"This way," he said. "Right this way, Sheriff. The body is in here."

While they were crossing the hall toward the library he gave orders to Frazier, over his shoulder.

"Get the gentlemen some Scotch. Better make some coffee and sandwiches, too. We've a lot of work ahead."

He turned back to the police.

"You'll notice I've had the library door locked, so that no one could get into the room."

The last thing I saw as we left the hall was Lottie Dukes. She was biting her lips and twisting her hands, like she wanted to choke him.

But that was Q.—getting the jump on the dicks like he'd got the jump on every one else. When he said "we" it meant him and the police against all the rest of the house. He's a smart baby, and no mistake. I was proud of him.

Only, I didn't like the look that girl threw after him. I didn't like it at all.

10

There were just three dicks who really counted. The others were roust-a-bouts they'd picked up to drive the car and take care of the body.

Sheriff Milpotts was a slab-sided down-easter. His hair needed cutting and his clothes looked as if they'd been made for McKinley's funeral. He breathed slow and heavy, like a horse. When he wasn't chewing a straw he was munching a toothpick.

Handy was round and fat. It didn't take long for me to see the Sheriff used him like a wall to throw ideas against. If they were good they bounced back. If they were punk they fell with a thud. About the only words he knew were "Un-huh" and "Huh-nh." But he was the world's champion long-distance listener.

The third fellow was named Bill. I never did learn his last name. They just yelled "Hey" or "Bill" or "C'mere" and he came. I suppose he was a deputy. He had red hair and a cast in one eye. The back of his neck was sunburned, where it wasn't freckled, and he was always looking for a good place to spit.

They were just three hicks. Nothing to be afraid of, you'd say, for a guy like Q., who'd given New York dicks the run-around and put Scotland Yard on its ear.

But there was something I didn't like about that granite-faced down-easter. It was the way his teeth closed on whatever he was chewing. Or the nasty way his eyes bored into you while he talked to some one else. It made you feel like he was doing two things at once, and doing 'em both better than was healthy. I guessed right away he wasn't anybody's fool. I didn't make any mistake, either.

If Q. felt the same, nobody could know it. He was friendly and helpful as a bird-dog in quail season.

He showed Milpotts the library, the strong room, and the body. He held a light while the Sheriff looked down into the vault, and told him about how the murder had been discovered by Frazier, and all about the Borgia Blade. When I say "all" I mean all it was safe for him to know.

The police surgeon was also the coroner. He ran the hospital and was the only doctor in town.

Some woman in the village was having twins so they couldn't bring him along, but after Milpotts had taken a look into the strong room he seemed willing to take Dr. Jaffee's word for it that Welch had died from having his throat cut.

The Sheriff shambled around and poked into things, asking questions while he walked.

Q. answered them all—snappy and businesslike.

Milpotts took Q.'s notes on the women's testimony for a starter, but he called the men in and gave them the once-over himself.

I got in on it because I was the only one who could take shorthand. I picked it up in Auburn on. Q.'s advice, last time I did a stretch. It's come in handy more than once, letting me in on stuff I'd otherwise have missed. Like now.

"Bring 'em in one at a time," Milpotts said. "We'll start with the fellow who found the body."

That was Frazier.

He didn't have much to tell. Just that he'd last seen Mr. Welch about midnight, when he'd been sent for to bring some charged water.

"Was he alone?" Milpotts asked.

"No, sir. Dr. Jaffee was with him when I came in. But he left soon after."

"What was Mr. Welch doing?"

"Sitting at his desk, sir. Reading a document. Something legal-looking, it was. Something with printing."

"Is this it?" Milpotts held up the will we'd seen in the strongroom.

"Yes, sir."

"Did he say anything about it?"

Frazier shook his head.

"No, sir. Just told me he was going to stay down awhile longer. He told me he'd close the strong room and turn out the lights when he went to bed."

"What lights were on?"

"The light on the desk, sir, if I remember correctly."

"The same as when you found the body?"

"Yes, sir."

"The light in the strong room was burnt out," Q. put in. "At least, it won't go on from the switch."

"Make a note of that," Milpotts said, and finished with the butler by asking him if Dr. Jaffee had said anything before he went upstairs.

"Nothing in particular. Mr. Welch had been having one of his spells, a sort of a heart attack, and Dr. Jaffee had given him some medicine. That's why they sent for the charged water. The Doctor wanted Mr. Welch to go to bed, but he wouldn't. He was stubborn like that sometimes. He got Dr. Jaffee to give up his apartment and live here, so as to watch out for his health, and then he wouldn't take his advice."

"Has Dr. Jaffee lived here long?"

"Several years. He and Mr. Welch were old friends."

"Anything about him in the will?" Q. asked.

The Sheriff took a slant at the paper.

"H'm . . . twenty thousand cash, and a collection of old watches. Not much, considering the amount he had to leave."

"Who gets the rest of it?"

"Some to the servants. Some to the Metropolitan Museum. Most of it to Roger Storey. He's the nephew, isn't he?"

"Yes, sir. But I think—", Frazier cut off short, like he'd changed his mind about saying anything. Milpotts cracked down on him.

"*What* do you think?"

"I was going to say, sir, I think perhaps Mr. Welch was planning to make another will. I got the idea from something he said."

"When was this?"

"Three—maybe four days ago. He and Mr. Roger weren't getting along so well."

Q. asked: "Do Dr. Jaffee and the boy get along?"

"Yes, sir." Frazier nodded. "Dr. Jaffee gets along with every one. Many's the time he's kept Mr. Welch and Mr. Roger from splitting up, if you'll pardon the expression."

That was all he let out, barring the fact he'd gone straight upstairs, after Welch had dismissed him, and shut himself in his room.

He was just getting ready for bed, he said, when the shots outside brought him downstairs.

What he had to say about the finding of the body didn't mean anything, because we all knew it anyway.

Milpotts called Dr. Jaffee next.

If I haven't said much about the Doctor before now it's because everything had been going too fast for me to get a good slant at him. Now, when he came in and sat down across from old Horse-face I thought I'd never seen a better-looking man. He was about as tall as Q. but much heavier. Not fat, you understand, built square and strong, with a close-cropped mustache, and hair that was just turning gray.

He was a nifty dresser, too—the kind that wears the best of everything, but doesn't look flashy. Q. said he ate and drank the same way.

We doped it out that the reason Welch liked him around was because he could appreciate good things. Everybody else seemed to like to have him around, too. I gathered that the house wasn't any too easy to live in and the Doctor kept things smoothed down—partly by kidding and partly by keeping Welch and Roger apart.

Usually he was full of fun, Frazier told me, always thinking up laughs for Welch. I wouldn't know about that, of course. I didn't see him until Welch was dead, and he was pretty well sunk.

But even then you could see by the wrinkles at the corners of his eyes that he was a hearty laugher.

He had only one thing to tell, and I got the idea he didn't want to tell it. He'd come in—like the butler said—to spend a few minutes with Welch before he went to bed.

"What time?" I asked, for the sake of the record.

He thought it was about midnight.

"Probably Mr. Creel can tell us," he said.

"Creel?" Milpotts began to sit up and take notice.

The Doctor repeated: "Creel. They were having an argument when I went into the room. Nothing serious. Just about a watch that Mr. Creel insisted Mr. Welch had stolen from him."

Milpotts said: *"What?"* And Handy choked on his quid.

But neither of them saw Q. and me look at each other. Then we weren't the first that Welch had propositioned to do dirty work! He'd had stuff lifted before.

The Doctor didn't seem to notice anything. He went on, slow and thoughtful:

"It's not an ordinary watch. It's an antique. Very valuable. I don't like to tell you this, but I suppose I must. Neither Mr. Welch nor Mr. Creel had any right to it. It's reputed to have belonged to Napoleon, and if it's genuine it must have been stolen from a museum in Paris."

It had been. Le Coq showed it to us when Q. and I were on the continent, in '26. He wanted to turn the museum stuff over to Q. but Q. told him to sell it straight to collectors. He'd make more that way, with less chance of getting nabbed. The bulls might be watching a fence, but the collectors were mostly too rich for any one to put the works on.

I saw, now, that Le Coq had taken Q.'s advice. He must have sold Creel the watch before he pulled the fast one with the three Medici buttons.

Milpotts chewed some on a match he'd whittled down for a toothpick.

"You mean somebody stole the thing from Creel?" he asked.

"That's what he claimed." The Doctor nodded. "He thought Vincent—I mean, Mr. Welch—had put some one up to it."

"What made him think that?"

The Doctor squirmed, and his voice sounded regretful. He said:

"I suppose it was because Mr. Welch wasn't always particular about how he came into possession of the items in his collection. No real collector is." He smiled, in a nice kind of way. "We're all a bit balmy."

"You collect, too?"

"Some. Mostly clocks and watches. Of course, I can't begin to afford real treasures, like Mr. Welch and Creel."

I thought about that line in the will giving him the collection. Q. must have been thinking of the same thing. And Milpotts. But none of us blinked an eye.

Milpotts asked a few more questions about what Creel had done after the Doctor came into the room.

"Not much," Jaffee said. "Vincent worked himself into such a rage that he had a heart attack."

Q. sat forward.

"The butler told us about that. Did he have them often?"

"Not very. Once every few months. Usually they came when he was emotionally upset."

Q. didn't ask anything more, but Milpotts wanted to know what had happened after Welch had his attack and Creel left the room.

The Doctor said: "Vincent felt better, and insisted on going upstairs and getting into a dressing gown. I tried to persuade him to go to bed, but he refused to listen to me. He said he had some business he wanted to attend to before he turned in. I talked with him for a minute or two after he came back from upstairs. Then Frazier came in with Vichy water and I left."

"Did you go to bed?"

"No. The cook was hysterical and I went up to quiet her. I stayed in her room for about three-quarters of an hour."

"What made her hysterical?" Q. wanted to know.

"Nothing of importance. Just a servant's quarrel—a row with one of the housemaids. I gave her a bromide, and while I was waiting for it to take effect I heard the shots and a yell from outside. I was called to dress Mr. Creel's shoulder and," he shrugged his shoulders, "you know the rest."

That settled the Doctor. Milpotts sent for Creel.

He was looking green from losing so much blood. It hadn't improved his temper any, either. To begin with, he was sore as a boiled owl at missing the Silo sale. To hear him squawk, you'd think Welch had got himself bumped off just to keep him from getting some antique he wanted to bid on.

Prying information out of that bird was about as easy as drawing teeth from a mule. And just as profitable.

Looking over my notes, and boiling them down some, I can see that Q. and Milpotts, between them, dragged out the news that he'd come in to talk to Welch about breaking through the quarantine and getting home that night. This was a little before twelve. How much before he couldn't say.

What he *did* say was a lot of cuss words.

Welch wasn't there when he first went to the library. Out in the conservatory somewhere, he thought. But pretty soon he came in, and the two got to talking.

He admitted the talk was plenty hot, what with Welch's refusing to help him get away. One thing led to another, until they got to jawing over the watch.

He wouldn't have told us all this himself, you bet. But Milpotts took Dr. Jaffee's tip and used it on the old boy like you'd use a can-opener on a can of sardines. Told him he knew about the Napoleon watch and that the two had been rowing.

In the end, he had Creel squealing with rage.

"He got that watch! He put some one up to stealing it! Don't tell me he didn't! I've talked to those who've seen it. He showed it to every one! The—"

There is a blank here. I didn't bother to put down in my notes what he called Welch, but I remember it was something smelly.

Q. asked: "How'd you get the watch in the first place?" sweet and sympathetic, and that stopped Creel short.

He couldn't just remember where he'd got it. From some dealer in Europe. He'd have to look it up.

"Dealer named Le Coq?" Q. asked.

After that, Creel was eating out of his hand. There wasn't anything he wouldn't tell us. Only, he didn't know much. The Doctor had broken in on their argument. Welch had pulled that heart attack, and Creel had gone upstairs to get ready for his disappearing act. Or so he said. He'd no intention of spending the night in that house, not by a damn sight! Of course, he never dreamed there'd be a Greek with a gun at the gate, and willing to use it.

"How about Mrs. Statts?" Q. wanted to know. "Why didn't you pick her up the way you promised?"

Creel actually winked. He put his finger on his nose, which was long and sharp.

"I should help her get away! *Yes,* I should—with that auction to-morrow! Can you imagine the nerve of the she-goat—asking me to help her get to town, so she could bid against me?"

Knowing the Statts woman, I could imagine it. And, knowing Creel, it was just as easy to figure him leaving her waiting out in the cold while he went tootling off. Which is what the old buzzard would have done if Politos hadn't got busy with his rod.

That cleaned up Creel. We went back to the question of what Welch was doing in the conservatory a little before twelve.

"The butler called him out," Q. remembered. "He said something was wrong with the hot-water pipes in the conservatory.

"There wasn't anything wrong," I said. "Creel tipped Frazier to lie about it."

Milpotts took the match out of his mouth and looked at me like I'd told something he didn't know.

"Probably wanted him out of the room," he said slowly. "Maybe he thought he could locate that watch."

"Yeah—*maybe.*" Q. seemed to have something on his mind.

Whatever it was, he didn't get it out, because right then the Statts woman came into the room. Just sailed past the deputy with a wave of her hand.

"Police," she said to Milpotts, glaring down at him, big and black-browed, like she was paying him off for something he'd done to her, "if you're the police, there are things you ought to know."

Milpotts slanted the chewed end of his match stick up at her.

"Such as?"

"That blonde woman! Duchene! The older one. She had a hell of a row with Welch to-night."

Q. sat up and looked interested.

He said: "What time?"

"Between eleven-forty-five and midnight."

"Where?"

"In the conservatory. She was dummy at bridge. When the hand was played, I went out to find her. They were having it hot and heavy—out there near the pool."

"Why are you so sure of the time?"

"Because I was dummy for the last hand. We stopped playing just before twelve."

Q. asked: "Who's *we?*"

"Dr. Jaffee. The Duchene woman. Me. Creel, part of the time. You, yourself, took his hand at the last."

"Yes." Q. turned to the Sheriff. "That's while Creel was in the library with Welch."

"Was *that* where he was?" Mrs. Statts snapped. "What was he doing?"

"It doesn't matter," Milpotts told her. "Stick to your story about Mrs. Duchene. What were they rowing about?"

"How should I know? I didn't listen. They stopped the minute I came in. She went back to the bridge table."

Q. asked: "How about you?"

"I stayed and said a few words to Mr. Welch."

"Such as?"

"Such as: 'You've had good luck with your plants this year' and 'How *do* you manage to raise such orchids?'"

"Nothing else?"

"Nothing else." She shut her jaw like it was a rat trap.

Q. and Milpotts both saw they wouldn't get any more out of the old girl. All of which meant there wasn't much more to be learned, because we knew what had happened earlier, before Welch was called into the conservatory by the butler. Lottie Dukes had told us. She'd been in the library with him, getting the necklace, and, before that, there'd been the talk with Roger Storey.

It all hitched up with the testimony Q.'d taken from the women, and fixed everything ship-shape back to dinner.

Milpotts didn't seem to want to go earlier than that. I gathered he wasn't any crazier about straight detection stuff than we were. He'd his mind made up pretty clear by then. Although he didn't say much, I guessed he was splitting the difference between Creel and Roger Storey. Anyway, he went off to do some sleuthing on his own, while Q. and I went upstairs.

The door to Q.'s room was unlocked.

Lottie Dukes was sitting beside the fire. Q.'s dinner coat, the one I'd washed the blood stains out of, was lying across her lap.

11

Q. asked: "So what?" Short. Snappy. Defiant. Like he saw there was no use trying to stall.

The coat hadn't had time to dry. Lottie Dukes must have guessed right off that we had been washing out stains.

"So *you* did it!" she said.

Q. pulled his lips back in a kind of smile.

"Maybe I spilled wine on my coat."

"Or butter. Or marmalade. Don't be a clown! I suppose you were cleaning him out and he caught you."

"You can suppose anything you like," Q. said. "There's no law against it. Have a drink?"

She would, and did. Q. had one. I had two. I needed them.

Q. asked her: "What are you going to do?"

"What have you already done? Laid the blame on me?"

Q. said: "I haven't laid it on any one."

"That's likely, isn't it?"

"Likely or not, it's the truth."

She looked at him for a minute. You could see she was trying to dope out what he was thinking.

"Why should you suck around the police," she wanted to know, "if you weren't trying to frame some one?"

"I might be trying to find out who did the murder."

She didn't say anything to that, just turned and looked at his coat.

Q. laughed.

"There's that. I'm not going to try to explain it. You wouldn't believe me."

"How well you know me," she said.

"Better than you think."

She lifted her eyebrows.

"You really want to believe I didn't do it," Q. went on, "only, you're afraid to."

"Why?"

"Because if I didn't, some one else must have done it."

"Of course."

"And it might be some one who would upset your plans."

She put down her glass so hard it splashed over. "You mean Roger?"

"Roger—or your mother."

That was a new idea to her, I could tell by the way she screwed up her forehead.

"My mother? Why would she—"

"You tell *me*. She had a row with Welch early in the evening. Statts caught them at it, in the conservatory, after you'd gone to bed."

That brought the hot-water bottle back to my mind. I'd remembered it once or twice during the evening, but things had been moving too fast for me to do anything. While the girl was arguing that the Statts woman was crazy, or drunk, or both, I crashed in with:

"After the old boy was dead I saw your mother hide something."

"Where?"

"In the pool—a hot-water bottle."

"A hot *what?*"

"Is it a gag?" Q. asked.

I told him no. I'd seen her just like I said. Also, what I'd done with the bottle.

"Why didn't you tell me?" Q. snapped.

"When?" I wanted to know. "In front of the coppers?"

There wasn't anything he could say to that.

The girl was repeating: "A hot-water bottle. A *hot-water bottle!* But why in the name of—"

"It's clear enough," Q. told her. "You use a bottle to keep water in, don't you?"

"Yes, but—"

"It works the other way around, doesn't it? You can use it to keep water from getting in."

"I—"

He nodded to me.

"Go get it," he said. Then to the girl: "She's hidden something in it. Do you know what it is?"

"No—yes—she couldn't be such a fool. . . ."

That's the last I heard until I got back with the bottle under my coat. It was right where I'd hid it; but I had a little trouble getting it, because some one was in the conservatory when I got there, romping around in the dark.

Once I thought I heard a kind of a splash, but it might have been one of the big gold fish. I didn't see any one except Bill, the deputy, sitting on the other side of the plate-glass window, with a bottle of beer and a chicken leg. It made me think of something, and I went back through the pass pantry where there was still part of a bottle of Scotch.

When I got upstairs, Q. and Lottie were scrapping again.

"—trying to frame mother to get out of it yourself," she was saying as I came into the room.

Q. said: "Some people go looking for trouble. Have another drink?"

She said she would. He gave it to her. I took one, too.

We unscrewed the hot-water bottle. Q. pulled out the necklace, then he dumped out the knife. Last, he reached in and got hold of three letters that had been rolled around the ivory handle.

First I thought Lottie Dukes was going to faint, then I thought she was going to have apoplexy. She turned white. She turned red.

"The fool!" she said. "The brainless cow!"

Suddenly she came to herself and made a grab for the letters, but Q. got them first. He held them to the light. I looked over his shoulder.

There were three letters, all to Pearl Dukes, all signed by Welch, all hot stuff. The kind of mush and goo that would look like hell in print, I mean newspaper print.

Q. read them and laughed.

"Pretty fair. Didn't know the old boy had it in him! How much was she asking for the lot?"

Lottie was looking sulky.

"How should I know? It was her game, not mine. I thought I'd called her off. She must have sneaked around behind my back."

Q. said: "Start at the beginning."

"Beginning of what?"

"How come she met him? When and where?"

"Name three good reasons why I should tell you."

"I can't name one—unless you think you may need help."

"You'd be likely to help me, wouldn't you?"

"Well—if you know a better 'ole go to it."

She took a long swallow, and looked at him over the top of her glass.

"I wish I knew—" she began, then settled back in her chair. "Oh, I might as well. . . . Mom knew Welch years ago. Out West somewhere. When she and Pop were playing small time."

"They never played anything else but."

"They *did*," she began, then laughed. "What difference does it make? Anyway, she met him out there. She cheated on Pop, I guess. But, then, that was nothing new. He did the same on her. She got a near-sealskin coat, some almost-diamonds and those letters, before she had to move on with the show. She hung on to the letters and, last summer, when we were in Cannes, she read somewhere about the way Welch had made money and was chucking it around. At that time he was buying antiques in Italy, whole churches at a crack. She hauled these letters out and showed 'em to me. I didn't think much of the idea, but she was dead set on trying it, so I came along to keep her out of trouble."

Q. asked: "How'd she get in touch with Welch?"

"We fixed it so we came back on the same boat. He didn't know she still had the letters, and was nice enough at first. Roger was with him. . . ."

"And fell for you," Q. put in.

She shrugged.

"Yes. After that the letters didn't matter."

"I can see why."

"I thought Mom had sense enough to lay off. She *would* gum the works for a few thousand. I suppose she thought she could pull it off without my knowing."

"But all this doesn't explain the knife."

"That?" She didn't seem worried. "That's just a fool thing Mom picked up in Paris. She'd a crazy idea some one might attack her. I wouldn't let her carry a gun, so she carried that in her bag. Used to put it under her pillow at night."

"Not a bad idea." Q. tried the blade with his thumb. "It's sharp enough to slit a throat."

She jumped and glared.

"You're not trying to pull *that*?"

"I still don't know why it was in that hot-water bottle."

"That's easy. Mom didn't want it found in her things, in case the police did some searching. The letters, too. Any fool can see why she wanted to get rid of them. They might drag her into the case."

"Then why didn't she burn them? Or tear them up and run them down the toilet? She couldn't use them after Welch was dead."

"I don't know." She meant it, too. You could see that by the kind of helpless look she had on her face. "They wouldn't be any use now, would they?"

"Unless—" Q. had an idea. You could feel him pulling it out of the air a bit at a time. "Wait a minute. Let me see." He picked up the letters and shuffled them. "They're not dated. You don't suppose she was hoping to claim you were his daughter?"

"That's a crazy idea."

"Sure it's crazy . . . but it's been done. Look at that case in San Francisco."

"But I was two or three years old when she met Welch."

Q. said: "How can you tell what was in her mind?"

"Maybe that's the reason she bumped him off," I said, and took what was left in the bottle.

"She didn't!" The girl flared up like we'd set her afire. "Just try that on the police, Q. Silver, and I'll tell them your right name! They'll have lots of fun with the stains on your coat."

"And if I don't?" Q. asked.

She didn't say anything for a minute, just frowned like she was thinking things out. After awhile she said:

"I'll keep my mouth shut, as long as you do. Is it a bargain?"

Q. gave her a chance to get nervous while he blew smoke out of his nose.

"Is it a bargain?" she asked again, and he nodded.

"All right. You can count on me."

Lottie got out of her chair. She picked the hot-water bottle and the knife off the table like they didn't really mean anything and she was just tidying up.

"I'll take these," she said, "and the letters."

"You're wrong," Q. said. "They stay with my coat."

The girl opened her mouth, but she didn't have time to say anything, because just then her mother galloped in. She was breathing through her mouth and her face was mottled, red and white, like an Easter egg that hasn't been dyed right.

"Get to hell out of here!" she yelled at Lottie. "And get out quick!" She glared at Q., who was standing with the letters in his hand, then turned on Lottie again. "I just told the police who *he* is. They're coming to arrest him!"

12

Q. said: "Well, that's that!" and sat down on the edge of the bed.

Lottie said: "You fool! You God-damned fool!" And when her mother tried to argue she told her to shut up.

Pearl got mad. Then she began to whimper.

Q. told me to go down and try my luck at getting another bottle of White Horse.

"I guess I know what I'm doing," Pearl Dukes was saying when I left the room. "I had my reasons."

I didn't need to stay and listen. I knew what her reasons were. She was the one I'd heard in the conservatory when I went down earlier. She'd been looking for the hot-water bottle, and she'd seen me carry it upstairs. She'd figured Q. would take the stuff straight to the police, and she'd tried to beat him to it.

She was still sniffing when I got back. When Q. poured her a drink, she grabbed it like it was a lifeline and she was drowning.

"I did it for you," she told her daughter. "And all the thanks I get is a cussing out. How could I know he wasn't going to squeal to the police?"

"I'd have handled it!" Lottie was mad clear through, so mad her hands were shaking. "Haven't I always handled everything? But you wouldn't keep out of it. No! You had to go spill your guts to the dicks. And all because you double-crossed me with those damned letters!"

"You wouldn't give me any money."

Lottie cracked back with: "You know why!"

Her mother didn't say anything to that. She stopped sniffling and looked squint-eyed at the letters in Q.'s hand. She seemed to be thinking about something.

"Well," she said, "we can talk that over to-morrow. You'd better come out of this room and go to bed."

She was moving toward the door as she talked. Suddenly she made a grab for the letters. She got them, too, and bolted for the grate.

Q. dived and caught the back of her kimono. It came off in his hand, leaving her in a thin pink nightie, but that didn't stop her.

She'd have thrown the letters into the fire if I hadn't skipped around the table and caught her wrist.

I had lots of chance to be sorry. She fought like ten wild cats, and Q. wouldn't help me. He just stood there laughing, with his drink in one hand and the red kimono in the other.

Pearl was yelling: "Let me go, you louse! You dirty son-of-a—" Then she broke off short and began to scream: "Help! Help! Sheriff!"

I saw the door was opening. The Sheriff came in with Handy.

The Dukes woman stopped wrestling with me. She went over and draped herself on Milpotts.

"Thank God!" she said. "Thank God you came!" She hung on to him with one arm and tried to stuff the letters down the front of her nightie with her free hand. But she didn't get far, because the thing she had on was thin as tissue paper.

The Sheriff said: "Let go of me," and pushed her off.

Lottie grabbed the red kimono from Q. and threw it around her mother,

Feeling I was going to need it, I poured myself another drink.

Milpotts saw what I was doing. He took the glass with the hand that wasn't holding a toothpick and drank the stuff himself. He was blushing bright red and trying not to look at the old hell-cat, who was talking and sniffling, and trying to get her hands in the armholes of her kimono all at the same time.

"He threatened me!" she told Milpotts. "Both of them threatened me, because I told you who they were. If you hadn't come in I don't know what might have happened. He's a dangerous criminal, Sheriff," she said, pointing at me. "Both of 'em are dangerous criminals."

She had the kimono on now and was squirming around trying to get close to the table.

I saw what she was after. I picked up the tray of glasses and put it down on top of the ivory-handled knife.

Milpotts didn't pay any attention to us. He was looking at Q.

"How about it?" he asked.

Q. didn't answer, just looked back at him with his eyebrows up high.

Milpotts pointed at Pearl Dukes with his toothpick.

"She says you aren't Bleigh, you're a crook named Q. Silver. Is she telling the truth?"

The Dukes woman broke in.

"What's the use of asking him? He'll deny it. He's Silver, all right. My daughter and I saw him on the Riviera when we were—"

"When you were what?" Q. asked, and she skipped a breath.

"When we were *visiting*. All you have to do is cable the Paris police. They'll give you an earful. He came with letters to Mr. Welch. I'll bet dollars to doughnuts they're phony! He came here to steal, Welch caught him red hand-ed, and he bumped him off!" She was sure anxious to get us in bad, the old so-and-so, talking faster and faster, higher and higher, like she had to get the words out before they choked her.

Milpotts held up his hand. He was still looking at Q.

"What have you got to say?" he asked.

"Not a word." Q.'s face didn't show anything. He was looking big and blank and like a wooden Indian. "I'm lis-tening, not talking."

Pearl Dukes went on:

"I tell you he killed Welch! That was his knife you found on the floor! He's the only one could have done it! The only one who had any reason!" She moved quick, and the letters crackled in the front of her nightgown. "Isn't he, daughter? *Isn't he?*"

If I'd had time to be sorry for anyone else but my-self I'd have been sorry for Lottie Dukes. Plain as day, I could see what she was thinking. If she said "Yes" Q., like enough, would tell her right name. If she said "No," they might find out who she was anyway, and she'd lose her chance to throw the blame on us. That much was clear. If I'd known all she was thinking I'd have understood even better. I'd have understood why she finally made up her mind to throw us to the wolves.

"Yes. It was his knife, and he's Q. Silver," she told Mil-potts.

I started pussy-footing toward the door. The windows were no good, because there was a drop of a hundred feet to the river. I found the door wasn't any good either, be-cause Handy was there.

Q. was standing near his suit-case. He reached into the pocket of the lid. I guess Milpotts thought he was reach-ing for a gun.

He said: "Drop that!"

But Q. brought out a leather folder.

"You might take a look at this," he said, and tossed it to the Sheriff.

Milpotts looked at it, then at Q., who winked one eye and went toward the dressing-room. The Sheriff followed, and, after staring a minute, Handy went, too.

The door closed after the three of them.

Pearl Dukes said: "Well, for God's sake, can you tie that?" and reached for the bottle. But I got it first.

Lottie didn't say anything. She was tiptoeing over to the dressing-room door, trying to hear what was going on inside.

The look on her face made me begin to feel better. That and the drink.

She took two jumps from the door, just before it opened.

Milpotts came out, looking about the same as usual, only he was chewing his toothpick a lot faster.

Handy was goggle-eyed.

He kept saying: "Well, well, well!"

Q. said: "I'm here on the quiet, you understand."

The two dicks nodded and looked solemn.

"I understand," the Sheriff told him, and handed back the leather folder.

I didn't need to look at it to know what was in it. At that house-party, where Q.'d won the money from the guy with the apartment in New York, there'd been a fellow from Scotland Yard. Not an Englishman either. An American they used for cases on this side. Pyle his name was. Henry Pyle. His room was robbed one day while he was out swimming. When he got back his studs were gone, along with his watch, his passport, and his identification papers.

There'd been a lot of rumpus at the time. Q. got considerable fun out of it. He also got the papers.

He put the folder back into the suit-case and winked at the sheriff again.

"Not a word to any one," he said.

The sheriff winked back.

"Not a word."

"Aren't you going to arrest him?" Pearl Dukes squealed.

Milpotts didn't say anything to that. Just grunted sort of disgustedly and started for the hall door, but Q. took Pearl's arm and grinned over her head at Lottie.

"You'd better put your mother to bed," he said. "She's had a bit too much to drink. What she needs is a good long sleep." He turned. "Before you go, Mrs. Duchene, I'll just relieve you of these."

Pearl Dukes made a clutch at the front of her kimono with one hand and slapped him across the face with the other, but when Q. straightened up he was holding three letters.

Milpotts was gone by now, and Handy with him.

Lottie Dukes looked at Q. like she was looking at a rattlesnake ready to strike.

"What are we to do now?" she asked.

Q. picked up the water bottle and the knife. He put them in his suit-case along with the letters and his folder. The necklace he handed back to Lottie.

"I don't know what *you're* going to do, but I'm going to sleep," he said.

13

He meant it, too. Funny thing about Q., he can drop off
to sleep standing up in the middle of a boiler factory, and
he wakes just as easy as he drops off, with his brain all
clear. Not foggy and thick like most.

I wanted to sit up and talk. He said no. Milpotts and
Handy had gone to take the body to town but they'd be
back in a few hours. We'd better get a rest while we could.

Q. slid into bed.

I stretched out on the couch in his dressing-room.

I didn't sleep much. Just lay and went over and over
things in my mind. I'd a lot to think about, and none of
it made much sense.

The more I chewed on it the dizzier I got, until, finally, everything went black and I fell into a nightmare
where Creel was chasing me around the conservatory while
Mrs. Statts and Pearl Dukes threw orchids that turned into
green and yellow snakes when they hit me. Margot came
up with a big hot-water bottle and we both climbed inside
and held 'em off with the Borgia Blade until all the clocks
in Welch's collection began to strike at once. Then the
hot-water bottle blew up and landed us in the pool.

I woke up and found Q., slapping my face with a dripping wash-rag.

"Wake up," he said. "It's seven o'clock and Milpotts is going to want those notes of yours."

The only typewriter in the house was in Welch's library. Bill was guarding the door, but he let us in. While I pounded the machine, Q. walked around the room, looking at this and that. Part of the time he spent in the strong room. Then he went into the conservatory, and came back almost immediately. He sat down in front of the fire Bill had made and began to smoke. He was still sitting there when Milpotts came in with Handy.

Milpotts was looking some brighter than he had the night before. He wasn't chewing a match or a toothpick this time, but a witch-hazel twig he'd cut off a bush outside.

"Had any ideas?" he asked Q.

"Nothing to brag about."

"H'm."

"But there's some stuff we might talk over. First we'd better run through these notes."

I gave Milpotts a carbon copy, and a third carbon to Handy. It never does any harm to make small-timers think you believe they're somebody with a capital S.

Right away he swelled up like a frog. Then he pulled a pair of nickel-rimmed spectacles out of his pocket, took out a big blue pencil and sat frowning while Q. looked through the typewritten pages.

"There's lots of stuff we still don't know about," Q. said. "But this is a starter. It will give us some idea of what went on last night."

I had put the time out in the margin like a train schedule. Q. read it out loud:

"7:30 to 8:30 Dinner

"8:30 to 10 Every one looking at collection in
    Welch's library. Visiting. Walking through
    the conservatory, etc.

"10 House notified of quarantine."

"I meant to speak about that," Milpotts said. "The fellow didn't have smallpox."

Q. said: "No?" To look at him you wouldn't guess he'd heard it before.

"No," the Sheriff explained, like he was pleased to be able to tell us something we didn't know. "Dr. Ascher—he's the health officer—says it was just chickenpox, but Welch offered him a hundred dollars to say it was smallpox. Some sort of a joke he was playing on his guests."

Even Q. looked surprised.

"You mean the Doctor admitted it?"

"Sure." Milpotts chuckled and spit out some witch-hazel bark. "If you knew the Doc you'd understand. He's always trying to get money for some of his charities, and Welch never'd come through with a dime. He didn't see any harm in it, and he was in a hundred dollars."

Q. didn't say anything to that—just went on reading:

"10:30 to just before midnight The Doctor,
      Mrs. Duchene, Mrs. Statts, and Creel played
      bridge in the drawing-room. Welch left."

"Where'd he go?"

"Places. Part of the time he was with Miss Duchene in the conservatory."

"Duchene's the good-looker?"

"Yes; it was her mother who tried to turn me in last night." Q. grinned.

Milpotts grinned back, and Handy laughed, like he felt it was his duty.

"She's engaged to Roger Storey," Q. explained, and I saw he wasn't going to give Lottie away, at least not yet. "She went to bed early. Around eleven. With a headache."

"But I see by the notes, here, that she came downstairs again," Milpotts said.

Q. nodded.

"About eleven-thirty. She came down the private stairs over there. Welch had asked her to come. He wanted to give her something . . . a sapphire and diamond necklace."

"Whew!" Milpotts whistled. "What for?"

"*She* says it was an engagement present."

"It could have been."

"It could. Sometime between eleven and eleven-thirty, Welch had a talk with his nephew. Roger claims it was all sweet, and friendly. Nothing said about the will. And maybe he's a little George Washington. There's nobody to contradict him."

"No one heard them talking?"

"I can't find any one who did. Perhaps later . . ."

Milpotts nodded.

"Yeah. Things have a way of showing up."

Q. went on:

> "11:45 Miss Duchene went back to her room
>   with the necklace.
> "11:46 Frazier, the butler, called Welch out to
>   the conservatory to look at the steam pipes."

"What's the name Creel doing in parenthesis there?" Milpotts wanted to know.

"Creel bribed Frazier to call Welch out of the room. Remember?"

"I remember." Milpotts nodded. "So Creel could take a look for the Napoleon Watch. Welch came back and caught him. There was a row."

"Yes. But before then, while he was in the conservatory, Welch had a row with Mrs. Duchene. That's what the Statts woman told us. Maybe one with Statts as well."

"Busy evening," Milpotts said.

"Medium lively. But the old man was asking for it." Q. went back to the notes in his hand. "Duchene, Mrs. Statts, then Creel. After that, the Doctor. All of 'em around twelve. Something must have upset Welch by then, because Frazier says he was fooling with his will."

"Frazier was the last to see him alive?"

"So far as we know. But any one might have come downstairs after Frazier left. We know Creel and Mrs. Statts were somewhere about, getting ready to break quarantine. Roger and the Duchene girl may have been in bed, and, again, they may not—then there's always the Doctor and Mrs. Duchene."

Milpotts said: "You can have her. I'll take Creel."

"Why Creel?"

"I don't like the cut of his jib. Besides, we know they didn't get along. They were rowing earlier in the evening, and Creel was caught trying to escape."

"He wanted to go to an auction. Mrs. Statts was trying to get away, too." Q. pointed out. "She didn't like Welch any better than Creel did."

"What in thunder were they doing here, those two?"

"Search me. For that matter, you might ask what I was doing here."

"I was just getting around to that."

I'd been wondering what Q. was going to say when the Sheriff asked that question. Now, we were to have it. Q. was looking as cool as a cucumber, but the palms of my hands were sweaty.

"I'm here because Mr. Welch sent for me."

"The butler says you wrote Mr. Welch, something about a dagger—the one used in the killing."

So he had been checking on us in spite of those Scotland Yard credentials! Just like I'd feared, the old bird wasn't as dumb as he looked.

"That was a blind," Q. told him. "I did bring down the Blade for him to see, but what he really wanted was some help in a business way."

"You mean detecting?"

"I'm not sure. I've had dealings with most of the big museums abroad." (Q. never said a truer word.) "Welch probably wanted me to look up something for his collection."

"Frazier says you had a talk with the old man early in the evening."

"I did, but we were interrupted. He was to explain fully later on. That was how I happened to be the one to find him dead."

Milpotts jumped. He had nothing on me. My jaw dropped a foot and I nearly swallowed my upper plate.

"Yes," Q. said casually, "I found the body half an hour earlier than the butler did."

14

I thought Q. had gone nuts. The Sheriff looked like he thought so, too.

"If you found the body why didn't you report it at once?" he wanted to know.

Q. said, smooth as silk:

"I did try to call the police, but the phone was out of commission. So I decided to wait until the body was discovered by some one else, and, in the meantime, watch and try to catch the killer off his guard. Sorry I didn't tell you all this last night," he said, and you'd have sworn he *was* sorry, "but they'll tell you at Scotland Yard I'm a Lone Wolf. Like to work things out by myself. Of course, I'd no idea you fellows up here would be so intelligent. Now that I've had a chance to see you—"

Milpotts coughed, and threw what was left of the witch-hazel stick into the fire so he could use both hands to pull down his vest.

"I guess we'll be able to work together," he said. "I haven't always lived here in the backwoods. I used to be a deputy up in Bangor."

"I could tell you came from a big place," Q. said, serious and solemn. Then, in a low voice: "Is that some one in the shop?"

I moved over to the shop door. Handy moved with me. He managed to fall over a chair and drop his blue pencil on the way.

By the time I'd reached the door nobody was there. But a window was open on to the garden. It hadn't been open the night before. Maybe one of the servants had tried to air the place—and maybe they hadn't.

I came back and told Q. He was talking to Milpotts again and didn't seem interested.

"Welch had been dead about five minutes, when I found him," he was saying. "The blood was still running from the wound. I got some of it on my coat."

So that was why he had spilled the stuff about finding Welch! I began to see light, and kicked myself for not seeing it sooner. If the girl told about the stains on the coat, he had his alibi all ready.

I wanted to jump up and down and yell. I wanted to sing songs. It was those damn stains that had me down. And now he'd made it all right! At least it would be all right until Milpotts looked us up and found those Scotland Yard credentials were phony.

I decided I didn't want to sing after all.

"You're going to have a lot of trouble holding 'em all here," Q. said. "Creel has influence. So has Mrs. Statts." The Sheriff set his jaw. It was long and lean, with the same kind of lower lip a horse has.

"They'll do as I say. If Creel kicks too hard I'll clap him in jail as a suspect. He can yell his head off for bail if he wants to—the judge is my brother-in-law. I guess the rest of 'em won't put up any back talk if I tell 'em they can have their choice between staying here comfortably, or being held down in the jail as material witnesses."

"Will the District Attorney stand for it?"

"The D.A.'s away getting his appendix out. Handy, here, is the deputy."

We looked at Handy, who blushed, grinned, and scratched the stubble on his chin with the blue pencil.

"I took law onct," he said, like he was apologizing. "Anyway, we don't get many murder cases up this way."

I heard some one at the door and opened it. Frazier came into the room. He looked more like an undertaker than ever.

He told us breakfast was ready, and asked us would we like it served in there.

Q. and Milpotts both said we would.

Frazier came back a little later with another man and some trays. While they were bringing in the food, Q. and the Sheriff talked about dogs, and neuritis, and inflation, and what the hell Roosevelt was going to do about the strikes.

The other man had gone out, and Frazier was leaving when Q. stopped him.

"Just a minute," he said. "About the knife—"

"You mean the one you brought, sir?"

"I mean the one used to kill Welch. I left it in the library with him before dinner, when we were there looking at his collection. It was lying on his desk. Did you see it when you were in the room?"

"No, sir. But I saw it earlier. Right after dinner when I came in to look at the fire. Mr. Welch picked it up and showed it to me. He said it was hundreds of years old . . . and that nobody knew how many men it had killed. He said it had originally belonged to the Borgias, and they didn't think anything of polishing people off, if I may use the expression."

"You may," Q. said. "Anything else you can think of?"

"Not right off hand, sir. Except—"

"Yes?"

"When I left Mr. Welch, he was gathering up several things from his desk as though he meant to lock them in the strong room."

"What were the things?"

"That paper I spoke of, sir. The one that was made out in legal form."

"The will?"

"Yes, sir. He had that, and a watch."

"What kind of a watch?"

"An old one. Gold and enamel."

"Napoleon's watch!" I said.

Q. asked: "Did he have a clock, too?"

"Not at that time, sir, but he may have picked one up later. I didn't actually see him go into the strong room."

"The clock's in there now," Q. told Milpotts.

The Sheriff said: "Yes, I saw it. Smashed. Works all over the place."

Q. said: "Thank you, Frazier. We shan't want anything more for the present."

Frazier eased himself out. When the door closed behind him, Milpotts asked:

"What's the idea? Something on your mind?"

"No. But the less he hears the better."

"You don't mean you think—"

"Not necessarily. But he was the last person with Welch, except the murderer. You said something about bequests to the servants in that will, didn't you?"

"H'm . . . that's right. There was something for him. Ten thousand. I noticed particularly, because that's pretty big money. And a piece of property. A farm not far from here."

"Know anything about him?"

"Not much. They don't like him in the village. He's—"

"Tight as a spigot," Handy put in. "Grafts on all the tradesmen."

Q. swallowed a mouthful of coffee.

"Which may not mean a thing," he said. "If you're going by character, there isn't any one in the house you could pin a rose on."

"Except Miss Duchene," Milpotts said. "She seems a right nice young lady."

"Of course, I'd forgotten Miss Duchene." Q. grinned at me and I grinned at my buttered toast, remembering Lottie's language the night before.

There was a knock on the door. It opened.

A round-faced, round-bellied man, with pink cheeks and gray hair, stood on the threshold. He had pale blue blinking eyes and old-fashioned gold-rimmed spectacles. He was wearing a baggy gray suit that was thin at the knees and had ashes spilled down the vest. His tie was pulled out of place so it showed a big brass collar button. You liked him, and trusted him, the minute you saw him.

"Goot morning," he said, in a sort of thick German voice.

Milpotts's face broke into a grin.

"Morning, Doc." He beckoned with his fork. "Come on in. This is Dr. Ascher, the coroner," he explained to the rest of us. "Sit down and have a bite."

"I haff had my breakfast, but I will take some coffee." The Doctor drew up a chair. "It is raining und I had been driving like mad to get here."

"That means all of twenty miles an hour." Milpotts winked at us. He loosened up and acted like he was human with the old boy. "Did you finish your post mortem?"

"Ja." The Doctor poured himself a cup of coffee. He added cream and three teaspoonsful of sugar, all slow and careful, then he said "Ja" again like he forgot he'd said it before.

"What did you find out?"

"Dot Mr. Velch . . . he iss dead," he said between gulps.

"That's a help!"

"He died from loss of blood. Also, because he could not breathe mit his windpipe severed. I will haff, too, a piece of coffee kuchen. The round vun mit raisins. *Danke.*"

"You think the murder could have been committed with that Italian knife I showed you?" Milpotts asked.

"It iss possible. The blade iss sharp. But it vould take much force. The neck, it hass been cut half through."

Q. asked: "Does that mean a woman couldn't have done it?"

"*Nein—nein*. Not possible," Dr. Ascher said. "Unless she wass strong like a horse. No . . . it vould take a strong man, a very strong man to cut so deep."

Q. looked at Milpotts.

"That's the first helpful information we've had," he said. "It knocks off half our suspects at one blow."

"Not for me."

"Why not?"

"Because I never suspected any of the women."

"*I* did. I suspected every one."

The Doctor said: "Dis iss goot coffee, *nicht wahr?*" He poured himself another cup and began shoveling in sugar.

Q. got up from the table and walked toward the strong room, talking as he went.

"Let's work out just what happened last night. Welch was sitting at the desk, here, looking over that will. Just before Frazier went out of the room, he gathered up the document, the watch and, possibly, the clock and the Blade. Then he went toward the strong room. Frazier says the door was open, but it was dark. Probably Welch snapped the switch here at the door. Something was wrong. The light didn't go on." He stopped. "By the way, what *is* wrong? It was O.K. when we looked at the collection earlier in the evening."

The Doctor went on drinking his coffee, but Milpotts and Handy went over to the strong room.

Q. pushed the button at the door, then jumped down into the room, climbed the wooden steps and reached up.

"It's the bulb," he said. "Unscrewed."

Milpotts asked: "Think it was accidental?"

"Not a chance. Too much coincidence. Whoever committed that murder loosened the bulb so Welch wouldn't be able to see into the room."

"Sounds as though some one was hiding in there."

"If you look at it one way. On the other hand, the killer may have wanted Welch to start fussing with the light, and so give him time to get into the room."

"That would also explain the steps being out of place," Milpotts pointed out. "Welch might have shoved them over so he could climb up and reach the bulb."

"That makes sense—but there are things which look queer."

"Such as?"

"That clock. It's smashed into so many pieces it must have been dropped violently."

"It was," Milpotts put in. "From the top of the steps."

"But a clock's a damned awkward thing to hold while you climb up to screw in a light, especially when you already have a watch, a knife, and a large legal paper. Why didn't Welch put the stuff down on the table before he began fooling with the light?"

Handy said: "That's right," and Milpotts nodded.

"Then you think the murderer was hiding in the strong room and jumped on Welch as he came in?" he asked.

"It's a possibility. The steps might have been pushed to one side in the struggle over the knife."

I put in my oar.

"That means the murderer knew Welch was going to bring the Blade with him into the room, and counted on using it."

"No." Milpotts shook his head. "He might have had some weapon—a gun, or another knife, but decided not to use it when he saw the Blade. Naturally, he'd prefer using something that wouldn't point to him as the murderer."

Q. grunted, but didn't say anything. I gathered he wasn't particularly crazy about either theory, but he hadn't anything better to offer.

Dr. Ascher looked into the strong-room alcove from the other side. He was carrying his cup and munching another wedge of coffee cake.

He asked: "Who do you t'ink hass killed him?"

"Search me," Milpotts told him, "but your cutting out the women narrows it down."

Dr. Ascher suggested: "Some vun from the outside it wass maybe."

Q. told him: "You can forget that. First, there is the wall around the place, with charged wire on top. Then, two guards were watching the house. The only windows into this room are barred, and, finally, Mrs. Statts was on the terrace outside, waiting for Creel. If any one had come in or out that way she'd have been sure to see him."

"That leaves us with Creel, the nephew, Dr. Jaffee and Frazier—with a possibility of it's being one of the servants," Milpotts figured.

Q. said: "Possible, but not likely," and climbed back into the library again.

"How do we stand on motives?" Handy wanted to know.

"They're the best things we have. Creel and Welch were old enemies and had a row only last night. Frazier, Jaffee, and the nephew all have money coming to them by the will."

"How about opportunity?" Milpotts snapped up the list and took a slant at it. "All of 'em seem about equal on that, too. Creel was running around somewhere, getting ready to light out. Frazier says he went upstairs, but we've only his word for it. The same goes for the nephew and the Doctor."

"Hold on!" Handy said. "Wasn't Dr. Jaffee with some one who was sick?"

"He was with the cook."

"That's what *he* says," Q. told them. "But I'm going to look it up. You'll notice he was giving her a sedative. She might easily have dropped off to sleep long enough for him to slip out of the room."

"Check that," Milpotts said to Handy.

Handy looked important, hitched up his glasses and made a note in a big blue scrawl on the back of a gas bill.

Q. was walking around the room.

"There are three entrances into the library," he said. "The one from the conservatory. The door into the shop, and the private stairs. Not one of them was locked last night. Any one could have come down from the second floor, or in from the conservatory, without being seen."

"Hang it all," Milpotts said, "there isn't anything to help us." He took out a fresh match and began to whittle at it with his pocket-knife. It seemed to remind him of some things.

"What did you do with that knife after you got through with the post mortem, Doc?" he asked.

The Doctor said: "I haff it in my bag. Do you vish I should get it?"

"I'd like to take another look at it, yes."

"Vun minute und I go." The Doctor knocked the crumbs off his mustache on to the front of his vest. He sure was a sloppy old geezer. "Dot iss a fine dagger. Very fine," he said to Q. "Fifteenth century, Italian, *nicht wahr?* Florentine vork?"

Q. told him: "First quarter of the Cinquecento. Supposed to have been made for one of the Borgias. How did you guess?"

"About art I used to know somet'ings ven I wass in Germany. Der iss no time for keeping up mit such t'ings in a general practice, but sometimes Dr. Jaffee vould permit dot I look through Mr. Velch's collections."

"You know Jaffee well?"

"He iss my friend, yes. A fine man. A most brilliant doctor! A shame it iss he hass left his profession." The old guy waggled his head. "Vatching over a rich man's belly. . . . Gott! Vat vork for a surgeon!" He swallowed the last of his coffee and got going. "I vill bring you dot knife."

Milpotts said: "Funny cuss, the Doc. Kind of a Red, but he's harmless. Raises roses. Has over three hundred varieties. 'Specially climbers. They grow all over his house and barn, and the hospital, too. It's a sight worth seeing in the summertime."

The Doctor came back. He was looking sunk.

"My bag—it iss gone!"

"Gone?"

"*Mein Gott,* yes! On the bench just outside dot door it wass. I vill show you."

We followed him and looked. He pointed to a swell seat of carved-up marble in the conservatory. It stood against the wall next to the library door.

"Right dere! I put it down mit my coat as I came in, because dey vere both vet."

"You mean you didn't come in the front way?"

"*Nein.* Through the conservatory. It iss nearest the drive, vere I left my car."

Q. was looking around. He opened a door close to the one into the library.

"That's the other door to the shop," I said. "I looked in there when you thought you heard some one."

Q. said: "I was right! Whoever it was, must have been listening to us!"

"But my bag," the Doctor was still stewing around, "I tell you it vass dere—under my coat!"

Frazier came in from the entrance hall. He was carrying a leather bag that was worn brown-black. One clasp was broken, and the handles were mended with adhesive.

"Were you looking for this, sir?" he wanted to know. Ascher grabbed it.

"Dot iss it! Dot iss my bag! *Gott sei danke!*"

Q. asked: "Where did you find it?"

"In the entrance hall, sir. On the table."

"You must have left it there when you came in, Doc," Milpotts said.

"But no! I haff not come dot vay. As I tell you, I come in through the conservatory." The Doctor was looking through the bag. He gave a kind of a snort. "The knife! It iss not here! It iss gone!"

Milpotts said: "It *must* be there. Look again."

"I tell you it iss gone! It wass on the top, wrapped in a towel, and now—"

Q. asked sharply: "Anything else missing?"

The Doctor went through his bag again.

"*Nein—ja!* Dere wass a tube of cocaine. It, too, hass been taken!"

15

Milpotts ordered the whole dump searched from top to bottom, including every one in it. A lot of the guests were just getting up. Or pretended like they were. Others were breakfasting in their rooms. But he routed them all out, and put them through the wringer along with the servants.

They made me think of those three monkeys you buy down in Jap Town. None of 'em had seen anything. None of 'em had heard anything. None of 'em had anything to say. I mean, anything worth listening to.

Usually there would have been a lot of servants around at that hour, Frazier told us, but Milpotts had ordered them to stay in the service wing unless they were sent for. Frazier, himself, was superintending the breakfast trays that were being sent up to the rooms.

The outdoor men all claimed they had been sitting in the garage out of the rain, except Politos, the big Greek who had potted Creel the night before. He said he'd been crossing the lawn outside the house a little earlier and thought he'd noticed some one in the conservatory.

"Man or woman?" Milpotts snapped.

Politos couldn't say. The palm leaves and ferns were thick inside the glass, and he hadn't taken a good look. He just had a hunch some one was there.

"What were *you* doing on the lawn?" Q. asked. "Singing in the rain?"

Politos shook his head and grinned. But not like he was amused.

"No, boss, not singing. Dr. Ascher, he leaves his car outside. Water is dripping in. I think I run it under shelter. I cross the lawn and try to start the damn thing. But no key. I think, I go into the house and find Doctor maybe. Then I think, No. Doctor is busy. If he want car in garage, he put it there. So I go back to the garage, then I have breakfast. Two eggs, four piece bacon—"

Milpotts cut him off with:

"All right . . . all right! That's enough. If you can't help, shut up. And that goes for the rest of you! When I want to know anything more I'll call you. In the meantime, stay in the house, or you'll land in the hoosegow."

He went off with Handy to start casing the joint for the Blade. The others went back to their rooms, or into the living-room, where there was a fire.

Lottie was one of them. She tried to give Q. the eye, but Roger Storey got there first. He sure was goofy, that guy.

If he'd been hitting the hop he couldn't have been any worse. All he could see was that Dukes doll. He pulled a chair up to the fire for her and slogged it full of pillows. He sent a maid up for her scarf, and Frazier for some sherry—because, he said, she looked pale.

She didn't look pale to me. Just part mad and part worried, like she had something on her mind and wanted to get rid of it.

Q. and I started upstairs. When we hit the upper hall we found Creel on the watch. He called us into his room, then shut the door. He was still in a dressing gown. One sleeve was off the shoulder because of his bandaged arm.

He had deep circles under his eyes, but he wasn't the sort you could feel sorry for.

"Listen," he snapped, the minute the door was shut, "that Duchene woman says you're a crook."

Q. didn't say anything. Just stood there looking at him, poker-face.

Creel went on: "Frazier tells me that you're a detective, and Welch introduced you to us as a collector. Mind saying which you are?"

Q. forked out a cigarette. He lit it with a match from the bedside table.

"Which would pay the best?"

Creel grinned. I could see he was all for business, and that he liked the way Q. talked turkey without stalling.

"A little of each," he said, and looked at me.

"Lynch is safe," Q. told him. "What do you want?"

"I want you to pick up something. Something Welch stole from me." He stopped and studied Q. with his mean little eyes. "You can't believe that, can you?"

"I might be able to." Q.'s face was turned away, but I knew he was getting a kick out of it.

This was the topper, all right. Welch asking us to lift something from Creel and now Creel wanting the same thing.

He said: "That's God's truth! It's a watch that belonged to Napoleon. Gold and enamel, with rubies. You'll know it by the 'N' on the back."

"And then?"

"Return it to me and I'll give you two hundred dollars."

Q. started for the door. I followed.

"Five hundred!"

Q. kept on going.

Creel yelled, "A thousand!"

Q. stopped and turned half around.

"Why do you want the watch?"

"Because it belongs to me! Never mind where I got it. But I paid for it—plenty."

"I'll bet you did," Q. said, and I thought of Le Coq. "How'd you lose it?"

"Welch sent a crook named Weston. An out-of-work actor, I found later. He pulled a yarn about writing a book on watches. He'd been coached until he sounded like an expert. He wanted photographs of my collection. Like a fool I let him look through it. Next day the Napoleon watch was missing." He stopped short. "What the hell you laughing at?"

"Nothing." Q. wasn't laughing, there was just a twitch at the corners of his mouth. "Nothing at all. What makes you think Welch was responsible?"

"I don't think. I *know!* He was after that watch! Ever since he heard it was missing from—never mind about that. When he found I'd cornered it he almost burst a blood vessel. He'd have tipped off the police if he hadn't known they would send it back to Europe and he'd lose his chances of nabbing it. So he sent Weston."

"You're sure the watch is here?"

"Dead sure. I've seen it."

"When? Where?"

Creel didn't seem to want to tell, but he saw he had to. He fiddled a minute with the bandage on his arm, then: "When Welch showed us his collection, last night, there was one place empty," he said. "The mark on the velvet was about the size of the Napoleon watch. I knew he'd taken it off the hook and hidden it away to keep me from seeing it."

"So you slipped something to the butler to get Welch out of the library and into the conservatory."

"How the hell did you know?"

Q. didn't answer that one. Just went on talking. "Then you sneaked in to take a look-see."

Creel's mouth squeezed tight. Then he opened up:

"The watch was mine!"

"Did you find it?"

"Yes. It was in the top drawer, to the left of the safety boxes, in the strong room."

Q. started crowding him.

"Then you were in the strong room?"

"You bet I was in the strong room. I knew the watch wouldn't be anywhere else."

"Was the light all right? Were the steps in place?" Q. poured out, and Creel looked foggy.

"So far as I know. The light was burning, and I walked down the steps."

"Which means everything was normal at midnight," Q. told me over his shoulder. "That was the time Welch came back into the room from the conservatory, wasn't it?" he asked Creel.

"Just before midnight, yes, I remember a clock struck while we were having our argument."

"He caught you in the vault?"

Creel cracked out: "Yes, damn his soul. Just when I found the watch—but before I could get my hands on it. We had it hot and heavy for about five minutes."

"Did you stay in the strong room?"

"No. We went back into the library."

"What happened then?"

"Welch worked himself into such a rage he almost had a stroke. Dr. Jaffee came in and started calming him down. I went on upstairs."

Q. reminded him, "But not to bed."

"No. I intended to get the watch and light out. Didn't take any stock in that quarantine business. Suspected Welch was up to some dirty work. When I saw I couldn't get what I was after I decided to go anyway."

"And do what?"

Creel's eyes squinted and he showed his teeth. They were sharp and yellow, like dog-teeth.

"Well, if you must know, I decided to tip off the police as to the whereabouts of that watch."

"You were going to tell them it was stolen from you?"

The old buzzard winked.

"Not on your life. Just intended to say Welch had it, and that I'd seen it. He'd have had a lot of explaining to do. Because of the museums, you know. He wouldn't be the white-haired boy with the curators in London and Paris . . . when they found he had stolen goods in his collection."

"Little spite work, eh?"

"Call it what you like. I was fed up with his dirty methods. But now, things being as they are, I'd like to get the watch back. How about it?"

Q. said: "That depends upon whether I'm a crook or a detective."

"I'm betting on the first," Creel told him. "I'll have a check waiting for you."

Q. got up and started for the door. I went after him.

Creel was beefing behind us. Scared, I guess, that we were going to spill what he'd told us to the dicks.

Q. closed the door in his ugly face.

There was no one in the hall, except Margot, who gave me the office.

I stopped a minute, behind some curtains that cut off an upstairs window seat.

Margot said: "Why you have not seen me zees morning, eh?"

"I've been busy," I told her. "*Très* busy."

"*Tiens!* You have foun' out something?"

"Nothing," I said, but she wouldn't have it that way. "You 'ave jus' say zat, because you do not trus' me."

"Why the hell should I? Your mob tried to put the finger on us, didn't they?"

"Zat was not me. It was the old woman."

"Same thing. You're all in it together."

But she hung around my neck and spouted a lot of stuff in French. Q. called to me to hurry. I got myself unwound. But not too fast. She was a damned swell-looker and no mistake.

"See here, sugar," I said, "I got a hen on just now. I'll see you later."

"*Alors!* I weel be waiting." She gave me a kiss. A hot one.

I followed Q. down the stairs. Not the front stairs. The narrow stairs that led to the library.

Q. was at the strong-room door again. It had been shut but not locked. He swung it open, turned on the light, and went down the steps.

The room was just about as we had seen it earlier. The body was gone, and the floor had been cleaned up some. Everything else was left as it had been, except for the Blade and the will. Nobody had bothered to pick up the clock. It was still lying smashed, all over the floor.

While I stood guard, Q. opened the drawer Creel had talked about. There wasn't any watch in it. He opened all the others, and rummaged about, but he didn't find anything.

I heard him say "Damn."

After a while he came back into the library and looked around the desk. I helped him. We didn't find what we were looking for.

"Maybe Welch was afraid Creel was coming back to take another look," I suggested, "and hid the thing."

"Maybe. But the butler saw him carrying the watch toward the strong room—" He didn't finish, just stood thinking. "Look here," he said finally, "have you got the servants spotted? I mean, do you know which is the maid that takes care of the bedrooms?"

"There're two of them," I told him. "A skinny shad with gray hair, and the cute blonde."

"It's just a chance, but you might tackle the blonde. Nine out of ten people who have something to hide put it somewhere around a bed. Ask her if she's noticed anything. If not, tell her to keep her eyes open. Tell her there's a sawbuck in it if she finds the watch."

"I'll take the sawbuck—she'll do it for love."

He started to say something, but some one was coming into the room.

It was Milpotts shooting a string of good old down-east cuss words at Handy and Bill, who were tailing him. Seemed they'd looked everywhere inside the house, and hadn't found a trace of the Blade.

"There isn't a square inch of this place we haven't covered," Bill said. "I'm plain wore out crawling under beds and shinning up curtain poles."

Q. had an idea.

"Look here," he said, "while you were turning things out did you happen to run across a watch?"

"What kind of a watch?" Bill wanted to know.

"Can't describe it exactly, but it's an antique. Gold and enamel, with rubies. The initial 'N' on the case."

"'N'?" Bill asked. "Yeah. I saw it."

"Where?"

"It's under the mattress in that front room upstairs. The room with the blue curtains."

My jaw dropped so I could almost step on it.

Q. was old poker-face, like always, but I knew he was knocked for a loop.

That was the room we had just left. The one that belonged to Creel.

16

"Now what in hell does *that* mean?" I said the minute Q. and I were back in his room.

"Go there and find out," he growled, by which I knew he was as mixed up as I was.

"Why should Creel spring that song and dance about the watch if it was under his mattress all the time?"

"Your guess is as good as mine."

"Haven't you any ideas at all?"

"Well, just off hand, I'd say Creel might have swiped it, been afraid some one would find it was missing. Dr. Jaffee, perhaps—and report it to the police."

"Where would that get him?"

"Don't you see? If he got to us first and pretended he wanted the watch and couldn't find it, we might not suspect him."

I had to admit that sounded as good as anything I could think up, but it was pretty screwy at that.

"The watch was there in the library after Creel had gone upstairs," I reminded Q. "The butler saw it."

"That's right!" He stopped and looked thoughtful. I brought out what was left of the bottle we'd had the night before, and poured him a drink.

He swallowed it like he didn't know what he was doing.

"Suppose," he figured, "Creel left the library just as he said—went upstairs, packed his things, got ready to clear out, then came back to make another try at getting the watch."

"You mean he planned ahead to go in and bump the old man off?"

"Maybe. I wouldn't put anything past him."

"Me, neither. But I dunno—to kill a man, just for a watch . . ."

Q. said: "There's a hell of a lot more to it than that. They'd been scrapping for years, and we don't know what was said between them during that row. It must have been pretty damned hot to throw Welch into a heart attack."

"Um. And that lineup would explain why Creel was so anxious to take it on the lam."

Q. said: "It would not."

I saw he was thinking, so I didn't butt in.

"When you come to look at it," he went on, "you'll see that's the last thing he'd do—kill a man, then run away. If he stayed, there wouldn't be any more reason to hang the murder on him than any of the rest of us. If he scrammed, the police would take it for granted he was guilty and finger him for sure."

"You're right." I sat down next the bottle.

Q. picked it up and put it on another table, kind of as if he was absent-minded and didn't notice what he was doing.

He said: "I wish I hadn't thought of that."

"Why?"

"I hate to drop Creel off our list. It leaves only Roger, Frazier, and the Doctor."

I said: "I choose Roger."

"Why?" Q. sounded like he really wanted to know.

"Why not? The guy's nuts. You can see it first glance. He'd knock anybody off if he thought they were standing between him and Lottie."

Q. puckered up his lips.

"Maybe," he said slowly. "But when we saw them in the conservatory last night, he didn't think his uncle was in his way. He thought the old man was all for the marriage."

"But how do you know what happened later—when they had their talk? Welch may have said he was going to change his will. Or maybe he spilled the fact he was after the girl himself. Or—hold everything—here's an angle. Why couldn't Roger have been hanging around the keyhole when Welch gave her that necklace?"

"If he was, he certainly heard plenty," Q. said. "I'll bet that scene was hot!"

"Hot enough to set the kid on fire, providing he was listening in. He could have sneaked back afterward and had his say with the knife." I was beginning to be proud of my own case. "That's better than anything you can dope out against Frazier or the Doctor."

Q. said: "I'm not so sure. There may be lots of reasons why Frazier would want to wipe out the old boy. He looks like a sulky devil."

"And that's no lie."

"Dollars to doughnuts, Welch was hell to work for. Got insulting, and treated the servants like dirt under his feet. You could tell it to look at him. Then there's that legacy. Ten thousand's real money."

"How about Jaffee?"

"The Doctor's our dark horse. I've looked him up plenty, and from everything I can find out he's a good guy. The servants say he and Welch were always friendly. Jaffee's the only man the old boy never quarreled with. But how can we be sure? The Doctor's evidently a liberal tipper and they all like him. They may be shielding him with lies. Even if they aren't, he and Welch may have had a quarrel nobody knew about. Oh, there's a lot I mean to find out about Jaffee before I'm through!"

"You talk like we were going to stay here forever," I said, discouraged.

"We're going to stay until this thing is cleared up. If we don't, we're sunk. Once give Milpotts reason to check with Scotland Yard—" He stopped, then went on in the same voice: "Certainly the Doctor is the logical man for us to suspect. Except for the butler, he was the last one with Welch."

"Except you."

"Except me—and, oh, Lynch, lay out my tan suit for pressing. The collar is wrinkled, and remind me to order some new ties when we get back to town."

I said: "Yes sir. Very good, sir."

Milpotts was opening the door. He was chewing a cigar.

I didn't like the way he busted in without knocking. But I judged I'd better not take a poke at him.

"You don't need to worry about the Doctor," he said. "We've just checked on him."

"Yes?"

"H'm. He went straight from the library to the cook's room, and stayed there. One of the maids, that skinny one, was in the room with them. She says he never left, not for a minute, until those shots were fired outside and they all went down to see what had happened."

"Well, that's that," Q. said. "We can cut the Doctor off our list."

"And that isn't all," Milpotts went on. "That little blonde floosy of a maid came and confessed. . . ."

"You don't mean she—"

"No such luck! What she told us was that Frazier came straight to her bedroom after he left the library last night. He was still there when Creel was shot in the shoulder."

Q. laughed at that.

"The old devil! Didn't think he had it in him!"

"Me neither. Of course the girl made me promise to keep it quiet. Said Frazier wouldn't tell, because he didn't want to get her fired. But she thought we ought to know he had an alibi."

"*Is* it an alibi? She may be lying because she knows Frazier was the last one to talk with Welch."

"But he wasn't!"

Q. whistled. "You mean that?"

"Yes. Later he talked to Politos through the window. Mrs. Statts saw him. What's more, she saw Welch after the Greek had gone."

"How'd she happen to do that?"

"She was waiting outside the library for Creel. She saw Welch through the window, as he went toward the strong room."

"She didn't see anybody else?"

"No. She says she didn't want Welch to notice her, so she went back and sat in the shrubbery."

"Why didn't she tell all this before?"

"Because she was afraid. She finally decided it would be safer for her to come through."

Q. said: "Better have a talk with the Greek."

I went to get Politos. He was out by the gate taking money off one of the dicks with a pair of dice. I didn't like his looks any better than before. He sure was a hunk of beef, that baby. And mean.

But because he had big black eyes, and his hair was curly, the women fell hard. I even caught Margot looking at him like he was something she might go for later—if Lottie copped Roger and they all settled down at Sant' Angelo.

Politos knew the women were nuts about him, too. You could tell it by the way he kept flashing his white teeth at 'em. Even at old battle-axes like Pearl Dukes and the Statts dame.

And men didn't faze him, either. Not even dicks. He stood straight and square and stared into Milpotts's eyes like he was laughing way down in his guts.

He said yes, he'd talked to Mr. Welch the night before. Just after midnight.

No, he hadn't said anything about it. He didn't want to be the last one who'd seen him alive. Anyway, Welch hadn't said anything important. Just told him to watch the gate extra well. He didn't want any one getting out.

He said: "That why I shoot Creel. I know if he run away my job, it run with him."

"You like your job?" Q. asked.

"Sure—certainly—I like. Good pay. Good food. Pretty girls. Why shouldn't I like—Goddamn?"

He had a funny way of talking, thick and fast, so you could hardly understand him. Sometimes I thought he made it that way on purpose when he was talking to the dicks. With women you could understand him lots better.

Milpotts asked: "What did you do after Welch closed the window? Stick around awhile?"

"No, sir. Not me. No! I go back to the gate, damn fast you bet you. Mr. Welch tell me to watch—I watch."

"And you didn't see what he did in the room?"

"Not me. Nothing. Nothing after he talk."

Milpotts wanted to see where he'd stood when he talked with Welch, so he took him out. I went along.

When we came back, Q. was counting on his fingers.

"We've eliminated Dr. Jaffee, Frazier, and Creel." He told how he and I had figured Creel wouldn't have done the murder and then tried to get away.

Milpotts agreed it made good sense.

Q. asked: "You see what that leaves us?"

Milpotts said: "Yes, the nephew. He's the one I've been suspecting all along. He stood to lose the most if Welch changed his will, and he stands to gain the most now that the old man is dead."

"If that was the latest will."

"What do you mean?"

"I mean there may have been another. That will is two years old, isn't it? How do we know Welch didn't make one later, and that he wasn't getting out the old one to destroy it?"

"We don't." Milpotts was chewing on the idea like he chewed the end of his cigar. "But no other will has turned up."

"It may be in one of the locked boxes. Or his lawyer may have it, or Jaffee." He turned to me. "Go and look up Dr. Jaffee, will you? Ask if he minds coming down for a minute."

I started out to round up the Doctor, but Margot got hold of me first.

She was worse than an octopus, that skirt. And it wasn't on account of I was such a treat to her, either. I'd long ago made up my mind to that. It was because she had orders from Lottie Dukes to get the latest dope, even if she had to strangle me to do it.

Now she jumped out from behind the curtains in the hall and glommed on to my arm.

"You 'ave promise to come back, an' I 'ave' wait' an' wait'," she complained. "Why you treat me so, eh?"

"Listen, baby," I said, "I got work to do. That's the way it is, I got work to do."

"What work?"

"Things."

"What t'ings?"

"Business for the big Chief and the Sheriff." That was a mistake. It set her itching for information.

"Why you don' trust me? 'Ave you forgot las' night?" She cuddled up and whispered some words in French I

couldn't understand. She acted like things had gone a lot
farther the night before than they did. Maybe she wished
they had.

I tried to get untangled, and lowered my arm—but she
grabbed herself another hold.

"You can stay wiz me long enough for one leetle drink?
Jus' one."

"Where you got it?"

"In here." She led me toward the door of Lottie Dukes's
room, which was close by. "Zere ees nobody an' eet weel
tak' only one minute."

I didn't really want the drink, but I thought it would
be a good way of getting rid of her. So I went along.

Margot poured out two tall ones. The only chairs were
across the room, so we sat down on the edge of the bed.

"It mus' be won'erful to be a great beeg detective," she
cooed, "like you an' Mr.—Mr. W'at-is-his-name?"

I knew she was putting all this stuff on, but I didn't let
her know I knew.

"Bleigh, to you," I said. "H. Findley Bleigh."

We had another drink, and she asked some more about
what we'd found out, and who Q. thought had done the
murder.

I didn't tell her a damn thing. That is, nothing much.
Just enough so she could see I was pretty high up on the
inside of things, to let her know I was somebody, the way
a guy does when he's talking to a good-looking doll. But
I warned her I couldn't spill the most important parts because they were secret.

There was still another drink in the bottle. I thought I
might as well have it before I went. Q. wouldn't know but
what I was still looking for the Doctor. He'd think I was
having trouble finding him. I'd earned a little rest after
the day and night we'd put in.

Margot made me put my feet up and sort of lay back on the pillows while she rubbed my forehead. She was a cuddly piece, and that's a fact. Her hands were soft, and she smelled like a bunch of flowers. Her skin was more like satin to touch than any dame's I've ever known—and I've known plenty.

She stopped trying to pump me when she found I didn't like it, and began telling me what *she* thought. She gabbled a lot about whether this one or that one was guilty, and I told her why she was on the wrong foot. Not giving anything away, of course, just letting her think it was my personal opinion. Like Creel, for instance. When she said it looked mighty suspicious to her, the way he and Welch didn't get along, I told her I didn't think he'd have killed Welch and then tried to make a get-away. He'd be more likely to stick around so he wouldn't look guilty.

She was interested in what I had to say. We went over every guy in the house, her telling me what she thought, and me telling her my views.

When we were finished, she said:

"If you t'ink Monsieur Creel did not keel him, you mus' t'ink ze same about Madam Statts. She was trying to make ze get-away, *aussi.*"

"Sure she was. But we know she didn't kill him, without that."

"*Comment?*"

"We know damned well it couldn't have been a woman, because a woman wouldn't have been strong enough."

"You are ver' sure?"

"Sure I'm sure. The coroner himself said so."

Margot jumped off the bed and did a dance step, then came back and kissed me so many times I broke out into gooseflesh all over.

"Zat ees for telling me!" she said.

I guessed she'd been worried about Lottie Dukes, and perhaps Ma Dukes as well.

Of course what I told her made her feel both of them were safe, but I saw I'd spilled more than I'd meant to. I knew if Q. found out he'd be sore, so I made her promise she wouldn't say a word. Not to Lottie. Nor to Pearl Dukes. Nor to any one else. What I'd told her was a secret between us two, because of last night, and because of some other nights we might have together when things got quiet again.

She looked solemn and swore on a cross she had around her neck she wouldn't tell a soul.

I saw by the clock near the bed that it was four-thirty. I'd been there over twenty minutes.

I started to get up, but Margot laughed and held me down. We had a tussle, with me hanging on to her wrists and her pulling my hair. Both of us were laughing like loonies.

Right in the middle of it I looked up and saw Q. standing at the foot of the bed. That put a stop to things, you bet.

I sat up and tried to straighten my tie. Margot sat up, too. She was mad as hell.

Q. said: "How much dope did the little fool kiss out of you?"

"Nothing," I told him.

He said I was a liar, and Margot was something worse.

That got my goat. I told him what little I'd spilled she'd promised to keep to herself.

"Swore it on a cross," I said.

Q. didn't answer. He hurdled the bed, quick and quiet, and threw open a closet door.

Lottie Dukes was kneeling on the other side, close up, like her ear had been pressed to the keyhole.

17

When Lottie saw she was caught, she didn't look silly or mad. Just laughed and stood up. She stretched herself, and threw her arms over her head. A way she had that always made her look like she was just going into a dance.

"So you found a woman couldn't have committed the murder?" she said to Q. "Very comforting."

Q. frowned.

"That doesn't let *you* out," he said. "There's still Roger."

"You don't think he did it."

"You don't know what I think. All you know is what Lynch, here, *thinks* I think. I'll tell you this, if Roger did it, you're more than half responsible. With your record, the dicks won't let you slip out of it, you bet. You'll be held as accessory."

Her eyes flashed. "You haven't told them?"

"Not *yet.*" The way he said it meant a lot.

"We made a bargain—" she began.

"We did . . . and you know what happened to your side of it."

"Well, I couldn't strangle my mother, could I?"

"It's an idea!"

I knew Q. was mad. He'd been cagey enough to save himself with that letter from Scotland Yard, but he had nothing to thank Pearl Dukes for, or Lottie Dukes, either.

If they'd had their way, the two of us would have been headed for the hot seat long before now.

"I'm sorry, *truly* sorry," Lottie said. "You understand, don't you, that mother told them without my knowing? I wouldn't have had it happen for worlds!"

Q. said: "You bet you wouldn't. I'm your ace card—and her squealing on me has put you in a hell of a hole."

"But you can't mean to give me away just because my mother double-crossed me."

"Why not?"

"Because it wouldn't get you anywhere, and for me it would be—the end. Finis."

She was looking up at him. Her big, brown eyes had tears in them. Her lips were puckering like a baby's.

"You've no idea what it's like for a girl left alone," she said. "I've *had* to do the things I've done. There wasn't any other way—with mother on my hands—and everything against me. I've hated it. *Hated* it! Now I see a chance to go straight, to marry and settle down. Don't you realize what it means to a woman to have a home?"

"And kiddies," Q. said. "Don't forget the curly-headed little toddlers that will call you 'mama.'"

She said: "You louse! Get out of here!"

Q. just stood there grinning at her.

"Did you pull that act on Welch last night?" he asked her. "You couldn't have practiced on Roger—he doesn't know about your past."

"He does!" she spat. "I told him. Everything!"

"*Every*thing?"

"Well . . . almost everything. I wanted to play straight. Since we are going to be married, I thought it was only fair."

Q. snapped: "That's a lie, too. If you told him anything, it's because you were afraid Welch would beat you to the draw. It wasn't a bad idea, at that. I suppose the kid's getting a kick out of playing Knight Errant."

Lottie changed suddenly. She quit looking mad and laughed.

"He's saving the fallen woman," she said. "You ought to see me doing Magdalen." She stopped short in the middle of her laugh.

I could see she was sorry she'd been human, even for a split second. If she'd been with Q. as long as I had, she'd have known it was the best way of handling him. But she hadn't, and didn't. Instead, she started moving in again.

"Please be just a little bit kind. Tell me what they have on Roger."

"So you can decide whether it will pay better to string along with him or to forget the home and kiddies and do a bunk?"

"You don't give me credit for anything decent, do you?"

"Why should I? In the first place, you came along with your mother to put over a blackmailing scheme on Welch. You didn't chuck that until Roger fell for you, and you figured marrying him would pay better. I'll swear, last night you were ready to give Roger the go-by and take on the old man—only, you weren't quite sure just how far he meant to go. You were stalling for time until you found out. Now he's dead, you're back with the kid again. But if you find he's likely to be nabbed for the murder, you want to know it in time to get clear of him. Am I right, or am I right?"

"Near enough," she admitted. "But you forgot to accuse me of a few things like murdering Welch and shooting Creel."

Q. said: "I was coming to that."

"You mean you think I shot Creel?"

"No, the Greek did that. But you could have murdered Welch."

Margot said: *"Mon Dieu!"* and grabbed my hand.

I guess they'd forgotten all about us. At least they hadn't paid any attention to us, which was natural, because Q.

was as used to me as he was to his right hand, and I guess
the Dukes girl felt the same about Margot.

"Why in hell do you figure I killed him?" she wanted to
know. "And when? And how?"

"You could have had several swell reasons. When you
talked with him last night he might have gone on with
that conversation you had in the conservatory."

"He did. On . . . and on . . . and on. . . ."

"He might have made it clear that he wouldn't let you
marry Roger. That he'd put a stop to it by force."

"He said just that."

"He might have told you he was going to cut Roger out
of his will, and if you married the boy you wouldn't get
anything."

"He told me something like that, too."

"You may have decided that a few months' gallivanting
around Mediterranean sea-port towns with Welch wouldn't
pay as well as marrying Roger, providing Roger got the
fortune."

"I did a little thinking along those lines."

"And you decided?"

"To postpone everything until morning and get some
sleep."

"Maybe you're telling the truth. Then, again, maybe
you made up your mind last night. You knew about the
stairs into Welch's library. You may have waited, listened
to make sure no one was there, then slipped down just as
he was going into the strong room. You could have followed him there, got into an argument with him, picked
up that knife of mine and cr-rr—"

Q. brought his forefinger across his throat with a nasty
gurgling sound.

"You're raving! I couldn't have done it! The coroner
told you no woman had the strength."

"I've just realized the coroner's wrong, sweetheart. You could have done it easily enough. Your mother could have done it. Even Margot, here."

Margot gave a screech like a cat that has been stepped on, and shot from the bed.

"*Non! Non!* I did no such a t'ing! *Jésus Christ, non!* Me—I did not even know heem!"

"Keep your shirt on, sister," I said.

Q. told her: "I didn't say you did it. I said you could have done it." He turned back to Lottie. "To cut that deep isn't a question of strength if he happened to fall on the knife."

Lottie was looking like she'd seen a ghost.

"I get what you mean," she said slowly. "After he was hit, if he fell forward—" She didn't finish.

Q. said: "You have it. He was probably standing on the steps. He was a heavy man, and his weight would natural-ly—"

"Don't!" she shuddered. "Don't talk about it! Remember, I saw him!"

I remembered she'd been with us on that second trip into the strong room. She had tried to be hard-boiled about it then, but the scene had stuck with her, you could see that plain enough.

"You—you really believe a woman could have killed him?"

"I'm sure of it. When the coroner thinks it over, he'll be sure, too."

"Oh, my God!" All Lottie Dukes's cockiness was gone. She dropped down on a chair and began to cry. "You'll go to the police with that story, and you'll make them believe you. They'll believe it—because you're louse enough to tell them I've got a record."

The door opened. Roger Storey looked into the room. Then he came in.

"What's the matter?" he asked Lottie. "What's he been doing to you?"

Lottie didn't say anything for a minute, just cried some more, first into her handkerchief, then on his shoulder. I guess that dame never had to think quicker in her life.

If she didn't hand out some sort of story the whole thing would look funny to Roger, Q. being in her room. And me.

But if she said anything dirty about Q. he might spill a lot of stuff she didn't want Roger to know.

I didn't take much stock in what she'd said about telling him everything. Like hell she had!

"What have you b-b-been doing to her?" Roger said. This time it was to Q., but Lottie answered:

"Accusing me"—she choked on a sob—"of horrible things! Of killing your uncle!"

Roger didn't wait for any more. He tore away from her and swung on Q.

Q. stepped back, but he was too near the bureau. The kid caught him on the cheek. He kept right on coming, too. Not like he wanted to fight, more like he wanted to kill. It took both Q. and me to hold him. And all the time he was yelling words. Most of what he said you couldn't understand, but what little got through would take the hide off an elephant.

We got him down on the bed at last. He was still screeching, but suddenly he shut up. His teeth locked together and I saw bits of foam at the corners of his mouth.

Lottie'd been saying "Hush!" and "Don't Roger!" and "Please, dear," and trying to get between him and Q. Now she sat down beside him and put her arm under his head.

I brought a wet towel and Margot dug up some smelling salts.

Q. stood and watched, grinning.

He said: "There's your bridegroom. I wish you joy of him."

Lottie threw him a look, then went back to wiping Roger's forehead with a towel.

He was beginning to groan and try to sit up.

"You'd better get out before he comes to," she said to Q. "Seeing you, will make him worse again."

"I wouldn't intrude for the world," Q. told her. "Come on, Lynch."

We were starting for the door, but it opened again. This time it was Pearl Dukes came staggering in. Her face was white and her hands were shaking.

"Give me a drink!" she yelled. "God damn it to hell, why don't one of you move? Give me a drink, *quick!*" Then she saw Q. "Oh, so *you're* here? Well, you'd better go down-stairs. They want you."

"What's the matter?"

"Nothing much. Only somebody's killed Dr. Jaffee."

18

Dr. Jaffee wasn't dead. We found that out when we reached downstairs. And his throat hadn't been cut, like I'd somehow expected. When Pearl Dukes said he was killed, I'd thought of the Borgia Blade and pictured him lying, like Welch, in a pool of blood. But nobody'd used the dagger. This time it was cocaine.

It had all happened about twenty minutes before.

"I was walking along the hall in the west wing, sir," Frazier was telling Milpotts when we came into the drawing-room. "I heard most peculiar noises coming from the Doctor's room. Oh, *most* peculiar, sir. Laughing—or more like howling—you might say—and muttering and groaning. It sounded so strange that I knocked on the door."

"Go on."

"The noises went right on. So I took the liberty of entering. I saw right away something was wrong. The Doctor was acting sort of—if you'll pardon my saying so—sort of drunk. He was staggering up and down the room, laughing and groaning. Fortunately Dr. Ascher was still in the house. I called him."

"He says Jaffee will pull through all right," Milpotts told us. "Lucky Frazier found him in time."

Q. asked: "Do you know how the stuff was administered?"

"In hot-whiskey lemonade, sir. Dr. Jaffee felt a cold coming on, and asked me to bring him a glass. I made it myself, because I didn't want to trust any of the servants with the whiskey. It's been disappearing very strangely the last twenty-four hours."

Q. looked at me.

I looked out the window.

Frazier went on: "The Doctor said he didn't want any dinner. He was planning on drinking the lemonade and then going to bed."

"Did you take the drink to his room?"

"No, sir, to the conservatory. He carried it upstairs himself."

"Any one know you were making the lemonade for him?"

"Yes, sir. Quite a number of people were present when he asked for it."

"Who?"

"Mrs. Duchene. Miss Duchene. Mrs. Statts. It was Mrs. Statts who suggested his taking the drink. She told me exactly how to brew it—with lemon peel and honey instead of sugar. Better for the throat, she said."

"Were the women still there when you brought the glass into the conservatory?"

"Just Mrs. Statts. The other two ladies had gone. But I met Mr. Roger in the hall, outside the conservatory door."

"Alone?"

"Yes, sir. But I think he had just been talking to Mr. Creel."

Q. hadn't seemed to be listening. Now he asked:

"Did any of them have a chance to get near the tray?"

"Not while I was carrying it. But, what happened afterward . . . you'll have to ask Dr. Jaffee about that."

Q. wanted to know when we could see him.

"Shortly," Milpotts said. "Ascher is going to let us know."

Dr. Ascher was coming in as he said that. He looked pretty well sunk. I thought about his being up all night with the dame having twins, then the autopsy, and on top of them Dr. Jaffee.

Milpotts asked: "How's he making out?"

Dr. Ascher said: "He vill recoffer. Cocaine, it iss quick. Either you go like dot"—he snapped his fingers—"or you are vell again in half—three-quarters of an hour, und, *Gott sei dank,* he did not drink all the lemonade."

"Where is what's left of it?" Q. asked.

"In his bathroom. I'm keeping it for analysis, but dere iss no doubt about the cocaine. I haff only to touch it mit my tongue!"

"Bitter, isn't it?" Milpotts asked.

"Bitter, *ja.* But in lemonade—I do not know—mit lemon peel and a goot deal of viskey the bitter vould, maybe, not be noticed. Then, too, it wass hot . . . und the Doctor, he iss coming down mit a cold. His sense of taste vould naturally be not so goot. He can tell you himself more better than I, und soon you should be able to talk mit him."

As it turned out, it wasn't until after dinner that we had a chance to talk with Dr. Jaffee. He didn't pull through as soon as the old Dutchman had hoped. His heart cut up rough and we had to let him alone.

In the meantime, more dicks arrived. And a lot of reporters with them.

Q. and Milpotts cleaned the newspaper guys out as quick as they could. Sant' Angelo being private property they couldn't stay without the Sheriff's say-so, and the wall helped. Most of their dope they picked up from Bill and the Greek. At that, it was about as good as they'd have got anywhere. Nobody knew anything for sure.

Milpotts had sent for the dicks before he knew about Q. being from Scotland Yard. He explained this like he didn't want to make Q. sore. He said the D.A. was almost splitting his stitches trying to get out of the hospital, and he had to do something, so he'd phoned for help from the city.

There was only two dicks, both specialists. One was a fellow who ran around blowing powder on fingerprints and taking pretty pictures. He was tall and wore thick glasses.

The other was short and had warts on his hands.

He kept saying: "Take it from me, brother, it's an outside job."

He spent all his time in the garden, slopping around with an umbrella over his head to keep off the rain. He was looking for footprints he could take up with plaster-of-Paris and glue.

There were hundreds of footprints and thousands of fingerprints. I never saw two guys have a better time.

Me—I wasn't so, happy, because I had some prints in the file at Auburn. And one or two other places besides.

I did my best to get Q. to take it on the lam while our credit was still good. I knew Bill Mowbrick, well heeled, would be waiting to take us over the border in the plane. Once off, we'd be out of it before they found out who we were. But Q. wouldn't listen.

He argued: "There's lots of things I'd rather do than spend my life dodging a murder charge."

"Maybe you'd like to rot in Sing Sing," I said. "Or fry."

Q. looked me up and down, kind of slow and scornful.

"You poor God-damned shrimp," he said, "You still think I did it, don't you?"

I told him: "It don't matter what I think. It's what the dicks'll think."

"But you can use your mind."

"I am."

"Shut up! How do you think I could have slipped Jaffee that drink? And why?"

"I'm not figuring on why. If you want to know *how*—you didn't butt into that room where Margot and I were sitting . . ."

"'Sitting?'" He grinned.

"All right, we weren't sitting! You didn't come in until just about the time the Doc must have been drinking that poison. How do I know what you'd been up to before?"

"If you want to know, I was with your little blonde . . ."

"What little blonde?"

"The maid. Incidentally, she's the one who slipped me the news that you were in Lottie Dukes's room with Margot."

I marked one up against the blonde for that. Yet it was flattering, too, having her keep tabs on me that way. It showed she cared.

"How'd you happen to tangle with her?" I wanted to know.

Q. said: "She looks bright. There are things she can find out. Some things she's found out already."

"Such as?"

"Such as—old lady Dukes is a dope."

"What?"

"Fact. I suspected as much last night, from her voice, and her complexion, and her eyes. The way she was excited, then jittery, then blew up. Didn't look like booze to me. You heard what Lottie said."

"Not that I remember."

"I mean about money. She said, 'You know why I won't let you have any.' And her mother closed her trap like a clam."

"What does she take?"

"Coke. The little blonde found some snow when she was doing the room."

"Cocaine!" I said. "Why, that's—"

"Yeah," he nodded. "You get it! Cocaine's what some one slipped the Doctor. It all ties together."

Right then Frazier came to tell us dinner was served.
He was all in a sweat about me. Ever since he'd heard Q.
was from Scotland Yard he'd been looking me over, kind of
worried and nervous. You could see he didn't know whether I was a detective like Q., or an honest-to-God valet. He
was the kind of guy that had to know what you were before
he knew how to treat you.

He coughed, sort of embarrassed, and asked me: "Would
you rather I brought your dinner up here, ahem, sir? Or
would you prefer to eat downstairs?"

I looked at Q., not knowing what he wanted me to do.

Q. said: "Lynch will eat with the other servants."

"Thank you, sir. That's *all* I wanted to know." Frazier
wasn't trying to be funny. He meant it.

After he left the room, Q. said:

"You'd better keep your eye on the service wing while I
watch the front of the house . . . and lay off the booze and
women, or I'll brain you."

19

I sat between Margot and the blonde at dinner, and held hands two ways at once.

Q. didn't have as good luck in his part of the house . . . so he told me later. We'd purposely kept the news about Jaffee from the crowd. It wasn't hard, because the Doctor had already told most of them about his cold, and how he was going to stay in bed.

Just the same, everybody was feeling glum. The women hadn't bothered to put on evening clothes, except Lottie Dukes, who was dressed in a tight jade-green thing that made her look like she'd been taken up raw and dipped in green paint from the shoulders down. She was a swell-looking dame and no mistake.

Roger Storey was on his feet again. He was a little yellow about the gills, but still able to sit up and look at Lottie.

Q. said he stared like he wanted to eat and drink her instead of the food.

The rest of the company talked about the murder, and who could have done it, all casting sidewise looks at each other. All, that is, but Roger, who didn't open his trap, except when he offered Lottie the salt, or ordered Frazier to fill her glass, before it was anywhere near empty.

Nobody kicked about being kept at Sant' Angelo. Maybe they were glad it wasn't jail, or maybe they were afraid if they seemed too hot on leaving it would make them look guilty.

Anyway, every one tried to act natural, and the result, Q. said, was like each of them was playing a part in a different show.

Mrs. Statts was trying to be coy and kittenish with Handy and Milpotts. It didn't go with her make-up, which was large and bony.

Pearl Dukes was doing Lady Vere de Vere. Very reserved and dignified, until she got to dipping her beak too often. Then her voice went shrill and her eyes
goggled.

Q. said he expected any minute she'd start seeing pink lizards on the table-cloth.

Lottie Dukes was quiet and watchful, keeping an eye on Q. and Milpotts, like she wasn't sure how much they'd talked her over. Every now and then she'd sort of remember and start being sweet to Roger. When she did, the poor goof almost choked on his wine.

Everybody drank a lot, Frazier told us, and everybody tried to pump what they could out of Milpotts. But nobody got much.

Along about dessert, Creel got the hiccoughs. Nerves, mostly, I guess, but they stayed with him the rest of the night.

When dinner was almost over, Dr. Ascher came down from upstairs. He called Q. and Milpotts out into the hall. He told them Jaffee was well enough to talk.

Milpotts sent the Doc in to get some dinner while he and Q. went up to see Jaffee.

Q. sent Frazier for me. He said it was because he wanted me to take some shorthand notes, but I knew it was because I sometimes caught things he missed.

When I got to Jaffee's room, I saw he was still looking weak and sick. He sure had a swell room to be sick in. All the other bedrooms I'd seen in the joint were like funeral parlors—cold white walls and heavy pieces of carved-up furniture that hurt you to sit on.

The Doctor showed more sense. He had a small cozy fireplace and, big, soft, comfortable chairs that had cushions you could sink into. There were low tables, lamps just right to read by, and a kind of high-topped desk with glass-doored shelves where he kept his collection of watches and clocks.

His bed didn't cover ten acres like the one in Q.'s room, and it wasn't painted all over with cupids like Lottie Dukes's. It was just a bed, with a lot of fat pillows and a blue satin quilt. He was dressed in a swell blue-brocaded dressings gown, over silk pajamas that had a monogram embroidered on the pocket. He was sitting up in front of the fire, but he didn't look right. His hands shook and his eyelids were heavy. While he talked clear enough, he seemed to be having trouble with his breathing.

"I didn't drink much of the lemonade," he was saying, "because it had a bitter taste. At first I thought it was the whiskey, but my mouth began to burn and I became wildly excited. I heard myself talking, and thought there must have been more liquor in the glass than I realized. After that everything blurred and I don't even remember Frazier's coming in."

Q. asked: "Any idea when the cocaine could have been dropped into the lemonade?"

The Doctor shook his head.

"Not unless it was done in the pantry. Hold on!" He thought for a minute. "I remember, now—when Frazier brought me the glass I was in the conservatory with Mrs. Statts. I intended to carry the drink upstairs to my room, but I remembered I hadn't checked the barometer in the workshop window. While I was attending to it, I left the glass of lemonade on a table by the pool."

"Was Mrs. Statts near the table while you were gone?"

"I don't know." He frowned. "I have a feeling she left when I did. At any rate, she was gone when I returned."

"How long were you in the workshop?"

"Oh, perhaps one minute, perhaps two. I remembered that the drink was getting cold, and hurried back to pick it up."

"Any one in the conservatory when you returned?" Milpotts wanted to know.

"Not near the lemonade. I believe Mrs. Duchene was somewhere at the far end. I noticed her, because she was trying to pick one of the orchids. I was going to stop her. I knew Vincent wouldn't like it. Then I remembered he was dead and it didn't matter. I took the glass from the table and came on upstairs."

Q. asked: "As a doctor, have you noticed anything abnormal about Mrs. Duchene?"

Jaffee said: "I know what you mean. She's a drug addict. I spotted it the first time I saw her."

"A dope?" Milpotts looked like he'd been handed ten bucks. You could tell he thought he was getting somewhere at last. "What does she take?"

The Doctor was worried.

"I shouldn't like to hazard a guess without observing her further."

Q. said: "No use trying to protect her. We know it's cocaine."

"I was afraid of that," Jaffee said. "But, of course, it doesn't necessarily mean she's responsible. Ascher tells me some cocaine was stolen from his bag. The fact she takes the drug may be only coincidence."

"What other poisons would Dr. Ascher be likely to carry in his bag?" Q. wanted to know.

"Morphine. Codeine. Some type of germicide . . . like bichloride. Possibly chloroform and atropine."

"With all those poisons to select from, why was cocaine chosen do you suppose?"

"Perhaps it was the first that came to hand."

"Perhaps." Q. didn't say anything more about that. Instead, he asked: "Have you any poisons in your possession, Doctor?"

"Nothing very much. A little morphine and codeine—and, oh, yes, some carbolic."

"Better turn them over to the Sheriff to be locked up," Q. said. He turned to Milpotts. "How about having Handy check over the drug cabinets all through the house? We don't want any more trouble."

"Right." Milpotts went into the hall and called Handy. I heard him tell him to make a search. Handy was to pick up anything he could find in the way of poison.

I went into the Doctor's bathroom. The glass of lemonade was still standing, about a third full, on a shelf near the washstand. There was a bottle of carbolic solution, a tube of morphine, and one of codeine on the top shelf. All of them had stood there long enough so they stuck a little to the paint. I went back to the bedroom. Milpotts was still missing, but Q. was prowling up and down. Now and then he'd stop and shoot questions at the Doctor.

He asked: "What do you know we don't?"

Jaffee looked dumb.

"I'm afraid I don't understand," he said.

"It's obvious," Q. told him, "whoever gave you that poison didn't do it for a joke. He—it might have been a woman, but we'll say 'he' for the moment—wanted you out of the way. There can be only two reasons: First, because you stood between him and, something he wanted. Second, because you knew something he didn't want told."

"But who could possibly—"

Q. looked like he wanted to choke him.

"That's what I'm asking you! If it's a question of money, it might have something to do with Welch's fortune. Do you know anything about the will?"

"A good deal. Vincent consulted me when he made it."

"How'd he happen to show it to you last night?"

I guessed Q. was sniping in the dark, but he made a bull's eye. The Doctor didn't even ask how he knew.

"Because he was planning to change it, and wanted my advice."

"And you didn't tell us," I could see Q. working it out, "because you were afraid it would direct suspicion at some one, eh? Who was it?"

"Roger." The Doctor looked like he saw he was caught and decided to come clean. "That will was made several years ago. It leaves the bulk of the fortune to Roger. But Vincent was annoyed with the boy. He was planning some changes."

"What were they?"

"Well, roughly, he said he intended to treble the bequest he had made to me and leave the rest to build and maintain a wing in some large museum which was to house his collection."

Milpotts came back into the room chewing a toothpick. He sat down on a chair at the foot of the bed and planted his number twelves on a padded stool. He put his thumbs in the armholes of his vest and listened.

Q. went on asking questions.

"What advice did you give Welch about the will?"

"I told him I thought he was making a mistake. After all, Roger was his own flesh and blood, and he was making too much of what was probably only a youthful infatuation."

"For Miss Duchene, you mean?"

"Yes. Mr. Welch had, or thought he had, some reason for believing she wasn't the right person for Roger to marry."

"Why not?" Milpotts asked. "She seems a mighty fine girl."

Jaffee shook his head.

"Undoubtedly. It was just prejudice on Vincent's part."

I marked the Doc up one for that. I'd have bet a million Welch had told him all about Lottie Dukes, but he was sport enough to keep his mouth shut.

Q. did the same.

Milpotts asked: "Do you think Welch told the kid he was changing his will?"

"Of course not." The Doctor was a rotten liar. It stuck out all over. "I'm sure he didn't. And even if he had, it isn't in Roger to commit murder. Why, I've known that boy all his life."

"So have I, more or less," Milpotts grunted. "You can't help hearing things down in the village. They say he's crazy. Didn't he get into trouble once for half killing a gardener?"

"It wasn't as bad as that. Roger merely gave him a hiding, when the fellow abused a dog."

"How about the time he was arrested in Boston?"

"That was just for a radical speech. You know how some boys turn red at his age."

"He's a swell one to be a Red—with all that dough coming to him," Milpotts said disgustedly.

The Doctor looked like he agreed.

"Vincent felt the same way," he said. "He and Roger were continually at odds. I was always making peace between them. You see, Roger's father died young. From the time he was a little boy, he's turned to me when he got into trouble."

Q. had been standing by the window looking out at nothing, so far as I could see. Now he fired a question.

"Then you don't believe Roger is the one who gave you that cocaine?"

"Roger? Why, the idea's preposterous!"

"Not so preposterous that you haven't been thinking about it."

"I've been thinking about every one in the house, but Roger's the least likely of the lot. Oh, I admit he might have killed his uncle. Not cold-bloodedly. But he might have done it in a sudden rage, if Vincent said something against Miss Duchene. When it comes to hurting me—it's out of the question. Why, there isn't anything the boy wouldn't do for me!"

The housekeeper came in just then with some chicken broth she'd fixed special for the Doctor.

She was a skinny old dame, with cast-iron hair. You could tell she had blue blood, by the veins in her hose, which was thin and bony. She seemed fond of the Doctor. I guessed she'd been with the family for a long time, because, except for him, she was the only one who admitted to being sorry about Welch. She said she was used to his ways and it 'put her out' having him dead.

Q. fished around some, but he didn't catch much. All he could find was that she thought the whole thing was scandalous, and something should be done about it. She'd always said no good would come of taking little blonde flibberty-gibbets as maids and then allowing them to carry on fast and loose with men old enough to be their fathers. Not naming any names, but there was no fool like an old fool, and a man in a butler's position ought to have more dignity.

Q. stopped her long enough to ask who'd been hiring blonde flibberty-gibbets. Didn't her job as housekeeper include hiring the help?

She said not the maids. The upstairs girls Mr. Welch picked out himself, and they had to be pretty—or what Mr. Welch called pretty. So far as she was concerned—

Q. shut her up and got rid of her, then came back to Jaffee.

He said: "There's one thing we still don't know. What it is the murderer doesn't want you to tell us."

"Yes." Milpotts finished off the toothpick and waggled his head. "If there's anything you're holding out on us, Doctor, you'd better spill it. For your own safety."

Dr. Jaffee looked scared enough to suit any one.

"Don't you suppose if there was anything I knew, I'd tell you?"

"Perhaps," I said, "it's just something the other guy *thinks* he knows."

Q. looked surprised, like he always does when I say something that makes sense.

"It might be, at that. Whatever it is, it didn't become important until this afternoon. Otherwise, he'd have made some attempt to polish the Doctor off before."

"He?" Milpotts asked.

Q. shrugged. "Or *she*. You'll have to take it either way. I wonder—"

"But I thought you'd decided a woman wouldn't have had the strength," the Doctor said, and Milpotts explained what Q.'d figured out about Welch's falling on the knife.

I could see Q. was thinking while they talked.

"I've a new idea," he said.

"What?"

"Some one might have thought of bumping off the Doctor in such a way that it would look like suicide. Every one would think he had killed Welch for the legacy, then gone panicky."

"I believe that's it!" Dr. Jaffee said, and even Milpotts looked pleased.

"In that case, the Doctor's safe. Whoever slipped him the cocaine wouldn't be likely to try it again," he said.

Q. pointed out: "At best it's only a theory. We'd better put a guard over the Doctor, just to be on the safe side."

"If you think it necessary," Jaffee said. "But I find it hard to believe any one really wants to kill me."

Some one knocked on the door. It was Roger Storey, come to see how the Doctor's cold was getting along.

It was the first time I'd seen him really look at any one but Lottie Dukes, and I began to take more stock in what Jaffee said. Maybe the boy did care about him.

Anyway, he looked all worked up. His eyes were twitching and he was stuttering worse than ever.

"I've g-g-got to see the Doctor," he said. "I m-m-must see him at once."

Milpotts didn't like the kid. You could tell that. It was kind of funny, too. First, he was sore at him because he'd inherited a pile of money, and, second, because he snooted money and was a Red. Why he should hate him both ways I don't know. But that's the kind of a guy he was.

"What do you want to see the Doctor about?" he wanted to know.

Roger said: "N-n-none of your business," and "This is my house and I'm n-n-not going to have a l-l-lot of insolent d-d-dicks around insulting the l-l-ladies," and some other things that didn't help him any with the Sheriff.

Milpotts was getting sore enough to throw him in the can when Jaffee called out from the room.

He said: "Roger! Stop that nonsense this minute!"

The kid quieted down like he'd been socked on the chin.

The Doctor said: "The Sheriff is only doing his duty. You ought to apologize."

The kid managed to get out a "S-s-sorry," but only to Milpotts. Not to the rest of us. He looked like he'd be glad to give half of what he was getting from Welch just to see Q. choke to death.

But Q. didn't let it worry him. He even argued the Sheriff into letting Roger see the Doctor alone.

He sent me to find the dumb deputy, Bill, and tell him to get ready to spend the night in Jaffee's room.

It took a lot of time to find him, because Margot helped me hunt, and we looked in all the darkest places first.

After a while we ran into him betting on cockroaches with Politos. They'd found two big fat roaches in the basement and had them lined up on a board like a whippet race. The Greek had cleaned Bill out of everything except his vaccination mark.

When we got back to Q. I found we needn't have hurried. Dr. Ascher had come upstairs and offered to spend the night with Jaffee.

"The Doctor, he iss out of danger," Ascher said. "But he iss not so young as once, und the after-effects of a shock—dey are sometimes more serious as the shock itself. Dere iss a couch in the room. I vill sleep dere."

"Well, that takes care of *him,*" Milpotts said.

We were in the upper hall. Roger, inside the Doctor's room, was talking loud and excited. You couldn't hear what he was saying because the door was too thick, but you could tell he was plenty stewed up about something.

Q. was tapping his knuckles on a big carved table. His jaw was set and there was a white line around his lips.

He said, "I wonder who'll get it in the neck tonight?"

"What d'you mean?" Milpotts wanted to know.

"Just that. Some one still has the Blade."

"You don't think—"

Q. brought down his hands on the table so hard Milpotts jumped.

"God damn it! Don't keep asking me if I don't think! Of course I think! If you'd do a little of it for yourself you'd see who ever stole that knife wasn't planning to use it for cutting his toe-nails!"

The cute little blonde came out of a room down the hall with some towels over her arm. She was breathing quick and her eyes were bright.

"Sheriff!" she squealed. "All of you! Come here!"

Milpotts sloped, double time. We all went after him, through the door and into the room. It was Mrs. Statts's bedroom. I saw her dressing gown over the back of a chair, and a wad of black hair stuck with wire hairpins on the dresser, but she wasn't there.

The little blonde led us across the room which was large and high-ceilinged, with windows on two sides. There was a bed, big as a Bronx flat, with four fat posts at the corners and red curtains hanging at the head.

The blonde pointed.

"Look!" she said. "Look at that!"

There was a thin black thread tied to the headpost. It stretched across the wall several feet, then it went out a window.

Q. pulled the thread, hand over hand, like a fish line. Something came up from below.

"I'll be damned!" he said, and threw it on the bed.

It was the empty sheath of the Borgia Blade.

The Blade itself was still missing.

20

After that, Milpotts went crazy. It was all Q. could do to keep him from cracking down on Old lady Statts right there and then.

Q. was for waiting.

"Why? *Why?*" Milpotts wanted to know.

"Until we learn more."

"More, hell! Want to wait until she does another killing? Who else could have hung that thing out the window?"

"Plenty could."

"For instance?"

"The little blonde."

"You're kidding."

"Listen, the butler's lost his head over that girl."

"You mean *Frazier?*"

"Frazier. I suspected it when the housekeeper began catting about blonde huzzies for housemaids. Then I checked up, and the old boy seems to have gone hog-wild."

"Where does that get us?"

"Places. Frazier's due to inherit under Welch's will. Ten thousand and some property—which would be a lot according to the blonde's ideas."

"You think *she* did the killing?"

"Not necessarily. There's a play called Macbeth, you know. . . ."

"Yeah, I saw it once."

We were in Q.'s room by now, sitting in front of the fire. Milpotts was fooling with the poker, shoving the hot coals back and forth while he thought things out.

"I get what you mean," he said, finally. "The dame that went walking around in her night-shirt with blood on her hands."

"That's near enough," Q. said. "But she merely *thought* it was blood."

"Yeah." Milpotts was still working at it. "She didn't do the murder, just jawed her husband until he did it to shut her up. You're arguing that the blonde and the butler—"

"It's a thought. The girl might have hung the scabbard from the window, then deliberately called our attention to it to draw suspicion away from Frazier."

"That's right, she might!"

"Yes—but, then again—somebody else could have slipped into the room. The blonde says the door wasn't locked."

"Well . . ." You could see Milpotts hated to give up the Statts dame. Same time, he didn't want to make a fool of himself. Especially in front of a guy from Scotland Yard. He was so worried he started to chew the poker before he noticed.

"If you're so sure Mrs. Statts didn't do it—" he began.

"But I'm *not* sure. The way I feel at present, the old hell-cat's as likely to be guilty as not. I just don't want to go off half-cocked."

"What do you think we'd better do?"

"Keep an eye on her. See that she doesn't make a move without our knowing it. Don't let her suspect we're watching."

"That's going to be tough."

"Not if you put the little blonde on the job."

"But I thought you said—"

"I'm apt to say anything when I'm arguing. The blonde's in on it already, so we might as well learn all we can from her. Put her to watching Statts—then we'll watch both of 'em. Maybe we'll get something. Then again, maybe not!"

Milpotts gave another swat at the fire and clanged the poker into the holder, but before he could say anything the door burst open and the Statts dame herself pounded in. She didn't walk in, she stamped in, bringing her feet down hard and flat, like she wished she was landing on somebody's neck instead of on the floor.

When she got inside she banged the door behind her and cracked down on the lot of us, playing no favorites.

She said Q. was a bastard, which he was, and a liver-gutted louse, which he wasn't. She said Milpotts would still smell bad if he was soaked for ten years in rose water, and she hoped he'd choke on his own bile. She said a lot of things about me which I don't clearly remember, and then wound up with:

"What the hell do you think you're doing, planting that scabbard in my room? And how the hell, do you think you're going to get away with it? I'll phone my lawyer. He'll see the District Attorney! He'll have you thrown into the gutter!"

She was talking to Milpotts, but Q. answered. Not mad, like you'd expect, but gentle and polite.

"I wouldn't send for a lawyer, Mrs. Statts. Not unless you want your name mentioned in connection with the murder."

The old war-horse snorted like he'd shot a gun over her head.

"Mentioned? *Mentioned?* What d'you think it's going to be when—"

Q. interrupted. "When what? Nobody is going to drag you into this, unless you drag yourself. I don't know how you found out about that scabbard."

"Maid," Mrs. Statts snapped. "Told me when I came upstairs."

Q. shook his head.

"That was wrong of her. Very wrong. We were so sure you didn't have anything to do with it we weren't even going to worry you by mentioning it. Isn't that right, Sheriff?"

Milpotts looked like it was news to him, but after he'd swallowed once or twice he managed to say: "Sure. That's right. We didn't suspect you. Not for a minute."

Q. said, just to make it good:

"In fact, if we *had* been suspecting you, which I assure you we weren't, finding the scabbard would have wiped you completely off our list. It's plain you're too clever a woman to hide anything so incriminating in your room, if you'd really done the murder. So you see . . ."

The Statts dame saw all right. She looked like she'd just stepped on a step that wasn't there. All the mad she'd got up was still bubbling inside her and she couldn't use it. She began to think about what she'd called Q. and Milpotts. And me. Her face got red.

"I'm sorry," she said. "Damned sorry. Made a fool of myself. I can see it now."

She waited like she hoped somebody would say she hadn't. Nobody said anything. She began backing away toward the door. She made me think of an ocean liner that's got put in the wrong dock.

"If there's anything I can do to help," she said, "I'll do it. I've had quite a lot of experience."

"In murder?" Q. asked, not nasty, but like he was really interested.

She said No, not murder, but with the law. She'd been through a lot of law-suits (I'll bet she had!) and she had a lot of influence in New York.

By now she was at the door and had it open. She said if they wanted her opinion—perhaps it wasn't worth much, but you never knew when a suggestion might be valuable— why, *she* thought they'd find it worth while to look up the past of a man who was right under the roof at the moment. She wasn't naming any names, but he knew a lot about murder. He'd killed plenty of men, not only on land, but on the high seas.

There was a kind of a screech in the hall and Creel bounded in under her arm.

I don't know what he'd been doing out there. Stretching his ear at the key-hole, like as not. But he was in now, and so mad he made the language the Statts dame had thrown around sound like a girl scout's pledge.

Only, what he said was to her, and not us.

I guess Q. and Milpotts got the same kick out of it I did. Anyway, they didn't say anything. Just let him rip until he ran down. It wasn't because he was out of words, either, but he began to hiccough and that spoiled what he was saying about what she was before she married Jake Carson (hic) who was the man she married (hic) before Statts. He said everybody knew about the kind of a (hic) house she'd kept. And not even first class (hic) either.

It was all news to me. Good news. It sent her out of the room as fast as she came in. Or faster.

Creel came down toward us, breathing fast and hic-ing between breaths. He said he'd been passing the room (hic) and he couldn't help hearing what was being (hic) said. So he'd stopped in to tell us his (hic) past was an open book.

Q. said, "Absolutely open."

Creel didn't know how to take that. His eyes shifted back and forth between Q. and Milpotts and he hic-ed once or twice more before he said:

"If you want to know what I think about this (hic) murder—"

Q. said: "We don't. All we want to know is whether or not you have any heavy black thread."

I looked at Creel quick. I knew what Q. was after. The scabbard was hung out the window with black thread and he wanted to catch Creel off his guard. See if he'd show anything.

But he didn't. Just looked surprised and said no. He didn't have (hic) thread of any kind. If Q. wanted to do some sewing he'd better call the housekeeper.

Q. thanked him for the suggestion and said it could wait until morning.

Milpotts said: "Well *I* can't." He got up and began walking toward the door. I guessed he was going to put the blonde to watching old Madam Statts, and Handy to watching the blonde.

But before he reached the door somebody knocked. It was a tall skinny maid. One that belonged in the kitchen. I'd seen her in the servants' quarters, but this was the first time I'd talked with her.

She said she had something to tell me. I went out into the hall. But she didn't tell me much. Just pushed a note into my hand, whispered a few words, and bolted, like she was scared to death.

I read the note, then went back into the room.

The Sheriff was gone. And Creel. Q. was sitting in front of the fire.

I said: "I'm walking out on you. Got a date."

"Blonde or brunette?"

"Red head."

Q. pulled up an eyebrow.

I said: "Weighs three hundred on the hoof. The cook. She just sent me this." I showed him the note.

It read:

*Can I see you? As soon as possible. It is some-
thing important I think you had ought to know.*

It was signed, *Miss Mary Fagan*. Under it was, *The Cook*.

"That tops the gag," Q. said. "Where're you going to
meet her?"

"Up in her room. She's the one Dr. Jaffee was with last
night. She's still supposed to be sick. The second cook got
dinner. Maybe there's nothing in it, but it won't do any
harm to go up and play her."

Q. asked, "Did you say play her or what? Remember
the age of consent in this state is sixteen."

"Well, I'm more'n sixteen," I said, and went out the
door.

21

Mary Fagan was waiting in her room, which was in the servants' quarters at the end of the third-floor hall.

I had to pass Margot's door to get there. It was open a crack, and I saw one black eye. It looked plenty mad.

I said: "Later," out the side of my mouth.

She called me a *"sale cochon,"* and banged the door shut.

All I needed was the blonde to make it complete. But she was downstairs somewhere with Milpotts. At least I hoped to God she was.

Mary Fagan was in a pink dressing gown with green and red cabbage roses sprouting all over it. I hadn't seen one like it since my grandmother died. Didn't know they made them any more.

The skinny kitchen maid with buck teeth, who had brought me the note, was in the room with her. She was saying:

"There, there, dearie," and "Don't take on so. You're doing it all for the best!"

When she saw me, Mary Fagan gave a sort of a gasp and clutched at her heart. The maid got a bottle of smelling salts, and stuck it under her nose.

"Sniff this, lovey!" she said, and right away the whole room smelled of ammonia and lavender. It made me think of my grandmother again. The old gal always used lavender salts for the hang-over after one of her bats.

"Well, I'm here," I said. "What you got to tell me?"

The cook took another sniff of the salts and waved it away. The pink and red and green thing she was wearing began to billow up and down.

"I wouldn't of told any one," she said, in a wheezy voice. "Not if they'd drawn and quartered me! Not if they'd poured me into boiling oil."

"You wouldn't have told what?"

"About last night. But the Doctor—" She began to cry, blubbering into her handkerchief. "It's on account of Dr. Jaffee."

"There, there, dearie," the skinny maid kept saying. "You mustn't give way."

"That man—you'd never have believed it—looking pious as a deacon and talking about us saving up and starting a little catering business in Hoboken!"

"The Doctor?" I said, thinking either she was nuts or I was.

"Not the Doctor, *him!*"

"Him? Who?"

The thin one spit out "Frazier," through her buck teeth, then snapped her lips shut and leaned back with folded hands.

I began to see light. But I knew better than to say anything. I just sat down in a chair and listened.

"I couldn't talk to the Sheriff, or that man you work for. He's got such a way of looking through you. It fair gives me the creeps. But *you're* different. I knew you'd understand how a girl feels at a time like this."

A girl. My God, she was fifty if she was a day!

"Of course he'll understand," the skinny maid said. "Won't you, Mr. Lynch?"

The two of them rolled their eyes at me, and I nodded.

"Sure I will."

The cook said: "It isn't him, really," mopping her eyes again. "It's that peroxided huzzy. He was perfectly respectable until she came slithering into the house."

"A better man you never met," the bean pole put in.

"Church always on Sundays. Prayer Meeting every Wednesday night he could get away. Never spending his money, except for a box of candy on Christmas and birthdays." She gave a gulp and pointed to a pink-satin-box on her bureau. "That's the last thing he ever gave me."

It wasn't much. Two pounds, maybe. With some pansies painted on the cover and a nasty little fat cupid that looked like he needed his nose wiped.

"Now it's perfume, and lingerie, and automobile rides."

"In a rented car!" said shanks.

"Movies. Theaters. He's even learned to dance. And him old enough to be her father!"

"Her grandfather, dearie!"

The cook laughed, sweet and nasty.

"Well, he won't keep her long. Not after he's spent all the money he's saved. She'll leave him like he was an ole shoe, for that oily Greek."

The other one said: "He knows it, too. I heard him tell her so. She just laughed and pulled his hair."

I began to get worn out between them.

"Say, you two," I said, "did you call me upstairs just to tell me the butler's a —?"

They both gasped and squealed. Such language! They wouldn't think of saying such a thing. And, anyway, he wasn't. Just misguided and led astray by a designing little tart. If they'd thought I was going to take it that way they'd never have sent for me!

"Well, why *did* you?" I got in.

Mary said: "Because I thought it was my duty to tell about last night. I wasn't going to breathe a word, but

now that some one has tried to kill the Doctor, and him so
kind, I hold it my Christian duty—"

"I feel the same way about it," the skinny one put in.

The fat one said: "No matter how much it hurts me,
I'm going to tell what I know."

"Which is?" I asked, but she wasn't going to be hurried,
not her. She began all over again.

"I had a nervous attack last night. One of my palpertations."

"Brought on," spare-ribs explained, "by worry over that
quarantine. She was afraid she might get smallpox and
spoil her face."

"That, and a little discussion I had with Frazier, *Mr.*
Frazier," the cook went on. "Maybe you don't know it, but
the room next door"—she pointed with her thumb at the
wall back of the bed—"is occupied by that blonde." (She
said "blonde" like she was saying something much worse.)
"Being only a second maid, she ought by rights to have
some one in the room with her, but Frazier, *Mr.* Frazier,
fixed it so she could sleep alone."

"Not *always,*" said the skinny maid, pulling her face
down until it looked like a dried prune.

"Be that as it may," Mary Fagan said, "I'm not one to
spread tales. But I've heard things."

"Springs?"

"*Things!* Just by accident. When I'm lying on the bed
with my ear near the wall I can't help hearing."

"She moved her bed special," the thin maid said.

"Because I felt I ought to know what was going on,
Frazier, *Mr.* Frazier, and me being practically betrothed,
until that trollop came along. Anyway, she wanted him to
get her a Ford."

"Can you bear it?" shrilled the skinny one. "Imagine!"

"She practically ordered him to get it, but he told her
he didn't have enough money."

I began to get interested.

"That was when?" I asked.

"Yesterday afternoon. I happened to run up for a clean handkerchief and heard 'em in there." She jerked her head toward the wall behind the bed again. "I got to thinking about it while I was getting dinner. Jennie, there, will tell you I nearly fainted over the soup. And by the time they came and said we were quarantined . . . Well, really, I went into a nervous collapse."

"Crying like she was crazy! Eight handkerchiefs she went through in no time."

"And hiccoughs," the cook added. "I couldn't stop."

Jennie explained: "That's when we sent Frazier for Dr. Jaffee. He came back and said the Doctor was with Mr. Welch, who was having one of his attacks, but he'd come right away."

"He did, too," Mary said, "and gave me something to quiet me. He stayed right with me until I went to sleep. Such a kind man."

"I stayed, too. Didn't I, dearie?" put in old horse-face.

"Yes. They both stayed with me, Mr. Lynch. But before I dropped off I heard something in the next room."

"Did you hear it, too?" I asked the totem-pole.

She said: "No, sir. Because the Doctor and I were sitting over there. Mary was there on the bed, with her head close to the wall."

"Just accidental," Mary explained. "It seemed to stop my hiccoughs when I pressed my ear up against something." She dabbed at her eyes. Her voice got sharp and shrill. "When your friend was asking questions after the murder I heard that little platinum drab say Frazier came right to her room after he brought the Doctor here. But she's lying. He did nothing of the sort. He didn't come up for at least half an hour. Just before I went to sleep he came in, and I heard her slanging him for being so late. Such language as she used! I wouldn't soil my lips!"

"What did *he* say?" I asked her, glad there was something worth taking to Q. *"What did he say?"* I almost yelled.

Her face turned spotty red. Her eyes were like shiny green marbles.

"He begged her to quit scolding and be nice to him. He showed her some money—I couldn't hear how much—and said she was going to get the Ford she wanted a lot sooner than she expected!"

22

God deliver me from women, was what I was thinking when I went out of that bedroom door. There's nothing they won't do for you, or *to* you, depending on how you happen to stand with them.

Just as I thought it, I ran into Margot, who was waiting to nab me.

"Which one was eet?" she asked.

"What you talking about?"

"Is eet the dried herring, or the red-headed peeg?"

I cracked: "Shut your face and let go of me! I got to spring something on the boss."

She went as far as the turn in the stairs, holding on to my arm. It was dark down there, and nobody around. I told her what the cook had said, and warned her to keep her trap shut about it. Then I sent her back and went to find Q.

He was still in his bedroom, sitting in front of the fire. He had a pad on his knees and was making notes. When I started my spiel he stopped writing.

"And I told you to stay away from dames!" he said when I got through. "If you take on a few more we'll have this case in the bag."

"*Will* have!" I said. "It's in the bag right now! It couldn't have been any one but Frazier."

"Yes? Less than an hour ago it couldn't have been any one but Mrs. Statts. And an hour before that it was Pearl Dukes."

He got up, went over to the wall and pushed the electric service button.

I asked: "What you going to do?"

"Have a pow-wow with Frazier."

"Think that will get us anywhere?"

"Your guess is as good as mine."

That's all I got out of him until Frazier appeared. While he was waiting, Q. got out his kit and began to shave. I knew he'd shaved before dinner. His doing it again didn't make sense.

Frazier came in looking suspicious and unhappy.

"You sent for me, sir?" he asked.

Q. stuck his face out the bathroom door, half covered with lather.

"Oh, Frazier," he said, "glad I could get hold of you. Will you do me a favor?"

"Certainly, sir." You could see he was beginning to let down a bit. His voice dropped two notes and the lines around his eyes smoothed out.

"I'll be glad to do anything I can for you, sir."

Q. said: "I hadn't expected to be kept here so long and I need some clean shirts."

That was a lie. He had two or three new shirts in his bag, but Frazier didn't know that.

"What size do you wear, sir?"

"Fifteen and a half. And if you could round up something for Lynch, here, I'd be much obliged. Size fourteen, isn't it, Lynch?"

"Yes," I said. "With extra long sleeves. And I'm partial to stripes."

Frazier said: "I shall send the car down to the village first thing in the morning. We have a haberdashery there which is quite satisfactory."

"That's a good fellow." Q. ran his razor over his cheek. "You might also pick up some socks. Light wool. Eleven. If you need some money—"

"Oh, *no*, sir. I shall let you know what it comes to when I bring the goods. Anything more, sir? Some Scotch, perhaps, for a nightcap?"

Q. said: "No," damn him, and "Thank you, Frazier," and "Goodnight."

"Goodnight, sir."

Q. went back to the bathroom. Frazier had almost reached the door when his voice called out:

"Just a minute."

Frazier stopped, sniffing a bit, and rolling his eyes.

Q. didn't come out of the bathroom, just went on shaving in front of the mirror. We could see him through the door. What he said was chopped up like he was working around his mouth.

"By the way," he said, "I've been making a chart of every one's whereabouts last night."

Frazier didn't seem to like that.

He said: "Y-yes, sir, very helpful—I'm sure."

"There are still one or two blanks," Q. went on. "Can you tell me where Mrs. Statts spent the time between midnight and one o'clock?"

"Sorry, sir, but I haven't the slightest notion."

"How about the Greek?"

"Politos?"

"What about him? Did you, by any chance, happen to run across him?"

"No, sir. I believe he was on guard at the gate, but I had no occasion to go outside. As I told you, after I left Mr. Welch, I went upstairs."

"Oh, yes." Q. stopped to wipe some lather out of his ears. "That's another thing we haven't filled in. I suppose you went straight to your room?"

"Yes—no, sir." Frazier began, to stiffen. His eyes moved back and forth. "I mean, sir, I didn't exactly go to my room—not at once."

"No?"

"I had several things to attend to."

"Yes, of course." Q. put away his razor and picked up a towel. "I remember, the cook was having an attack of some sort. You'd called Dr. Jaffee. Were you in her room?"

Frazier shook his head violently.

"No, sir. One of the maids was with her. I didn't think it necessary."

Q. came to the door, wiping his face with a towel.

"How," he asked, "did you expect to pay for that Ford?"

Frazier gulped. His eyes popped. His face quivered like he was going to cry.

"Wh-what do you mean?"

"You know damned well what I mean! How did you intend to pay for it?"

"I—I have a little money saved."

"*Did* have," Q. corrected. "You've spent most of it on that little blonde."

Frazier swallowed twice. "I'll tell you the truth, sir. I was lying to her. I didn't like her going out with Politos. He's a foreigner, not the sort for a girl like that. . ."

Quick as a flash Q. snapped:

"What about the money you showed her?"

Frazier went the color of pea soup.

"It was only fifty dollars," he said. "Mr. Creel gave it to me for fixing it so there would be a car to pick him up on the outside of the gate. He said he had to get away, had to be in town for that auction in the morning."

Q. said: "Fifty dollars won't buy a Ford. You told her she would have one—*soon.*"

"But I've told you I was lying."

"You're lying now!" Q. threw down his towel and came stalking out of the bathroom. His eyes were black as jet. They seemed to bore into Frazier. "Lying like hell! You didn't go straight upstairs after you left Welch last night. You didn't go up until half an hour after Dr. Jaffee. Welch was killed during that half-hour."

"But, sir—I give you my word—"

"If you weren't killing Welch, where were you? Who offered you money for the Ford?"

Frazier's Adam's apple went up and down several times, then he croaked:

"Mr. Roger."

"Where?"

"In his room."

"Did you go there, or did he send for you?"

"I went there." He began to talk faster and faster. "It's—that girl. She's done something to me, sir. I can't eat! I can't sleep! I can't do anything but think about her! When she wants something it—it seems as though I have to get it for her. I've bought her perfume, and silk stockings, and lingerie. Things I never thought of buying for any one before. Then she told me she wanted a car. Said if she didn't get it she'd go away with—with Politos. I had to do something, sir. I had to do something right away! Mr. Creel gave me fifty dollars. But that wasn't enough, not even for a down payment. So when I was with Mr. Welch I got up courage to ask him to advance me something on my salary."

"What did he say to that?"

"He said 'No.' He read me, sir, what you might call a lecture. I was upset. I'd been in his service a good many years. A man of my age feels a bit of a fool to be talked to like a school-boy."

"Go on. What time did you leave?"

"At the time I said, sir, just before twelve. But I didn't go straight to my room. I went to see Mr. Roger. I'd have gone to the Doctor if I could, but I doubted whether he'd have that much cash. Mr. Roger doesn't have any, either, most of the time. But when he has he's generous. I'd seen him loan it to others and I thought, perhaps, he'd do it for me."

"Did he?"

"Yes, sir. That is, in a manner of speaking. He didn't have any money just then, but he said he expected to have it in a few days—quite a lot. He told me he wouldn't loan, he'd *give* it to me. Several hundred dollars."

"For doing what?"

"For giving him the combination to the lock of the strong-room door."

"You knew it?"

"Yes, sir. I've been with Mr. Welch a good many years, and you might say he trusted me better than his own flesh and blood. He had a terror that some day the door might close on him accidentally. I believe he'd read somewhere of some one being shut into a vault and suffocating. So he had an electric bell installed. If the door closed on him all he had to do was to press the bell button. It rings in the servants' quarters. There's also a gong in the hall. I had the combination to the strong room so that I could let him out."

"Did he ever have to ring the bell?"

"No, sir. And I never used the combination."

"What is it?"

"I don't know as I ought to tell you, sir."

Q. shrugged his shoulders.

"Just as you like. The Sheriff doesn't know anything about this Ford business—*yet*."

Frazier looked at Q.'s face. He could see Q. meant business. He said:

"The combination is—"

Q. interrupted: "Write it down."

The butler wrote the combination on Q.'s pad.

Q. slipped the pad into his bureau drawer.

"Why did Roger want it?" he asked.

"I don't know, sir, but I believe it had something to do with money. He said if I'd just let him have the combination he'd be able to get a considerable sum, and I should have part of it."

"What do you think he was planning to do?"

"I've wondered myself, sir."

Frazier suddenly quit being a butler and turned human. His lips trembled. Big tears stood in his eyes.

"Don't you suppose I've wondered what the boy wanted? I worked for Mr. Welch twenty years. I won't say I was fond of him, but still, in his own way, he was good to me and I—I was used to him, you might say. To find a man one has known that long lying, the way he was, on the floor—with his—with his throat—" Frazier couldn't go on. He gulped once or twice, then his legs gave way. He dropped into a chair, covered his face with his hands and began to sniffle like a kid.

Q. didn't say anything for a minute, then:

"What did you *think* Roger was after?" he asked. "You must have thought something."

Frazier brought out a handkerchief and mopped at his eyes; his chin was shaking.

"I thought he wanted to use his Uncle's will to borrow on." (It sounded like he was telling the truth.) "There are men who loan on 'expectations,' as you might say. I thought he meant to show it to one of them."

"Welch kept it in the strong room?"

"He kept a copy there, yes, sir, but the original was with his lawyer in the city. He'd been talking a great deal about it with Mr. Roger of late. I overheard him several times."

"What was he saying?"

"He was threatening him with it. Mr. Roger has notions about being a Bolshevik. Nothing serious. Just the wild ideas a young man will get. Especially a young man that's a little unbalanced."

"You think Roger's unbalanced?"

"I shouldn't have used that word, sir. I should have said 'Nervous and excitable.' Mr. Roger has been that way ever since he was a child. He has fits of being very gay, and then, again, he becomes melancholy and morose. Used to talk about running away to sea and settling on some desert island, or about killing himself. Dr. Jaffee has done his best to help him. But nothing seems to do any good. That's the reason this Miss Duchene has been so bad for him."

"In what way?"

"Being in love with her, I mean, sir. It's made him even more excitable than usual. Almost crazy at times. Dr. Jaffee and I have worried about it, especially since she came here to visit."

"Did Mr. Welch seem worried, too?"

"No, sir, not exactly worried. That is, I don't believe it was Mr. Roger's health that upset him. He got the idea Miss Duchene wasn't the person for the boy to marry. Not that I mean anything against her. She seems to be a charming young lady, if I may say so."

"And a blonde," Q. said.

Frazier pretended like he didn't hear.

"Mr. Welch did everything he could to stop Mr. Roger," he said quickly. "Even before he became interested in the young lady himself."

"Oh, so you knew about that?"

"Every one knew about it, sir. I don't care for gossip myself, but the kitchen help . . ." (He coughed sort of apologetically.) "I can't always keep them in hand, and Mr. Welch's infatuation was the favorite topic of conversation."

"Did Roger know about it?"

"No, sir. I believe he was the only one in the house who knew nothing of it. He was just pleased and proud because he thought Miss Duchene had won Mr. Welch over, after he'd been so prejudiced against her."

Q. lit a cigarette and mumbled, "Pretty bad shock if he'd found out, eh?"

"I believe it would have been a terrible shock, sir. Knowing Mr. Roger as I do, I should say he would have been quite beside himself." Suddenly he stiffened. "Oh! I see what you are getting at, sir. You mean Mr. Roger may have had a talk with Mr. Welch late last night."

Q. said: "Something like that."

Frazier said: "But he wouldn't have harmed Mr. Welch. I'm sure!"

"What makes you so sure?"

"I don't like to say it, sir, but Mr. Roger is a coward."

"It was a cowardly murder—cutting a man's throat in the dark."

"Yes, sir, but it's not the sort of murder Mr. Roger could ever bring himself to do. The boy has always been afraid of his uncle. He'd have been too afraid to attack him. And then, the blood! Mr. Roger has never been able to bear the sight of blood. He might, possibly, have shot his uncle, but he never would have used a knife. *Never!*"

"Well, somebody used a—" Q. started to say, but he did not finish the sentence.

A bell started ringing in the hall below. A brassy bell, that kept on clanging and clanging.

Frazier turned white as a sheet.

"What's that?" Q. almost yelled it.

"It's the strong-room bell!" Frazier's voice was shaking. "The—the bell Mr. Welch had installed in case he was ever locked in the vault!"

Q. said: "Oh, some one has just pushed it by accident."

"But—but no one could get in there! The room is locked. I locked it myself. Sheriff's orders."

Q. didn't say anything, just made for the door.

Frazier and I followed him.

Every one was milling around in the hall and on the stairs.

Milpotts was below, looking sort of cross-eyed. He didn't know about the bell and couldn't understand the racket.

Q. didn't stop to explain. He was half pulling, half pushing Frazier toward the library door. It was locked. Milpotts brought out some keys. It took a minute or two for him to find the right one and I could hear Frazier's teeth chattering like he was having a chill.

Milpotts turned the key and Q. threw open the door. The same lamp near the desk that was lit when we found Welch, was on now.

The door to the strong room was open and the curtains were pulled back, but the room was dark.

Q. was the first to reach it.

Milpotts was second.

I was third.

Q. snapped on his cigarette lighter and held it up.

All crowded together, we looked into the vault.

Roger Storey was lying sprawled on the floor, face down, in a pool of blood. Lottie Dukes was crouched beside him. She was holding the Borgia Blade.

23

There were several other dicks besides Milpotts and Handy in the house. I haven't said anything about them because they didn't get in our hair, keeping mostly to the servants' quarters. I guess the idea of sleeping and eating in a place as swell as Sant' Angelo made them all want to come. Besides Bill and the two experts from town, there were a couple of men from the Sheriff's office and a comedy cop from the village, who watched the gate with Politos.

They'd all come tumbling into the hall when they heard the gong. Now, they were in the library fighting off the guests.

The women were squealing like mad. Pearl Dukes was the loudest of the lot. I could hear her voice above all the rest, yelling for Lottie.

"I can't find her!" she kept shrieking. "I can't find her. Oh, God! Somebody's killed my baby!"

Q. called: "Be quiet! Nobody's killed her!"

Milpotts and I reached down and pulled Lottie up out of the vault.

The steps were still at one side. Q. had moved them back there after he'd fixed the light, because Milpotts wanted everything left the way it was when we found Welch until after the inquest.

Lottie had dropped the Blade. She kept saying, over and over:

"He killed himself! He killed himself!" like a clock that's wound up and can't stop striking.

Milpotts yelled: "Everybody get to hell out of here! Lock the doors!" He turned the girl over to Bill, ordered Handy to fetch Dr. Ascher, then went into the strong room.

Q. was already inside. His cigarette lighter was flaming as he bent over the body.

"He's dead, all right," he said. "And that damned light is out of order again."

"Unscrewed?" Milpotts said.

"Wait. I'll see." Q. pushed the steps over and stood on them. "Yes; unscrewed."

The light went on again. You could see the room clear, now. A lot clearer than I wanted to. It was as bad as when we'd found Welch—or worse.

Dr. Ascher hurried in with Dr. Jaffee, who was white as a ghost and shaking so he could hardly stand up. He had insisted on coming. When he and Ascher started examining the body, I thought he was going to keel over.

"I'm to blame," he said. "I'm to blame for this! I should have kept him with me. Or asked you to put a guard over him."

"What do you mean?" Milpotts wanted to know.

"I mean he was talking wildly when he came to my room to-night. I thought his uncle's death had upset him, that he'd quiet down later. If I'd dreamed he would kill himself . . ."

Q. said: "This isn't suicide."

"What else can it be?"

"Murder," Milpotts said. "The girl killed him. We found her in here with a knife."

Jaffee went over flat on the floor. He was so heavy it took both Q. and Dr. Ascher to pick him up and carry him out.

They laid him on the couch in front of the fire.

Lottie Dukes was sitting in a big chair with Bill standing beside her. She didn't seem to pay any attention to the Doctor, nor to anybody else. Just stared around, sort of dull and stupid, like she had been having a bad dream and wasn't waked up yet.

Dr. Jaffee was coming out of his faint.

"Sorry," he said. "It's that cocaine."

"Take it easy," Q. told him.

But Jaffee wouldn't take it easy. He pulled himself up and looked at the girl.

"You didn't kill him," he said.

She turned around and stared at him.

"Kill Roger? Of course I didn't! He killed himself while I was in here."

"You expect us to believe that—" Milpotts began, but Q. stopped him.

"Better question them separately," he said.

"O.K." Milpotts had them take Lottie into the conservatory while he asked Dr. Jaffee about the talk he'd had with the boy in his bedroom. "What did he say that makes you think it was suicide?"

"Said he didn't want to go on living. Told me Miss Duchene didn't care anything about him. She was just marrying him for his money. Said nobody cared anything about him except for his money. That he didn't want the money. His uncle had stolen it from the Workers in the first place, and he was going to give it back. Nobody had any right to so much. Crazy things like that."

"He's always been a Red, hasn't he?" Milpotts asked.

Jaffee said: "Not always. Just lately. It was one of the symptoms of his disease."

"What disease?"

"Paranoia. Inherited from his mother. I've seen it coming on for months."

"How far had it gone?" Q. wanted to know.

"Not very far. Melancholia. Suicidal impulses. With occasional attacks of hysteria—"

"That the reason Mr. Welch kept you here?"

"Yes. That and his own bad heart."

"You believe the boy killed his uncle in a moment of homicidal insanity, then reacted and killed himself in remorse?"

Jaffee looked sick.

"No! I can't believe that! I don't know what to believe!" He turned to Dr. Ascher. "What do you think, Wilhelm?"

"Me? I should t'ink it vould be possible. *Ja,* but quite possible. Dis girl's coming, it hass unbalanced him. Any emotional excitement iss bad mit a mental case. More especially if he had the idea Mr. Velch wass trying to prevent the marriage. Den I can most easily imagine his becoming dangerous. Later, ven his homicidal fit it hass passed, it vould be quite natural for a paranoiac to become exaggeratedly remorseful."

"How well did you know Roger?" Q. asked Ascher.

"Intimately. Often und often down to my house he used to come mit Dr. Jaffee, here, for *wiener-schnitzel* und lemon *torte.*" The old boy looked pretty well cut up. "It iss too bad he had dot hereditary taint. His mind it wass brilliant. Not like most boys of to-day. *Nein!* Always reading. I gave him Marx, und Mills, und Nietzsche. . . ."

"So that's where he got it!" Milpotts growled. "Didn't know you were a Red, too, Doc."

Ascher looked sore as hell.

"It iss not being a Red to believe dot the world owes a man the right to earn a liffing, or dot it iss evil women und children should suffer und die mitout a hospital und medical care. Take it now our own town—"

I guess Q. saw the old guy was starting on something he could talk about all night if he wasn't headed off.

He said: "Never mind! Never mind! That's beside the point. Do you want to ask Dr. Jaffee any more questions, Sheriff?"

"A few." Milpotts looked at Jaffee. "With Roger talking like you say—in that wild way—why didn't you send for me?"

"Because I was convinced he didn't kill his uncle. I was afraid you might misunderstand his talk and think he was guilty."

"I sure would have," Milpotts growled, then seemed to snap out of it. "Oh, well, perhaps it's all for the best. If the boy committed suicide—"

Q. snapped: "The boy didn't."

"What?"

"He couldn't."

"How do you know?"

"Because his right hand is in his pocket."

"What?"

"Go look for yourself."

Milpotts hurried across to the door and looked down into the vault.

He said: "Damned if you aren't right!" then turned to the Doctor. "Was Roger left-handed?"

"No."

Q. said: "Then it's a cinch he couldn't have cut his own throat. Also, he couldn't have committed the murder."

"You think not?"

"I *know*. At the time Welch was killed, Roger was up in his room. Frazier was with him."

That was true enough. I don't know why it hadn't occurred to me before. No matter how guilty he looked, no matter what he had said about being sure of some money in a few days, Roger couldn't have done the killing. That is, if you believed what Frazier said, and I didn't see any reason for not believing him. He went straight up from the library to Roger's room and stayed there ten or fifteen minutes. Welch must have been knocked off during those minutes when Roger and Frazier were together.

Milpotts looked blank. He spit out the end of the pen he'd picked up from the desk and started in on a pencil.

"Then it must be the girl," he said. "Damn it to hell, I was hoping it wasn't." He got up, crossed to the conservatory door and called to Bill to bring her in.

Dr. Jaffee got up, too.

He said: "If you don't need me, I'll go back to bed."

Dr. Ascher said: "Goot! I vill help you upstairs."

The two went out.

Q. lit a cigarette.

"You might get some drinks," he said to me. "I could I do with a spot of Scotch."

The servants were all huddled in the butler's pantry and dining-room. Jennie, the skinny maid, was sniveling and the cook was having what she called "palpertations," but the little blonde looked excited and pleased, like somebody had made her a birthday present. I guess she figured this would clear Frazier.

Margot was sitting in a corner, looking around with her sharp, black eyes. When she saw me, she came over and backed me into a corner near the ice-box.

"W'at is zees?" she asked. "W'at is it zat has happen'? They tell me *she* has been arrested."

"Not exactly arrested," I said. "Where's Frazier?"

"Upstairs wiz Madame. Ze old lady, she is having ze fits."

"Why aren't you with her?"

The little wench cocked her head to one side.

"*Je m'en fiche!* Me, I am not hire' to tak' care of her. Only Mademoiselle." She came closer. "For why do zay keep Mademoiselle in zat room?"

"Oh, they're just playing a hand of bridge."

Frazier came in.

"The Sheriff wants some whiskey," I told him. "How's Mrs. Duchene?"

"Everybody wants whiskey," he beefed. "She's hysterical. I left Mrs. Statts with her. Scotch or Bourbon?"

"Scotch will do. I'll take a shot of Bourbon myself."

"Moi aussi!" Margot said. "Do zay t'ink he keeled himself, Mr. Roger?"

"We've counted six reasons why he couldn't of. He was murdered."

She gasped: "Murdered! Who do zay t'ink—"

I said: "When I left, they were betting on you," and took the tray of drinks from Frazier.

When I got back to the library, Lottie Dukes was talking fast and furious, like a patter act. She was on the couch in front of the fire.

Milpotts was sitting near her in a big chair. He'd finished chewing the pencil and was working on a splinter of willow from the wood basket.

Q. was standing by the grate, listening. His face was heap big Indian.

"I tell you I don't know what Roger was doing in here," Lottie said. "I don't know what either of us were doing. Roger just said there was something down here he wanted. He asked me to go with him to get it, and I did."

"How'd you get in?"

"He had a key to the library door. Give me a drink."

I poured a stiff one, and added some Vichy.

Q. handed it to her. She took it and drank it like she'd been lost for weeks in the Sahara.

Q. and Milpotts took theirs straight,

"Go on," Q. said. "Where were you when the boy told you this tale about wanting something?"

"Upstairs in my room."

"Anything seem wrong with him then?"

"Yes. He was terribly excited. Really wild. Kept asking me if I loved him . . . if I'd marry him even if he didn't have a cent in the world. Crazy things like that."

"What did you say?" Milpotts asked, when she didn't go on with her story.

"I told him," she lifted her chin and looked at Q. like she was daring him to contradict her, "I told him I loved him for himself alone."

"Did he believe you?"

"I don't know. Then he asked me to go downstairs to the library. I didn't know any reason why we shouldn't. The whole place belonged to him, didn't it? He had a right to go where he chose."

Q. said: "All right, we're not denying it. What then?"

"We went down the back stairs. Roger let himself into the room and turned on the light by the desk. He told me to wait. I sat down, while he opened the door of the strong room."

"He knew the combination?"

"Yes. He had it written on a piece of paper."

That much was true, anyway. Frazier had told us about giving it to him.

The Sheriff asked: "Did you see him opening the door?"

"No. He was in that alcove, and I wasn't particularly interested. I heard the door click and swing open. He called out, 'I'll be only a minute.' He snapped the light switch and said, 'The damn thing's on the fritz again.' Then he made a horrible choking sound and I heard him fall."

"What did you do?"

"I think I called his name. Then I got to my feet and ran across to the door of the strong room."

"Brave, weren't you?" Milpotts said, like he didn't believe her story.

I guess she thought he really meant it.

"I don't believe I was. I couldn't know anything serious had happened. My only idea was that Roger had tripped and fallen into the vault. I still thought that when I got to the door. It was dark inside, but there was a little light, enough for me to see him lying on the floor. I saw the steps weren't there. I thought he had stunned himself. So I jumped down inside."

She pressed her lips together like she was trying to hold something in.

"I put my hand down," she said after a little while, "to Roger's face—it was all wet! Sticky! I knew then he was dead! It never occurred to me he had killed himself. I thought the murderer was there somewhere in the room. My hand touched that thing you call the 'Borgia Blade.' I picked it up and crouched against the wall. I couldn't really think, but I suppose I meant to use it if the murderer attacked me. There was a horrible racket going on. It had been going on for some time. A clanging bell. People running back and forth and calling. I heard the door unlock and some one came into the room. Then you reached the door, and brought a light. As soon as I realized there wasn't any one else in the vault I knew Roger must have committed suicide."

"What started that bell?" Milpotts wanted to know. "Did you press the button? Or did he?"

"What button?"

"The one that rings the gong in the hall."

"Was that the noise I heard? I don't know anything about it."

Q. went over and looked into the strong room.

"The button is just inside the door," he said. "You may have unconsciously caught at the wall and pressed it when you jumped into the room. Once started it keeps on going automatically."

He came back to the fire, picked up a poker and jabbed at the log like it was to blame.

"Or—something else may have happened," he said.

"What?" Milpotts asked.

"It's possible, if the murderer really was in the strong room, that he slipped out while you," he pointed the poker at Lottie Dukes, "were bending over the body. That could have happened, couldn't it?"

She said slowly: "Yes. I suppose so."

"And his hand might have pressed against the bell as he pulled himself up out of the vault."

Milpotts looked a bit cross-eyed, like he always did when he was trying to take in a new idea.

"But in that case he'd have to have been locked in the strong room for hours," he said.

"Maybe he was."

"Sounds crazy," Milpotts said.

Q. said: "Sure it's crazy! Everybody's crazy! I'll be crazy myself if this keeps up much longer!"

I knew he meant what he said. He had more reason for going screwy than any one. We'd played into luck so far, but another twelve hours would be sure to turn us up—then blotto! They'd hang both murders on us somehow! I began to feel sick in the pit of my stomach.

Somebody started playing "Knock-knock" on the door.

"Come in!" Milpotts yelled. "And quit making that God-damned racket!" Which showed his nerves weren't so good, either.

Bill opened the door and stuck his head into the room. "The photographer's here," he said. "Bunch of reporters with him."

Milpotts snapped: "Tell 'em to go to hell!"

"They can get the dope from Welch while they're there," Q. said.

Milpotts changed his mind. "Bring the photographer in here. Take the reporters out to the dining-room and give 'em a drink."

"How about me?" Lottie Dukes asked. "I'd like to go to my room, if you're through asking questions."

Q. told her: "You're coming to mine. There are several more things I want to know." He looked at Milpotts. "That is, if you don't mind."

The Sheriff was wrapping up the Borgia Blade in a piece of newspaper.

He said: "Go as far as you like, but for cripe's sake learn *something!*"

Bill opened the door and sort of pushed the photographer into the room. He looked sleepy.

"What's the big idea?" he said out of the side of his mouth. "Isn't there enough hours in the day? Do you have to bump 'em off at night?"

Milpotts told him: "It's in there," and pointed toward the door of the strong room.

The photographer went over and looked down into the Vault. He twisted up his face.

"Christ!" he said. "It's sure juicy!" He began setting up his camera. He was whistling "One Night of Love."

Lottie grabbed Q.'s arm.

"Can't we get away?" she asked. "I—I can't stand much more."

Q. said they could.

The clock in the corner was striking eleven. I picked up what was left of the bottle and started after Q. and Lottie.

Q. took the bottle away from me. He said I was to cut along to the kitchen and assemble some sandwiches.

Lottie Dukes told him: "I couldn't eat anything."

Q. said: "I can. *Scram!*"

I scrammed.

When I got to the kitchen, Frazier wasn't there, but the cook was over her "palpertations" and she made up a Dutch lunch. All the time she was cutting bread she was flourishing the knife and talking about how it served some people right and the All-Seeing-Eye knew what was what and it just showed what the Lord thought of sin.

I didn't get rightly why she thought Roger's being bumped off was a good thing. But I didn't stop to argue, because I saw, out of the corner of my own all-seeing-eye, that the blonde was waiting on the back stairs.

I'm a fool for blondes. And, besides, I thought a word with that fluff might be interesting.

She just had time to take my arm and walk to the top of the stairs when Margot came clipping down the hall hotter than July.

She flashed her big eyes on us.

"I hope it is not zat I intrude," she said.

The blonde snapped, "You hope wrong, Frenchie. I was just going to tell Mr. Lynch something important. *And* private."

Margot looked like she was going to tangle with her.

I shoved the plate of sandwiches into Margot's hands.

"Hold these," I said. "This is business for the boss." I took the blonde down the hall. What she told me sounded like it might be important. Anyway, I grabbed the sandwiches and hot-footed it straight for Q.

24

When I got upstairs Q. and Lottie Dukes were at it again. You'd think they'd been married ten years the way they jawed each other.

"What business is it of yours whether I was in love with him or not?" Lottie asked.

Q. said: "None. I don't give a good damn one way or the other. All I'm trying to find out is what you were really doing in that room."

"You heard me tell the Sheriff."

"Sure. I heard you. But I still want to know *what you were doing in that room.*"

Lottie took a chicken sandwich and bit into it.

"I don't know why you think I'm lying," she complained. "I've always played straight with you. You know I have. Why, I've been counting on you—trusting you!"

"Have some bologna," Q. said, pushing the plate in her direction.

She threw down her sandwich, pulled out a handkerchief and began to cry.

"You *must* believe me," she sobbed. "You've got to believe me! If *you* don't, nobody will! Now that Roger's dead I'm so alone. And I'm frightened! Horribly frightened!"

Q. said: "If, you don't like bologna, take a green onion. It'll help you with those tears."

But Lottie didn't take an onion. She went on crying. After awhile she got up and went over to the bed. She buried her head in the pillow and cried a lot more.

Q. went right on eating for about five minutes, then he got up and walked over to the bed. He stood like he was listening for something.

"Look at me," he said; but she burrowed her nose deeper into the pillow. "Look at me!" he said again, and reached out. He took her by the shoulders, lifted her, and shoved her around so he could see her face. It was plenty mussed up, with lip rouge spread across one cheek and her nose all wet and shiny.

Q. grunted like he was satisfied she wasn't putting anything over. He sat down beside her.

"All right," he said, "I believe you. Now stop crying."

But Lottie couldn't. Not all at once. I guess the shock of what had happened down in the strong room was too much for her. Whether she cared anything for Roger or not, she'd had a damned bad jolt. Her face kept puckering up like a kid's.

Q. had to loan her a handkerchief. He even patted her shoulder and made her take another drink, which was going some for Q.

After awhile she got hold of herself enough to sit up straight. She took a look in a mirror, and from then on she got better fast.

When she'd straightened her hair and the line of her eyebrows, fixed her lips, powdered her nose and pulled up the strap of her green dress, where it had slipped off the shoulder, she was ready to talk again.

"You wanted to know what I was doing in the library," she told Q. "I'm perfectly willing to tell you. I followed Roger."

"Why?"

"Because I didn't want to marry him—"

"H'm?"

"—if he'd really killed his uncle. You can see that, can't you?"

"Sounds reasonable."

"He *did* come to see me. And he *did* ask all those crazy questions about whether I'd still marry him if he didn't have any money. He talked wildly about something he was going to do in the library. But he didn't ask me to go downstairs with him. I followed and watched. I wanted to know what he was up to."

"Did you find out?"

She shook her head.

"No. He just went in, turned up the light at the desk, and went over to the strong room. All I told that hayseed of a Sheriff from there on was true. Except—"

"Pass me a pickle," Q. interrupted. He'd gone back to eating.

"I wasn't watching from the desk. I was watching from near the door. That's the reason I couldn't see what happened. You believe me now, don't you?"

Q. took a bite of pickle and sandwich together.

"I'll try," he said, around the edges. "But it'll be a strain."

Milpotts came in, saw the sandwiches, and went for them in a big way.

"H'm, good!" he said. "We got the pictures, and they're taking the body into town. Find out anything?"

"Not much. But I can tell you Miss Duchene didn't do it."

Milpotts grunted, took a second sandwich in his other hand and went over to sit on the edge of the bed. I got the idea he was pretty sure Lottie wasn't guilty and didn't need much persuading.

"Then who did?"

Q. said: "Santa Claus."

Milpotts looked at him.

"Cut out the comedy. This is serious. The D.A.'s well enough to talk over the phone. He's damn near burned out the wire telling me what he thinks. If we don't get somewhere by to-morrow he'll bust open sure."

Q. went to the bureau, opened the top drawer and took out the yellow pad he had made notes on earlier in the evening.

"I hoped we'd get out of it," he said. "But not a chance. We'll have to do some sleuthing. An hour or so ago, I threw together a list of what is known as 'The Suspects.' After each name I put down the reasons for and against. Of course, as it stands, it's one murder behind, but perhaps if we bring it up-to-date we'll get somewhere."

"Your move," Milpotts said.

"I'd better go," Lottie Dukes put in, but not like she really wanted to.

Q. said: "Sit down. If you have any bright thoughts let us have 'em." He picked up his pad and studied it. "First on the list is Roger Storey. The fact he was due to inherit Welch's property made him look guilty. He's out now." He drew a line threw the name.

It made me sort of sick. I saw Lottie felt the same way. She closed her eyes tight and went green around the lips. Q. looked at her and said:

"Pull yourself together. You're next. There seems to be a lot *against* you—and just as much *for* you."

"What's against?" Lottie asked.

"You were planning to marry Roger Storey. Welch was trying to break up the engagement. You might have learned he was going to make a new will and have bumped him off so Roger would inherit!"

"What have you to my credit?"

"I wouldn't call it 'credit.' I've put down that Welch was making love to you on his own account. You'd have stood to gain more by marrying Welch than by taking the boy."

"That's downright insulting," Milpotts broke in.

"It's a damned-good defense," Q. told him. "And it's also the best reason we have why she didn't kill Roger. He wouldn't be any good to her dead."

Lottie said: "Thank you," in a nasty kind of tone.

Q. told her, "You're welcome," in a voice that was just as nasty.

"Who's next on that list?" Milpotts asked.

"Creel. In the 'against' column I have: Quarrel over watch. And the fact that we know he was wandering around near Welch's library last night. In the 'defense' column: The argument that he wouldn't be fool enough to murder Welch and then try to light out." He looked up from his notes. "By the way, where was he to-night when Roger was killed?"

"He says he was in his room. Nobody saw him, so we don't know whether he's telling the truth or not."

"Right. I'll put down a question mark." Q. turned to Lottie. "Now for your mother. She's next on the list."

Lottie kind of drew herself up. Plain as print I could see she was thinking about how her mother had been blackmailing Welch. Was Q. going to give her away to the Sheriff?

She said: "Do you have to drag mother into this mess?"

"Got to be fair with every one," Q. told her. He seemed to be studying his notes, but I could see he was playing with Lottie like a cat plays with a mouse. "There's only one thing against her."

"What?"

"She takes cocaine."

"Yes," Lottie admitted.

"And the Doctor was knocked out with coke," Q. went on. "Nothing else ties her into the case."

Lottie sighed. She tried to look grateful, but Q. wasn't paying any attention.

"Frazier comes next," he said. "For the prosecution I have down: He was one of the legatees. He was in need of money to hold that little blonde. Also, he had the best opportunity to slip that drug into Dr. Jaffee's lemonade. But the second murder throws him out. He has the best alibi I know. He was upstairs with Lynch and me when Roger was murdered."

"What next?"

"Dr. Jaffee. He's a legatee, too, and benefited by Welch's death."

"He certainly wouldn't poison himself," Milpotts protested.

"He might even do that—if he thought it would throw suspicion away from him. But he couldn't have done either of the murders, because when Welch's throat was cut he was up on the third floor with that hysterical cook and a maid. At the time of Roger's death, he was in his own room with Dr. Ascher. Or was he?" Q. stopped and looked at Milpotts. "Check on that, will you? We want to be sure."

Milpotts went to the door and talked to some one.

"It's being taken care of," he said as he came back.

I poured drinks all around.

Q. studied his list again.

"That covers everybody," he said, "down to Mrs. Statts. The main thing against her is the fact we know she was outside the library windows when Welch was killed last night. And that scabbard was found tied to her bed. We haven't checked on where she was to-night."

"Don't need to," I said. "I can tell you."

"Go ahead."

"That little blonde you set to watching her says she took some sedative tablets the Doctor gave her. She was asleep and snoring by ten o'clock."

Bill knocked at the door, then came on in.

"I got what you wanted, Sheriff," he said. "Dr. Ascher was with Dr. Jaffee from forty minutes before that gong started ringing until they went downstairs to look at the body."

"That's fine and dandy," Q. said, and picked up the list. He began to cross names off. "I was right the first time."

"What d'you mean?"

"I mean that wipes the slate clean. We've just proved nobody committed those murders. It *must* have been Santa Claus!"

25

It was along about there I began to get scared.

I'd been depending on Q. Figured he'd find a way out somehow, and pin the murders on the right party.

If he couldn't we were sunk. Here it was twenty-four hours after the first murder. Two men killed. Another poisoned. And no solution in sight.

I decided to forget what he'd said and light out on my own, first chance I got.

Q. stood up, stretched, and tossed his cigarette into the fire.

"I'm going down and take another look at that strong room," he said. "Want to go with me?"

Milpotts shook his head. Said he'd seen everything there was to see. From the way he said it, I guessed he wasn't as crazy about Q. as he had been.

"Go ahead and look at it if you want to," he said. "I've got to go back to town and settle some business."

He told Q. he was leaving several men on guard and would be back in the morning.

"A fat lot of good the guards have done so far," I said.

The Sheriff gave me a dirty look. I wished I'd kept my mouth shut.

"I guess there won't be any more murders to-night," he said. "I'm leaving Bill in the library."

Lottie Dukes began to laugh, high and shrill. She couldn't seem to stop. Just went on laughing and laughing.

"I—can't—help it," she told him. "Thinking about Bill in his shirt-sleeves—chewing tobacco—in the middle—of that—million-dollar room."

"Young woman, you're hysterical," Milpotts said. "You'd better get to bed."

He went out of the room. Q. gave her a look and Lottie Dukes stopped laughing like you'd turned her off with a spigot.

She said: "I'm going down to the library with you. Maybe I can help find something."

But Q. wouldn't let her go. When she tried to argue he shut her up and sent her to bed.

We waited until we heard Milpotts's car drive through the gate, then the two of us went down to the library. Bill was inside, with the door locked, but he let us in.

When I saw him I thought of what Lottie Dukes had said. He'd taken off his coat and hung it over the back of a chair. Sixteenth Century it was, Q. said, and worth a fortune. He'd taken off his shoes, and his socks were striped black and white. He was chewing tobacco all right, and spitting between the andirons into the fire. He looked like something that had crawled in through a crack.

Every one else in the house had gone to bed, except a guard in the hall and one or two that were scattered around the house—most of them within easy reach of the ice-box.

Q. sent Bill to get himself a cup of coffee. Bill didn't put up any argument about going. After he was gone Q. sat down on the couch in front of the fire. He put his hands in his pockets and stretched out his legs.

"Go on and say it," he growled.

"Say what?"

"That I'm losing my grip. That a louse could change brains with me and never notice the difference."

"I didn't say anything, did I?"

"No. But you've been thinking a lot, and you're right. Here I get me a European reputation—then come back to the good old U.S. and can't solve a two-by-four murder in a hick town."

"Two murders and a half," I corrected.

He groaned.

"Don't rub it in!"

"Maybe I'd better go up and pack, huh?" I was trying him out, thinking while he was discouraged he might fall for it.

He shook his head.

"Nope. If it meant frying, I'd still stick around. Just to find out who did it."

"We'll fry all right."

"Maybe." He seemed to go off into a haze. "Who the hell *could* have done it?" he growled. "It would have to be some one with a motive. An outsider or burglar might have come in and killed Welch. But he wouldn't strike twice."

"Then there's the dope that was slipped the Doctor."

"Yes. There's no doubt it's an inside job. But why? *Why?* Murder for revenge is out of the question. The three of them weren't tied up together in any way I can see. That leaves only money. The will. If we track that down, we find the boy profited by his uncle's death to a large extent, with the Doctor, and Frazier, and some of the other servants, in a lesser degree. But who would profit by the boy's death?"

"His mother," I suggested.

"Yes, but she's in an asylum. He wouldn't be likely to leave her much."

"He didn't have much to leave," I pointed out, "until his uncle died. Perhaps he hadn't made a will."

"Then that cuts off our last reason for his being killed. It isn't likely any one would bump him off just so his mother could inherit as next of kin."

I asked: "Lottie Dukes?"

"Maybe. But that would mean he'd made a will since he met her, and that's only a short time. Then, if she killed him she'd also have to be the one who killed the old man."

"You don't think she did it?"

"Not at the moment. But I *can* be wrong. She may be guilty as hell."

I offered another thought:

"There's her mother. If she knew money was coming to Lottie, she'd be willing to slit the throats of half New York State."

"Willing, yes. I wouldn't put anything past the old slut. But I still can't believe Roger'd made a new will. He's been here for ten days or two weeks and he'd have to have witnesses. Some one would have come forward to tell us about it."

"Who else would he be likely to leave money to?"

"Maybe to Dr. Jaffee. Maybe to some crazy Red organization. He might even have left something to Frazier."

I tried to do some figuring. "According to that, Roger, the Doctor, and Frazier are sure gainers by the old man's death. Lottie Dukes, and her mother, *or* the Doctor, *or* Frazier might have gained by Roger's death."

"Roughly speaking, that's it."

"But it doesn't do any good," I said, "because we've alibied all of 'em."

"Forget about alibis. We're talking about motives. Next comes Dr. Jaffee. Somebody tried to kill him. Who'd gain by his death?"

Without waiting for me to answer, he stuck his head out the door and told some one to call Frazier.

While we were waiting, he poked around the room. Tried the doors into the workshop and the stairs. They were both locked. He tried the bars over the windows and found they were solid.

Frazier came in, looking nervous and jumpy as a witch. Q. told him to sit down. He sat on the edge of his chair, his hands clasping and unclasping in front of him.

"What do you know about the Doctor?" Q. asked him.

"Which doctor, sir?"

"Dr. Jaffee. Has he been living here—I mean in the house—long?"

"Yes, sir. It's upward of five years now."

"Did you know him before he came?"

"Oh, yes, sir. Before Mr. Welch bought Sant' Angelo, Dr. Jaffee had an apartment quite near Mr. Welch's town house."

"How long ago did he give up his practice?"

"I can't quite say, sir. He didn't give it all up at once. Just a little at a time. Mr. Welch was rebuilding this place and he took more and more of Dr. Jaffee's time, until finally, when he come down here, he asked the Doctor to come and live with him."

"Was Dr. Jaffee ever married?"

"No, sir. He's always been a bachelor. He used to make rather a joke of it. About the five bachelors."

"Five?"

"Yes, sir. Mr. Welch. Mr. Roger. Himself, and myself."

"Who was the fifth?"

"Oh, Politos. Dr. Jaffee is always a great one for a joke, sir."

"Politos. How long has he been with Welch?"

"About four years." Frazier coughed and looked uncomfortable. "He was not one of the regular staff. Mr. Welch picked him up somewhere without telling me. He said he

needed a man to guard the place, some one who was good
with a gun and wouldn't mind using it."

"I'll say he wouldn't!" I put in.

But Q. didn't seem interested in Politos. He asked:
"Can you tell me who'd be likely to inherit Dr. Jaffee's
property in case of his death?"

"Why, yes, sir. As it happens, I can. Dr. Jaffee made a
will only a week or so ago. He was kind enough to consult
me about it." He pulled himself up short. "But I don't
know that I should be speaking of it. In a way, it's breaking a confidence."

Q. said: "I wouldn't let that worry me if I were you. It
may help save his life."

Frazier looked like he didn't understand.

Q. explained: "It's damned obvious some one is out to
get him."

"I see what you mean, sir."

"I'm trying to find out who it is before he succeeds in
bumping the Doctor off. It will help to know who would
benefit by his death."

"But I can't believe that any one mentioned in the Doctor's will—"

"I'm not asking you what you believe. I'm asking you
who's in it!"

Frazier looked so worried I wanted to laugh.

"I'm one of them, sir," he said. "But the Doctor hasn't
much to leave. Just his collection, and a few stocks and
bonds. He told me he was willing a government bond to
me. He'd been sick, you see, and he was good enough to say
I'd been kind to him. It was a pleasure. He's so generous.
Not only in the way of, ahem, money and presents, but
always pleasant spoken, and humorous. Every one likes to
do things for Dr. Jaffee. Mr. Roger and Dr. Ascher sat up
with him night after night."

"Dr. Ascher took care of him when he was sick?"

"Yes, sir. Dr. Jaffee was leaving a bond to *him,* too. Just by way of showing his gratitude. His collection of time-pieces was to go to Mr. Welch, and his books to Mr. Roger. There were a few small cash bequests to the servants."

"What servants?"

"Mostly those that have been here a long time. The cook. One of the housemaids. Politos. None of the legacies are very large, because the Doctor is not what you might call a rich man, sir. That is, he wasn't a rich man before Mr. Welch died. I believe Mr. Welch was planning to leave him something in his will."

"Did Dr. Jaffee know that?"

"Oh, yes, sir. Mr. Welch had told him. There was a provision in Dr. Jaffee's will in case Mr. Welch should die before he did."

Q. said: "Now we're getting somewhere. Who was to inherit?"

"No *one* person, sir. It was to start a fund toward building a hospital in the village."

"A hospital?"

"Yes, sir. While he was ill, I believe Dr. Ascher interested him in the idea. There isn't a real hospital here. Just an old house the Doctor fixed over with his own money."

"You say Dr. Jaffee was interested in the hospital project?"

"Yes, sir. He was trying to interest Mr. Welch, too."

"Did he succeed?"

"No, sir. I'm afraid not. Mr. Welch was not what you might call a humanitarian. He used to say the common people could be damned so far as he was concerned. He particularly objected to their smell, sir. I heard him tell Dr. Ascher so only last night."

"Last night?" I thought Q. was going to jump out of his skin. "Was Ascher here last night? Why weren't we told?"

"But you were, sir. I was sure you understood a doctor had come to attend the man who was taken ill. It was he who established the quarantine."

"Of course! I'd forgotten it was Ascher. You say he had a talk with Welch?"

"Yes, sir. Quite early in the evening. They talked in here. Mr. Welch sent me to fetch something to drink. That's how I happened to hear his remarks about the hospital."

"Anything else?"

"Yes, sir. I remember he said the noblemen in the Middle Ages had the right idea of how to treat the common people. One of the Borgias was riding out to a big affair. He came to a muddy place in the road. His horse's hoofs had been gilded with real gold leaf and he didn't want to get them dirty, so he made some of the peasants who were standing by lie down on their faces while he rode over their backs."

"Welch must have been sweet to work for!"

"He wasn't easy. But he paid very well. Somehow, sir, when you once worked for him you couldn't seem to get away. I left once or twice. The cook, too. But we always came back. It was the same with Mr. Roger. He was forever quarreling and leaving, then coming back again."

"Do you happen to know how Roger was leaving his money?"

"No, sir. I've been wondering myself. Now that Mr. Welch is dead, it would be a great deal."

"How much, do you suppose?"

"I couldn't say for sure, sir. We were always led to believe Mr. Welch was many times a millionaire."

"Would you say there was any chance Roger had left his fortune to Dr. Jaffee?"

"I shouldn't be surprised, sir. He was fonder of Dr. Jaffee than of any one. That is, until he met Miss Duchene."

"If that's true, all the money would come to Roger, and through Roger to Dr. Jaffee. If the Doctor kicked off—" Q. stopped. His eyes went sort of blank, and his nostrils twitched like he was on a scent.

I said: "But some one tried to bump off the Doctor *before* Roger was dead. If he'd died from the dose of poison his estate wouldn't have amounted to much."

"Yes." Q. was still looking blank. "We have to remember that. It must mean something, of course. But still . . ." He turned to Frazier. "You say there's a sort of a makeshift hospital in the village?"

"Yes. Just an old house that has rooms for contagious cases on one side, and a lying-in-ward on the other."

"Get the place on the phone for me, Frazier. That's a good fellow."

Frazier went to the telephone. The telephone service was about like what you'd expect in a small town at that time of night. He had a hell of a time getting what he wanted. Finally he talked to some one he called "Mrs. Peel."

"She's Dr. Ascher's nurse," he said over his shoulder, and handed the phone to Q.

Q. told her he was calling from Sant' Angelo and wanted her to know the Doctor was tied up and might not be back to the hospital until morning.

"How's the man who was sick?" he asked her. "The one with chickenpox. That's good. And the twins? Fine! Do you happen to know whether or not the Doctor got out last night to that rheumatism case? He didn't leave the hospital? You're sure of that? Of course. I understand. . . ." He said good-by and hung up.

"What rheumatism case?" I asked.

Q. grinned at me.

"How the devil should I know? There's always a rheumatism case around somewhere. But that doesn't matter.

What's important is that the Doctor didn't leave the hospital from the time he took the chickenpox patient down
from here until they called him back this morning to make
a post mortem on Welch."

"Then he couldn't—" I began.

"You're right! You're damned right! He couldn't."

Frazier's eyes were beginning to pop.

"But surely, sir," he said, "you aren't suggesting—"

Q. didn't let him finish.

"You heard me," he snapped. "I said it couldn't have
been Ascher!"

26

"Maybe a drink would help," I suggested.

Frazier had left us. Q. was tramping up and down the library like he was plugging out some idea.

"You and I are through with drinks," he said, "until we get this straight."

I said: "They always give you a drink the morning you're hung."

Q. didn't answer. Instead, he went over to the strong room, pushed aside the curtains and looked in, then he turned on the light and dropped down inside.

I stayed where I was. There wasn't anything about that room that made me want to look at it again.

Q. began talking. His voice sounded muffed.

"Nothing seems to be changed since the time we found Welch," he said. "That is, nothing of importance. The steps have been pushed a bit farther over, but Roger may have done that. The other stuff's still strewn across the floor. . . ."

I could hear him clearer, now, and I judged he'd climbed out of the vault. A minute later he came from the alcove. He was wrapping something in a handkerchief. There was blood on his hand. Blood that was bright red, not brown and stale.

I said: "What happened?"

He didn't seem to notice me.

"I cut my hand. Nothing serious. I found something."

"What?

"Oh, for God's sake, let's get out of here. I want some air!"

I hate walking even in swell weather, and it was drizzling outside. The ground was wet and sticky. But Q. made me come along.

We went out through the hall and cut across grass that squashed under foot, down to a drive along the river. It ran near the top of the cliff for a ways, then turned and followed the high wall that ran all around Sant' Angelo.

Q. walked in a quick, quiet way, putting his feet down one in front of the other, toes pointed straight forward, Indian fashion.

I tried to do the same, but my feet went wrong. After awhile the water got into my shoes. They began to squelch at every step.

I said: "What the hell's the big idea, and how long d'you expect me to keep this up?"

Q. said: "Quit bellyaching. I'm thinking things out."

After a long time he said:

"Nothing fits together. Not a damn thing! The only suspects with motives for committing the murder have airtight alibis. The ones who haven't any alibis haven't any motives. It's a hell of a mess."

I started to say, "And then some," but before I could finish a bullet went through my hat.

I sat down on my fanny.

Somebody said: "Put 'em up!"

Q. slipped around a tree. You couldn't see him leave. He just wasn't there.

A big guy came out of the darkness and tried to turn me over. Q. jumped him. After that everything was jumbled.

Mud. Trees. Stars. I couldn't tell which was which. Then somebody stepped on my face.

I heard Q. say: "I've got him. Hey, Lynch! Are you all right?"

I sat up. I couldn't see much but it looked like Q. had somebody by the neck and was rubbing his face in the mud. The fellow's fingers stiffened. A gun dropped from his hand.

Q. yelled: "Pick it up!"

I picked it up and said:

"Don't move or you'll be picking lead out of your rear fender."

Q. said: "That's me you're aiming at! Quit clowning and strike a light!"

The first two matches were damp. They went out. The third flared up.

In the yellow light I saw a face. It was the Greek.

When he'd spit out the mud and got his breath back, the story he told sounded straight enough. He'd been ordered by Milpotts to watch the grounds and not let any one make a get-away. When he saw some one on the road he let off a shot, so he told us, just to scare whoever it was and make them stop.

Q. said: "I see," and made me give him back his gun.

We started for the house. The punk went with us. First he was sulky, but Q. told him what a hell of a fellow he was. Quick on the trigger, and a swell fighter.

Soon as he saw Q. wasn't sore he began to brag. Most Greeks do if you give 'em half a chance.

"Where I come from we no use little guns much. Reffles. All reffles . . . or knives. I not learn to shoot until I am man full grown."

"I can't believe it," Q. said. "Look at the way you hit Creel last night. Right through the shoulder—when he was as much as ten feet away."

"Yeah. That's right, boss! I did that."

"And to-night, if I hadn't stopped you, it wouldn't have taken more than two or three tries for you to hit Lynch."

"Yeah. I am good shot, you bet you. Good at lots of thing. Good at shoot. Good at fight. Good at make love."

"Blondes?" Q. asked him, and the Greek laughed.

"That's right, boss! Maybe I marry onto one pret' soon."

"Let me know when you do. I'll send you a wedding present," Q. told him.

We were getting closer to the house. I wondered why he was taking so much trouble to butter up the Greek. He didn't seem important enough to be worth it.

Outside the conservatory door Politos stopped.

"Got to go back," he said. "Sheriff, he tell me to watch, and I watch, you bet you! Glad I no hit you, boss."

"Here's a fiver that's glad, too." Q. passed him a bill. The Greek looked like he was going to kiss him.

"Many thank. I buy that blonde two-three pair silk stockings. Last night, she tell me she want."

"About last night," Q. said, "I know you told the Sheriff you didn't see anything. But I wonder"—he winked—"if there wasn't' something you forgot to mention."

"No, by golly!" The Greek sounded sorry. "If I got somet'ing I sure tell you, boss."

Q. wasn't satisfied with that. He asked:

"When you talked to Mr. Welch through the window, just before he went into the strong room, did you notice if he had anything in his hands?"

Politos twisted his face and tried to think.

"A paper," he said finally. "He was carrying a paper—and somet'ing else. I no see what."

"A knife, perhaps? Or a clock?"

"Not a clock, boss. She is big. I would see. A knife, maybe. But I not know. Somet'ing smaller, I t'ink. I cannot say for sure enough. I do not look at his hands, boss. I just listen to what he tell me."

"What did he tell you?"

"He tell me watch gate. He tell me nobody must leave because of smallpox. Nobody at all. Then he close window. I go back to gate. Stay there. Pret' soon Mr. Creel come along. He try for to get out. I shoot. Everybody come down. I see not'ing else at all."

Q. sighed. "Oh, well, I suppose there wasn't anything to see." He started for the house.

Politos looked like he wanted to find something to do for his five spot. He said:

"If you want to know about to-night, boss, I see plenty."

"What?" Q. came back down the steps. He didn't seem to notice the rain, which was getting down to business.

"You like to know about?" The Greek asked.

"You're damn right I would!"

Politos smiled all over his face.

"Then I tell you somet'ing, boss. It was just before Mr. Roger, he got killed."

"How long before?"

"Ten—maybe fifteen—maybe twent' minutes. I am to watch in the woods, see? But I t'ink if I come back to the house a while I maybe see somebody." He winked. "She got yellow hair."

"Where did you come?"

"Over to that tree, boss. Sometime she come down on the outside stairs. From that balcony. She come when she finish work. You know, boss, opening up the bed and fixing water to drink. She come see me a litt' time before she go to bed."

"Did she come?"

"No. But somebody else come. Down those stairs."

"Who?"

"Sorry. I like telling you, boss. But I don' know."

"Was it a man or a woman?"

"No can say. Just somebody. It might be big lady or litt' man."

"Or a monkey on stilts. Hell! You're a big help! Where did he, or she, or it, go after coming down the stairs?"

"Into conservatory. The door open, then close, ver' soft. Poof! Nobody there!"

"See anything else?"

"No, boss. Sorry."

"All right," Q. started up the steps again. "If you see anything more, let me know."

The Greek patted his pocket.

"You bet you my life, boss. I come tell you quick."

Q. and I went back into the house. We hadn't been gone more than a few minutes. About ten, I think. Fifteen, at most, but you could have wrung me out like the week's wash.

Everything was just as we had left it, except that the man who was supposed to be guarding the door of the library was stretched out on a cushioned seat in the conservatory. He was snoring like a locomotive.

I thought: Anyway, we got a roof, over our heads, and I can have a hot bath.

I was wrong. As soon as Q. was sure the Greek had gone away, he turned around and went out again. I followed.

"Haven't we played tag with the pleurisy long enough?" I asked him, and he kicked my shin to make me shut up.

We went along the wall of the house to the stairs that came down into the shrubbery.

Q. walked like a ghost. I tried to do the same, but wasn't so good at it. My shoes were soaking wet and I slipped on a step. Q. stuck his elbow in my ribs and kept it there as a warning.

The stairs led to the balcony that was hung along the second story. The kind you see in jig-saw puzzles of "Venice at Sunset," or "The Grand Canal."

All the bedrooms on that side had windows opening on to it. Some of them had doors, too. Besides that, there was a door from the upper hall. We went in that way, and came dripping down to Q.'s room.

There was a light inside. Lottie Dukes was sitting in a chair by the fire. It made me think of last night, when we walked in and found her sitting beside Q.'s stained dinner coat. Only then, she'd been bright and snappy. Now she was asleep, curled up in the big chair. Her hands were under her cheek. Her lashes were so long they made a shadow on her cheek. Her lips were apart. You could see her breath moving the lace up and down on her thin dressing gown. That wasn't all you could see, either. But she didn't look smart or sassy. She looked like a tired kid.

Q. went over and stood in front of her. After a minute, he said:

"You can wake up now. I've had an eyeful."

She opened her eyes.

"When you play possum, you want to breathe slow and even, not quick and short," Q. told her.

She didn't try to deny anything.

"I was afraid you wouldn't like my being here," she said, and looked up at him through her lashes. "You won't scold, will you? I was afraid to stay in my room. I felt safer in here."

Q. said: "Yeah, just a little frightened fawn. Then again, maybe you thought you could get some dope when I came back—from wherever I was."

"And where were you?"

"Out and around."

"Learn anything?"

"Plenty." He took a cigarette from a box on the table.

Lottie struck a match and held it out to him.

"You don't need to do that," Q. said. "I'm going to tell you anyway."

She grinned and said: "You're poison, but I like you."

She lit a cigarette for herself, threw away the match and sat down.

"Go on. What have you been up to?"

"We've been knocking some one's alibi higher than a kite."

"Whose."

"That's the hell of it! We don't know—yet. But I'm willing to bet my left eye that somebody we thought was upstairs this evening slipped down the balcony steps, went through the conservatory, and into the library by the workroom door."

"Do you mean before Roger and I—"

"Yes. About twenty minutes before."

"But I'm sure the door was locked. I tried it when we went in."

"The murderer must have locked it after he came into the room."

"You don't think he was in the room when *we* were there?"

"Looks like it. It wasn't necessarily a man, either. The Greek says it might have been a woman. We'll just say 'he' because it's easier. Way I figure it, the murderer was hiding behind the velvet curtains in the alcove. When Roger went down into the vault he followed, bumped him off, then slipped out while you were bending over the body."

Lottie gave a kind of a choking gasp. The negligée thing she was wearing dropped down off one shoulder. "Don't talk about it! It gives me the creeps."

"Go on having 'em," Q. said. "They're becoming."

She pulled the negligée thing back in place, but it dropped down again. She got up and held her hands out to the fire.

You could see the blaze right through what she was wearing.

Q. said to me: "Get us something to drink. Whiskey's out. Try coffee. Frazier said he'd leave some in a thermos downstairs."

Lottie sat down on the arm of his chair. He didn't say anything, but he didn't move away from her, either.

"Margot is waiting for me in my room," she said. "You might stop in and tell her she can go to bed."

"You needn't wait to tuck her in," Q. said. "Make it snappy with that coffee." But he winked when he said it so I figured I didn't have to make it too snappy.

There was a dick in the upper hall. He got up and listened until he saw who I was, then he nodded and went back to his seat.

I slipped down to Lottie Dukes's room. I didn't want to wake anybody up so I went in without knocking.

Margot was there, all right. She'd peeled off her uniform and was holding up one of Lottie's evening dresses against the front of her to see how it looked in the mirror.

It looked swell from where I stood.

I wasn't on the mirror side, and she was wearing black georgette step-ins.

27

When I got downstairs, the kitchen and butler's pantry were empty. I could see Bill and another dick sitting in the dining-room. They were eating cold chicken and drinking beer.

I remembered we hadn't told Bill we were going out. He probably thought we were still in the library. It didn't seem important. I didn't want to talk with him or anybody else just then. I had a lot of things to think about. I've known plenty of girls, but never one that stayed in your mind like Margot.

I found the thermos jug and some sandwiches Frazier had laid out. There was cognac, too. I took it along, figuring Q. couldn't call it a drink if it was poured into coffee. I didn't dare stop to fortify myself, because, what with one thing and another, I'd been sort of delayed. I figured I'd better get back before Q. noticed.

I picked up the tray and started to climb the back stairs for about the hundredth time that night. Before I reached the top I knew something was wrong. A woman was screaming, highland shrill. I took the cognac bottle off the tray and stuck it behind a curtain on the window ledge, then went up two steps at a time.

Frazier and Mrs. Statts were hurrying down the hall. Frazier was still in his tux, but Mrs. Statts was wearing a wrapper. Creel came to the door of his room and looked

out just as Q. came out of the door next to Lottie's room
and crossed over to the Doctor's. He knocked.

"What's the matter?" I asked. "What's happened?"

Dr. Jaffee's door flew open. Dr. Ascher had opened it.

Q. said: "Something's wrong with Mrs. Duchene, Doctor. She seems to be delirious."

Ascher was wearing a pair of gray silk pajamas that
hung down in wrinkles, like the skin of an elephant. He
was trying to put on a green brocaded dressing gown that
would have gone around him twice. They both belonged
to Dr. Jaffee.

When he got his arms through the sleeves he grabbed
for his little black bag and ran across the hall to where
Q. was waiting. The door opened and we could hear Pearl
Dukes yelling something about a man in her room, a *great
big* man.

Creel and Mrs. Statts were listening like they were
stunned.

Dr. Jaffee came out into the hall. He looked sleepy.
"What is it?" he asked.

"A nightmare," Q. told him. "Or too much coke."

Pearl was screeching that the man was wearing a black
mask and had made a grab at her.

Q. said: "Better go back to bed, Doctor." He told me,
"Bring that coffee. We'll need it."

I followed him into Jaffee's room and put down the tray.

The Doctor had climbed back into bed. He was pulling
the satin comforter up around him like he was cold.

Q. offered him a cup of coffee, but he shook his head.
Said they'd filled him up with caffeine to counteract the
cocaine and he never wanted to taste coffee again.

Pearl Dukes was quieting down some. But you could
still hear her, even above the talk in the hall.

Frazier was out there with Creel and Mrs. Statts, also
one or two of the servants, and most of the men from

downstairs. All of them were listening, and trying to figure what Pearl Dukes could have seen.

My guess was—nothing. She was on the same side of the house as we were, and her room looked out on the hundred-foot drop to the river, same as ours. Nobody could have got into her room unless he had wings. I guessed Q. felt the same way I did, because he didn't pay much attention to her noise, just sat on the edge of the Doctor's bed, sipping his coffee and talking.

"Ascher will quiet her down," he said. Then, as though he was making conversation: "Ascher strikes me as a pretty good doctor."

"Very good," Dr. Jaffee said. "From Heidelberg."

"What's a man like that doing in a town like this?"

Jaffee shrugged. "The usual thing—a good doctor, but no bedside manner. He's a fool. He might have made a fortune in New York, or Boston, or Philadelphia, if he'd been willing to listen to rich women's troubles. But he manages to be fairly happy with his roses, his socialism, and his hospital plans. He's been drafting and re-drafting them for over ten years."

"Any chance of his ever getting the hospital?"

The Doctor smiled.

"If you'd asked me that yesterday," he said, "I'd have said not a chance in the world. But now, I don't mind telling you I've been thinking, as I lay here, that a hospital would make a very fine memorial to Vincent and Roger."

"Does Dr. Ascher know you are considering helping him?"

"I haven't talked with him seriously, of course. But he knows I've always been interested. I even tried to get money from Vincent for the project. Although I knew before I started it was hopeless."

I remembered Frazier had told us Mr. Welch used to say the common people could be damned.

Q. walked over to the tray. He picked up the coffee pot and poured out another cup.

Pearl Dukes had started yelling again. This time she said the man was all bloody. He had a knife in his hand, she said, a long shiny knife.

Q. went back to the bed, carrying his cup of coffee.

The Doctor said: "Have you talked at all to Politos?"

"The Greek?"

"Yes, I was thinking perhaps—oh, hang it all, I hate to accuse any one who may be innocent, but I've been thinking that he comes nearer to my idea of a murderer than any one on the place."

"Just why do you say that?"

"Because of his temper. Usually he's a peaceable chap, but when he goes into one of his rages—once he almost beat a dog to death. . . ."

"And Roger beat him?" Q. was guessing, but he guessed right.

"Yes. You heard Milpotts speak of that? Then he used to get furious at Vincent—Mr. Welch. Once he even struck at him. I can't think why Vincent kept him."

"I can't either," Q. said. "He might just as well have kept a gorilla. Except an ape has more brains."

"Then you've talked with him?"

"Yes." Q. didn't add anything more for a minute, then he said: "Doctor, your bed faces the window. I wonder if you happened to notice any one walking along the balcony about fifteen or twenty minutes before Roger was killed."

"Fifteen or twenty?" The Doctor thought it over. "No, I couldn't have seen any one. Matter of fact, I wasn't in bed at that time. I was taking a bath."

"You mean to say," Q. looked like he'd run into something in the dark and stubbed his toe, "you mean to say, you weren't in here with Dr. Ascher?"

"No. He was sitting in this room, but I wasn't actually with him. That caffeine they'd given me made me nervous and excited. The Doctor thought half an hour in warm water would relax me, make me sleep. As a matter of fact, I dozed off in the tub, I was still there when they came to tell me Roger had been murdered."

Q. put the cup of coffee down by the bed and started for the door. I started after him. When he had the door half open, he seemed to think of something and came back.

"By the way, Doctor, you know a lot about clocks. Can you tell me," he held out something wrapped in a handkerchief, I guessed it was the thing I'd seen him bring out of the strong room, "what part of a clock this is?"

It was a piece of wire, sharpened at either end, and bent into a sort of loop. There was a piece of adhesive tape wound around the flattened top of the loop.

The Doctor took it out of Q.'s hand. It seemed to me his eyes looked funny. Like he was surprised and didn't want Q. to know.

After a minute he said:

"It isn't anything I recognize. Where did you find it?"

"On the strong-room floor. It was part of the entrails of that smashed clock."

The Doctor handed it back.

"I can't tell you what part of the works it is. Those old clockmakers used whatever came to hand."

Q. asked: "Adhesive tape wouldn't be at hand, would it? Not at the time that clock was made."

The Doctor looked closer.

"No, of course not. But that doesn't mean anything. The wire was probably put in later. Perhaps it was to muffle the striker. Or it might have been used to hang the key in the case."

Q. said: "Of course." He took the thing from Jaffee's hand. "I'd better put it back where I found it, before Milpotts discovers it's gone."

He crossed to the door and was opening it.

The Doctor said: "You're not going down to that room again to-night?"

"Why not?"

"Because," he sounded like he was actually afraid, "because it's not safe."

Q. said: "It's safe enough. There are police all over the house."

"The police are numskulls. Morons. If you were to run into the murderer—"

"I won't. You see, I'm practically sure I know who he is."

Dr. Jaffee looked at him a moment. Then he shook his head.

"I think you're wrong."

Q. said: "I hope I am, but I've got to make sure."

"At least, you'll take Lynch with you?"

"I won't need him." Q. opened the door and bumped into Dr. Ascher, who was on the other side.

He said: "Hum-p-p-pp! *Schlemihl!*" Then he saw who it was and started apologizing in German.

Q. said: "Sorry, Doctor," and to Jaffee: "Don't worry about me. I've some writing to do first, but I'll go down to the library later. If there's still a light in your room, I'll stop in on my way back, just to let you know I'm safe."

Jaffee said: "Thank you," and Dr. Ascher asked:

"Vere are my pants? Dot voman she vill keep me all night!"

"What's wrong with her?" Q. wanted to know.

"Drugs, und drink, und damn foolishness. If you meet the murderer, tell him I haff anudder little job for him."

Q. laughed, and went out.

I followed him.

Creel and Mrs. Statts were still in the hall. They had made Frazier bring them a bridge table and were playing pinochle at a dollar a point.

Frazier was hanging around like he was itching to get into the game.

None of them were paying any attention to Pearl Duke's voice, which was still screeching fit to split your ears.

The old girl had changed her act. She was yelling something about a woman all in white, with long red hair, who was with the man in the mask.

Q. went over and touched Frazier's shoulder. The two of them walked to the alcove, where Margot had given me that kiss. On a chance, I went along.

Q. pulled the piece of wire out of his pocket and showed it to the butler.

"What do you make of this?"

"Sir?"

"Have you ever seen anything like it before?"

Frazier looked again.

"Yes, sir," he said. "It's one of Dr. Ascher's staples. He makes them himself, to hold up his climbing roses."

28

Creel and the Statts dame finished a game. Madam had lost, and she was bellyaching something fierce.

The dicks were ransacking the bedrooms and the shrubbery under the balcony, looking for the man Pearl Dukes claimed to have seen. They were turning their flash-lights across the lawn and down the cliff to the river. But not like they really expected to find anything.

I knew Politos was with them. I heard him yell when he fell into a thorn bush. What he said was Greek, but you could tell what he meant, all right.

Q. went out on the balcony and looked down for a minute. Then he came back.

"Let's get out of this," he said.

I thought he meant to take it on the lam, and nearly yelled for joy. But I got him wrong.

He headed for the butler's pantry. He opened the icebox and brought out a bottle of White Horse. He poured two drinks.

I swallowed mine before I said:

"Thought you weren't going to lift your elbow until you cracked through with the answer."

He said: "I've got the answer," and started walking.

I followed.

"That's what you told the Doctor. But can you prove it?"

He didn't say anything. Just turned in a door and punched on the light. It was the billiard room. He picked up a cue, then:

"I'm proving it now," he said. "I'll give you a handicap of six."

We played for ten minutes. He looked at his watch, then we played some more. When I tried to talk about the case he told me to shut up. I was so haywire he took three games off me running. After that he looked at his watch again.

"O.K.," he said, and put down his cue. "Let's go."

I asked: "Go where?"

He was already in the hall.

"To the library, to see if my hunch is right."

We went up two steps and came out in the conservatory.

Believe it or not, the guard we'd seen earlier was still asleep. And snoring.

Q. didn't try to go into the library through the conservatory door. He went down ten or twelve feet farther into the shop. It was dark, but Q. had a flash in his pocket. He turned the handle of the door that led from the shop into the library.

The door was locked, and the key was on the other side.

Q. handed me the flash and brought out a pair of nippers. He went to work, quick and quiet.

It wasn't any time before he had the key turned in the lock. He took the flash back from me and switched it off. Then he opened the door.

The library was dark. Even the desk light, which we had left lighted, was out.

I said: "There's no one here."

Q. whispered: "Keep your God-damned trap shut!"

There was noise, like some one running.

Then a scream and a thud.

Q. switched on the flash and we ran for the sound.

The strong-room door was open.

Q. turned the spot inside. The light hit Dr. Jaffee's face. He was lying on the floor—dead, same as the others.

That's when I went crazy.

Q. jumped down into the vault, but I went back into the library, switched on all the lamps and began looking behind furniture and into cabinets.

What I'd do if I met the man who murdered the Doc I didn't stop to think. I didn't have a gun, but I was mad enough to tear the bastard limb from limb.

I've seen fellows taken for a ride, I've seen 'em cut to pieces, I've seen 'em shot in the guts and left writhing—but this was different. They were mostly asking for it. The Doc was a swell egg. I'd liked him.

Somebody began pounding on the door and yelling: "What's happened? Who's in there?"

I ran over to the door and tried to open it, then remembered.

"It's locked on your side, you numskull," I yelled.

I guessed it was the guard and he was too sleepy to remember. He fumbled around and unlocked the door. Same time Milpotts came in through the shop with Bill and Handy. They both had guns.

I yelled: "Get the Doctor!"

"Dr. Jaffee?" somebody asked.

"Jaffee's been killed. Get Ascher!"

The guard disappeared like he was shot out of a gun.

Milpotts and Handy brushed past me and went over to the strong room.

Q. was just pulling himself up, looking sick. And when I say sick I mean *sick*.

"Nothing to be done," he said. "He's gone."

Milpotts snapped: "You're under arrest!"

Q. asked: "What for?"

"Murder."

"*What?*"

"You heard me! I just been talking with Scotland Yard. Keep him covered, boys, while I slip on the cuffs."

29

Q. and I have been in plenty of hot spots. There was the Wickersham blow-off. And a Paris raid. And the time Q. palmed the Maharajah's ruby. But compared to this, they were all like getting caught playing post office.

I was so sunk I didn't even try to blow. Just leaned up against the wall and waited for 'em to pick me off.

Dr. Ascher came running in with his little black bag. He made for the strong room. Handy was with him.

Bill stood back of me, holding a gun, kind of careless, in his hand.

The guard stayed by the door.

Milpotts was with Q. He hadn't slipped on the cuffs, because he was having trouble. He hadn't used them for so long the lock was rusty.

Q. said: "You're making a damn fool of yourself, you know."

Milpotts looked ugly. "I'll take a chance on that, after the earful I got from London."

"I suppose they told you they didn't know me?"

"You guessed it."

"What else did you expect? We're here on the Q.T. Nobody's supposed to know. They'd be likely to spill things to just any one who had the price of an Atlantic call, wouldn't they?"

The Sheriff didn't look like he was impressed. I couldn't blame him. The whole set-up was phony. Q. was just talking against time. Any one could see that.

"You'll be in a swell spot," he told Milpotts, "when the newspapers get hold of the story—'Sheriff Jails London Sleuth While Murderer Gets Away.'"

Milpotts showed his horse teeth.

"You're the murderer," he said. "You murdered all three of 'em."

"Talk sense!" Q. snapped. "What reason would I have for killing a bunch of people I didn't know?"

"That's what I'm going to find out!"

The Sheriff mightn't be a brain trust, but he was stubborn as a mule. He set his jaw. You could fairly see his ears lay back.

"Old Lady Duchene says you're a crook called Q. Silver, and she may be right. For all I know, you could have a hundred reasons. Listen, I'm going to lock you up until I find somebody looks more likely."

I knew we were sunk. Whatever Q. had in his mind when he came into that room had been wrong. I could tell by his face. He'd been knocked higher than a kite by finding the Doctor dead.

I began to wonder if you felt it when they shot the hot juice through you. And whether there was anything in this Heaven and Hell business.

Milpotts had the cuffs unlocked now, but he didn't snap them on. I guess he wasn't quite as sure of himself as he pretended. Anyway, he stopped to argue.

"Figure it out for yourself. It couldn't have been anybody but you who killed the Doctor. Those windows are all barred on the inside. The door on the stairs is locked, and the one into the conservatory. The only one open is the door into the workshop, and nobody went out that way."

"How do you know?"

"Because I was standing outside the window with Bill. We heard you pick the lock. I wanted to know what you were up to. Nobody came out after you went in."

"Is that the truth?" Q. stiffened like some one had shocked him with a battery. "You're *sure* nobody could have got out that door?"

"Sure." Milpotts said it so you believed him.

Dr. Ascher came out of the strong room. He was still carrying his little black bag, but his face wasn't red any more. It was yellow-white. He sat down on the big chair by the desk and mopped his forehead with a handkerchief.

"Dere iss not'ing I can do," he said. "He iss dead—killed same as the oders."

"'Same as the others,'" Milpotts repeated, and seemed to get an idea. "Did you find a knife?"

"No," the Doctor said.

Handy came in from the strong room and said "No," too. "There ain't any knife. Things are just the way they was after Roger was killed. You wanted them left. Remember?"

Milpotts went over to the strong room and looked down.

Q. stood without moving. You could feel he was thinking. Thinking so hard it *hurt*.

I thought I knew what was in his mind. If there wasn't any knife the fellow who'd killed the Doctor must have it. But nobody had left the room. And nobody was in the room—except us. Then who'd killed Jaffee? Who? Unless *we* did it. I began to think maybe we *had*.

Milpotts came back.

"No sign of a knife," he said. "And it couldn't have been the Borgia Blade. I got that locked up." But he didn't sound too sure. He went over to the desk and unlocked a drawer. The Blade was there all right. Wrapped in a piece of newspaper. "It couldn't have been *that*," he said. He turned to Q. "What did you do with the knife?"

"I was right the first time! *He* killed them." I heard Q.'s voice. It was talking, but it didn't make sense. "That's why nobody went out. Because there wasn't anybody to go out. Only the Doctor."

Milpotts seemed to think he'd gone off his nut. I thought so myself. He looked wild enough, with his black hair standing up, and his black eyes snapping.

"I know who did the murders!" he told Milpotts.

"Yeah? Well, call him in."

"It isn't anybody I can call."

"Why not?"

"You heard Dr. Ascher. He's dead."

Milpotts got mad.

"Are you trying to tell me it was Jaffee?" he asked. "That he murdered two men and then committed suicide?"

"He didn't commit suicide."

"Then who killed him?"

"No one killed him. It was an accident."

"An acci—"

"Yes. He stumbled and fell into his own trap."

Milpotts laughed, not like he was amused. Handy decided he'd better laugh, too. And Bill.

Dr. Ascher didn't laugh. He just sat and stared.

Milpotts asked: "If he stumbled and fell on a knife, where's the knife?"

"It wasn't a knife. The knife didn't kill any of them."

That brought them all up. Even Ascher.

"But of course it wass a knife," the Doctor said. "I myself—"

"It wasn't your fault, Doctor. I made the same mistake. If you find two men on the floor with their throats cut and a knife beside them, you're bound to think the knife did the cutting. That's what we were meant to think."

"But what? How?" Milpotts was stuttering like a kid. He'd forgotten all about the handcuffs.

"The clock hadn't any spring," Q. said.

"What clock?"

"The clock on the floor in there." He nodded toward the strong room. "I noticed it, but it never struck me as important until to-night, when I cut my hand. It was all a question of alibis, you see."

"I'm a hell of a long way from seeing!"

"Then sit down and listen."

Milpotts looked at him. Then he went over to the phone and called the village. He ordered the same photographer to come and take pictures. The poor guy was plenty sore at being routed out again, but Milpotts cut him off. He called the fingerprint man, too. And the dead wagon. He told Bill and the guard to watch the door, then he came back, took out a cigar, and sat down.

"Make it short."

Q. said: "It won't take long. Most of it is obvious. The motive, for instance. It's easy to see why Jaffee would profit by Welch's death. He stood to get ten thousand. It's my guess you'll find he was in debt."

"What makes you think that?"

"The whole character of the man."

Milpotts looked impatient.

Q. said quickly: "Listen. Unless you get the Doctor's character, you'll never understand those murders. Dr. Ascher, here, says he was a fine surgeon."

"He wass that," Ascher said. "A very fine surgeon. Most especially in orthopedic vork."

"Was there ever any scandal? Any reason for his leaving his profession?"

"Neffer! To me it wass always a surprise he should be villing to giff up his vork und stay here."

"There you are," Q. told Milpotts. "A fine surgeon doesn't give up his profession unless there's some reason. Jaffee's reason—he was lazy. Bone lazy. He loved luxury and physical comfort. You only have to look at his room to see that. Big lounging chairs with down pillows. A chaise longue fit for a woman. A down quilt on the bed. He liked good food and good wine . . . and soft living. A surgeon has to work hard and live clean, or he soon stops being a surgeon. When Jaffee saw a chance to slip out of it and live in luxury he took it. Am I right, Doctor?"

"In dot vay I haff neffer t'ought of it . . . but, now—I t'ink maybe you are right."

"Go on," Milpotts growled. I could see all this psychological stuff was getting his goat.

"He moved into this house with Welch. He was supposed to be a friend. Really, he wasn't much more than an upper servant. That's what made him hand out tips right and left. He wanted to keep proving to himself that he wasn't on the same level with the hired help. To keep his self-respect he pretended he wasn't loafing. He kept busy, tinkering with old clocks, making notes for a book."

Milpotts grunted and threw his chewed cigar into the fire. He pulled a straw out of the hearth broom and began on that.

"Go on," he said.

"The Doctor was perfectly happy living here in luxury, keeping an eye on Welch's heart and his diet, working a little at his clocks, and on his notes, loafing the rest of the time. But something happened to frighten him. Roger appeared with a girl."

"Miss Duchene."

"Yes. The way I read his mind, Jaffee'd figured on living with Welch until he died, then with Roger. You know what the boy was like. Not quite normal, easily led. The Doctor'd been working on him for years. He expected

Welch's money would come to Roger, and, after that, he'd be in control. That's the reason he fought so hard to keep peace between them. Then Welch threatened to cut Roger off and leave his money to a museum. He was even starting to make a new will. Jaffee had to move, and move fast. He had to bump Welch off while the money was still coming to Roger. Do you get it that far?"

"I get it!" Milpotts said. "But it's all guess-work. You haven't proved anything."

"Give me time." Q. got up and began walking around. Bill and Handy had forgotten their guns and were listening. Only the man at the door stood on guard. I began to wonder if Q. really meant what he was saying, or if he was just stalling, hoping something would turn up.

"Jaffee must have worried about the girl," Q. went on. "He knew if she married Roger she'd have everything in her hands and he'd be on his way out. Worse than that, the will Roger had made would be thrown out by his marriage, and Jaffee was the beneficiary under that will."

"Guessing again?"

"No. This much I'm sure of. When we talked to Jaffee in his room to-night, after Roger's death, he made a slip. He said he was thinking of endowing Dr. Ascher's hospital. Unless he knew a good share of the Welch money was coming to him, how could he hope to endow it?"

"But to endow a hospital, iss dot the vork of a murderer?" Dr. Ascher wanted to know.

"For this one it was. By passing on a few hundred thousand he could buy back his own self respect, and, at the same time, go on living like Lucullus."

Milpotts asked: "Who's that?"

"Sorry," Q. said, "you wouldn't know him. He was the original luxury boy."

Milpotts grunted and waggled the straw up and down in his mouth.

Q. went on: "I can't do more than guess how the Doctor's mind worked from then on. But I'm damn sure of one thing, when Roger went to Jaffee's room to-night I'll bet ten grand against a last year's hat he went to tell Jaffee he was going to be married."

"Is that the time he got hysterical and threatened suicide?"

"That's the time Jaffee *said* he got hysterical. Maybe he did. If so, it was probably because the Doctor tried to get him to call off his marriage. The Doctor'd run him so long it must have been hard for the boy to hold out. But he *did* hold out. That's why the Doctor bumped him off. It was either that or lose everything."

"But," I could see Milpotts was trying to figure back, he spit a mouthful of straw into the fire and didn't chew anything for as much as a minute, "the girl says Roger came down here alone. How'd he happen to do that?"

"Because Jaffee told him Welch had made a will later than the one we saw, and he'd better go down and destroy it."

"How can you prove that?"

"I can't. But nothing else explains what happened. We know Roger left Jaffee and went to the girl. She says he was all torn up. He kept asking if she'd marry him even if he was poor. She told him 'Yes,' but he probably didn't believe it. He wasn't going to risk losing her, so he took the Doctor's suggestion. He went down to find the new will and destroy it."

Milpotts took a pencil off the desk and began biting the eraser.

"Where is the new will?"

"Nowhere. It doesn't exist. Jaffee just used the idea to get Roger down to the strong room."

"But if the Doctor was waiting to kill him why didn't the girl—"

"He wasn't waiting." Q. said it so slowly we all saw it was important. Milpotts stopped chewing and Dr. Ascher leaned over his bag. "When Roger was killed, Dr. Jaffee was upstairs—soaking in the bathtub."

30

"If you want to know how those murders were done, come here," Q. said.

We followed him to the strong room. He jumped down into the vault.

"It was the clock that did it. And yet it wasn't the clock."

"You trying to kid me?"

"No. Just trying to explain. Remember, we couldn't figure out why Welch should carry that clock, which wasn't of any particular value, into the strong room. The answer is—he didn't."

"Then who did?"

"Dr. Jaffee. And it wasn't smashed on the floor. It had been taken to pieces beforehand."

"But, why in thunder—"

"I'm coming to that. Jaffee wanted Welch out of the way, but he wasn't going to use ordinary, obvious means, like a gun, or poison. He was going to make it hard for the police, and, at the same time, establish an alibi. First, he took the clock to pieces, then, while Welch was upstairs (you'll remember Frazier testified Welch went to his room for a short time just after his row with Creel), he went down into the vault and scattered pieces of the clock all over the floor. Next, he took the Borgia Blade from

253

Welch's desk and put it on the floor, just in front of the door. Then he took this clock spring . . ."

Q. reached down and picked up a spring which was lying on the floor with the other junk. He wiped it with his handkerchief, and handed it to the Sheriff.

"You might take a look at the edge."

Ascher and I looked over Milpotts's shoulder.

It seemed like an ordinary spring, made of steel ribbon. It was about half an inch wide and wound into a tight roll, like a clock spring would be.

Milpotts said: "I don't see anything wrong with it."

"Turn it over," Q. told him.

He did. The other side was different. Even rolled up, you could see the edge had been sharpened the full length. It was keen as a razor.

Q. said: "That's how I cut my hand to-night. It isn't really a clock spring. It's a special steel ribbon Jaffee sharpened for the purpose. But it looks like a spring. Any one would pass it over as part of the clock."

"I still don't—"

"Look here." Q. drew back the velvet curtains so we could see the frame of the strong-room door. The trim was wood to match the paneling in the library. A little over five feet up there were two tiny slits on each side. Above and below each slit was a small hole. None of it was big enough to notice, unless you looked close, and usually it was hidden by the curtains.

Q. took the spring from Milpotts. He pressed one end into the slit on one side. He took a staple out of his pocket. The one Frazier said was from Dr. Ascher's garden. The holes on either side of the slit just fitted the staple.

Nobody said anything. We just stared. You had to stare hard to see the ribbon. The razor edge was toward the library and, even with the lights on, it didn't show any more than a fine black thread running across the door.

"That's the way it was done," Q. said. "You can see the slits for Welch were two or three inches higher than the ones for Roger. There was about that much difference in their heights. Jaffee wanted to be sure of hitting the jugular vein."

He unscrewed the light so the room was dark. Then he moved the steps away from the door. He climbed back out of the vault into the alcove and stood with us.

"That's the way it was when Welch went into the strong room," he said. "You'll notice the spring is absolutely invisible against darkness. Now Jaffee knew Welch would go into that room before he went to bed, to put away his valuables. When he went he would fall into the trap. Jaffee made himself a perfect alibi by going straight upstairs to the cook's room and staying there until after Welch was killed."

Q. went over to a seat by the door and picked up a cushion. While he talked, he held it in his hand.

"Here's what happened. Part of it we know, part of it we can guess. We know Frazier was in the room talking to Welch for a few minutes after Jaffee left. When he was gone, we know that Welch talked out of the window to the Greek, then started toward the strong room to put away his will and the Napoleon watch. Now keep your eye on this!"

Suddenly Q. became Welch, talking each move as he made it.

"Welch walks into the alcove. The strong-room door is open. He reaches out to put on the light. The switch snaps, but nothing happens. He does what ninety-nine out of a hundred would do, looks up toward the light fixture and puts one foot down toward the stairs. But the stairs have been moved away. He loses his balance and falls forward."

The Doctor and I yelled like banshees. Even Milpotts jumped forward.

It was too late. Q. had gone over the edge.

There was a sharp crackle and a snap. There was a nasty thud. I jumped down into the room.

Q. was sprawled on his hands and knees. He was holding the pillow against his throat. The cover had been slit from seam to seam. The down was spilling out through the opening.

It was then I saw the spring. It was lying coiled up like a snake on the floor.

Q. said: "That's what was so damned clever. Jaffee put those staples in so they'd hold up to a weight of about a hundred and twenty pounds, no more."

Milpotts nodded.

"I get you. A man falling against the ribbon would slit his throat. Then his weight would tear the staples loose. The ribbon would spring back into a coil again, the way it did just now."

"That's right. If only one side tore loose, it would snap back behind the curtains. If both, it would fall on the floor and be mistaken for part of the clock. In either case, Jaffee knew, as a doctor, he'd be the first to be called and would have a chance to pick up both the spring and the staples. Remember, Lynch, after Welch was killed, Jaffee dropped his lighter on the floor and groped for it in the dark? I figure that's when he picked them up. When Roger was killed, Dr. Ascher was here, but Jaffee insisted upon coming down. He managed to palm everything except one cleat. That was under the body."

I said: "That's the one you found and showed to him!"

"Yes. He suspected right then I was wise. I wanted him to suspect, so he would try to put me out of the way and I could catch him red-handed."

"My God!" Milpotts said, and reached for a cigar. "My God!" he said again, and put it back in his pocket.

Q. said: "Murder's like dope. When a killer gets away with one death he thinks he can outsmart the world. Jaffee had everything on his side. He lived in the house and had access to all the keys. He knew how easy it would be to slip out on to the balcony and down the side steps without being seen. From there he could get into the library through the shop."

"Is that the way he went down when Roger was killed?" Milpotts wanted to know.

"Yes. Politos saw some one go down the stairs, but he didn't know who it was. Jaffee went down the side stairs while Dr. Ascher thought he was soaking in the tub."

"But he *wass* in the tub! Ven I vent to call him after Roger—"

"Certainly he was. But he'd been there only five minutes. Not twenty."

Milpotts was still scowling, like his mind wouldn't work to suit him.

"But how'd Jaffee happen to kill himself?"

"It was an accident. I told him I wasn't going to come down to this room until later, after every one had turned in for the night. That was to give him time to set the trap for me. But I didn't give him enough time to finish. I wanted to catch him in the middle of it. He probably heard us come in. His first thought was to escape. Then he realized he must get rid of the spring he'd stretched across the door. With that out of the way, he could bluff it. He ran back, but the room was dark. He hurried one step too far. . . ."

Q. got up and stretched his arms.

"That's all there is. There isn't any more." He walked over to the desk. The Borgia Blade was still lying where Milpotts had left it when he pulled it out of the drawer. "If you don't mind," he said, "I'll take this."

Milpotts said: "You can't do that! It's evidence."

"What evidence? It wasn't used for the murders. Jaffee merely left it on the floor to fool every one into thinking it was used. With a spouting jugular vein it was sure to get messed up with blood. Not that it was part of his original plan. It couldn't have been, because he didn't know about the Blade until I brought it down. Probably the first idea of using it came to him when he saw it lying there on the desk the night he killed Welch."

"And later," Dr. Ascher said, "he stole it from my bag!"

"Why'd he go through all that rigmarole?" Milpotts asked. "Any other knife would have done as well."

Q. said: "It wouldn't have cast suspicion on me." For the first time since we had come into the room he grinned. "Jaffee had a crazy idea the local police were—what did he call Mr. Milpotts and the others, Lynch?"

"Numskulls," I said without looking at Milpotts, "and Mormons."

Milpotts snorted: "I haven't even *one* wife."

"Not Mormons. *Morons,*" Q. told him. "He thought if he made it look as though the Blade had been used for the murder you'd be simple enough to suspect me."

Then I *did* look at Milpotts. He was turning red and beginning to swell up, but Q. went on quickly:

"He tried to confuse you by planting or giving out clues that made it look black for a lot of people."

"Such as?"

"Such as when he wanted to move himself over from the list of suspects to the list of victims. He didn't use morphine or codeine, although he had plenty in his possession. Instead, he used cocaine, a drug he knew would suggest Mrs. Duchene. He also saw to it that the lemonade in which he took the cocaine was handled by Frazier, which put the butler into the line of fire. After Welch's death, he threw suspicion on Creel by telling about the row over the Napoleon watch and then hiding it under his mattress. He suggested Roger by talking about his being mentally unbalanced. He dragged the Statts woman into it by hanging that scabbard out her window."

"How'd he manage to do that?"

"Easily enough. While we were at dinner he was supposed to be lying here, knocked out by the cocaine. Dr. Ascher was with him, but he came downstairs to get something to eat. Remember? Before we went up to talk to Jaffee, he had plenty of time to slip across the hall into Mrs. Statts's bedroom and hang the scabbard out the window."

"Go on!"

"I think by then it had become a sort of game and he got a kick out of it. He even called attention to the Greek, and brought *you* into it, Doctor."

"*Me?*" Dr. Ascher looked like he'd been stung by a wasp. "You are not saying he planted evidence—"

"Just that. He fastened that steel ribbon with staples from your rose garden."

Ascher didn't say anything, just sat with his mouth open.

"Then he made it clear his will was made out to you," Q. went on.

Milpotts burst in with: "You mean the Doc, here, gets all the Welch money?"

"Unless Jaffee was lying about his will, he gets most of it. You'll be building that hospital sooner than you think, Doctor."

(Q. was right. We heard later that the Welch relatives were trying to break the will. But I guess the jury didn't like their looks. Or maybe they liked the hospital plan better. Anyway, the bulk of the fortune went to Ascher, except what the lawyers hooked, which was plenty.)

"If it's all clear, I'll go upstairs and catch a few winks of sleep," Q. said. "I'm done in."

You could see Milpotts felt there was something wrong somewhere, but he couldn't quite smell out what it was.

"Hold on," he said, "you may have explained about the murders, and, mind you, I'm not saying I'm not satisfied. But you haven't yet straightened out who you are, and what you're doing here,"

Q. snapped: "Oh, for God's sake, get Scotland Yard on the wire. I'll talk to 'em!" He beckoned to me. "Come on. I need some coffee." He turned to Milpotts. "When the call comes through, let me know. But don't ask for just any one at the yard. Get Cholmondeley. C-h-o-l-m-o-n-d-e-l-e-y. Pronounced 'Chumley.'"

"C-h-o-l-m . . . Say! That doesn't spell 'Chumley.'"

Q. said: "It does in England," and went out the door.

We walked through the conservatory and headed for the stairs.

I asked: "Who's Cholmondeley?"

"God knows."

"Then how the hell can you be sure he's connected with the Yard?"

"He isn't. At least, I hope not. And even if he is, how long's it going to take Milpotts to spell C-h-o-l-m-o-n-d-e-l-e-y, *Chumley,* over the trans-Atlantic wire? Do you get it?"

I did. At last Q. was ready to scram.

31

I didn't ask any more questions. If Q. was going to take it on the lam, it was jake with me.

When we hit the upper hall everybody was gone except Creel and the Statts dame. They were in an alcove toward the front, still playing cards. The table was covered with greenbacks and silver, mostly in front of Statts. They were too busy quarreling to notice anything.

We got into Q.'s room without being seen. He grabbed his tool kit from the bag and took his hat and a leather coat. He gave me a cap and a sweater, because there wasn't time for me to go after my things.

We went back into the hall again and ran into Frazier near Dr. Jaffee's door.

He looked at Q.'s coat and my cap.

"Are you leaving us, sir?" he asked.

"You might call it that," Q. told him, and passed over a bill.

I couldn't see how much it was, but from Frazier's look it was plenty.

"Thank you, sir," he began, but Q. cut in with:

"There'll be twice as much if you get my car out of the garage and bring it to the main gate without being seen. Can do?"

"Yes, sir," Frazier said. "There's a service road at the back. I'll have your car there in five minutes." He went down the rear stairs.

We went out on the balcony. It was still dark, but dawn was near. I could tell by the way the trees were beginning to show against the sky.

I thought we were as good as off, but Q. stopped outside Lottie Dukes's room. We could hear Pearl Dukes. She was still at it. Not yelling any more, but moaning slow and regular, like a fog horn.

Q. said: "My God! I forgot to tell her she could stop!"

"You mean she was pulling a phony?"

He nodded and grinned. "Pretty good, wasn't it? I told Lottie they'd better *make* it good. They had to get Ascher out of Jaffee's room and keep him out, so Jaffee would have a chance to go down to the library and lay that trap for me."

He went through the French windows into Lottie's room. I went after him. Pearl was groaning fit to break your heart.

Q. crossed over and opened the door. Pearl was sitting on the edge of the bed, dressed in a green suit and hat. She was groaning, regular, like clock-work. Three counts, then a groan, three more, and a moan. Her face didn't show anything. She seemed to be making the noise automatically, like it had become a habit.

Margot was on the other side of the bed, packing a suit-case. She had her hat on, too.

Pearl was holding a hot-water bottle while Lottie picked up jewelry from the bed, wrapped it in toilet paper and dropped it in the top.

I saw a string of pearls and a couple of rings disappear before Q. said:

"You can stop that racket now."

Pearl Dukes cut off in the middle of a groan and dropped the bottle.

"You —!" she said. "It's about time! My throat's worn raw!"

Q. picked up the bottle and asked Lottie:

"Planning to make a run for it?"

"We can't be shot for trying."

"Can't you? Ask Creel about his shoulder!"

He held the bottle while Lottie dropped in a diamond bar-pin and a pair of earrings I'd seen on Mrs. Statts the night before. I figured she'd made a haul while the old girl was playing cards.

"You're laying yourself open for trouble," Q. said.

"Not me. By the time she finds they're gone that call will be through from the Yard, and Milpotts will be sure *you* took 'em."

"Who told you about the call?"

"A little birdie." (I looked at Margot. She winked.) "And I know about Jaffee, too."

"What about Jaffee?" Pearl Dukes wanted to know.

"He's dead, and Q.'s pinned the murders on him."

"My God! You let me go on splitting my throat—"

"It kept people out," Lottie said. She put a link ruby bracelet into the bottle and the necklace of diamonds and sapphires she'd got from Welch. Then she screwed on the cap. She ran a safety pin through the ring and fastened it under her coat.

"Ready," she said, "Got the Blade?"

"Right here." Q. patted the coat he was carrying over his arm.

I took the suit-case from Margot. Pearl Dukes straightened her hat. We all went through Lottie's room, out on to the balcony.

The fingerprint man, the photographer, and the dead wagon were arriving from town. They were milling around at the front of the house. There was nobody at the side.

We crept down the balcony steps and through the shrubbery to the pine woods. It was still wet from the rain, and
black as billy-be-damned.

Q. and Lottie were ahead somewhere. We saw them
for a little while, then Margot pressed against me and
we dropped back. She put her arms around my neck and
kissed me. I kissed her. Pearl Dukes came panting along and
swore at us. We had to pick up the suit-case and go on.

But when we reached the gate, Q. wasn't there. Nor
Lottie. Just Frazier with the car, and Politos, looking black
and mad.

He said he had orders from Milpotts. Nobody was going to get through. He said it waving a gun. The same that
had shot Creel. We didn't try to argue—much.

Then Q. showed up with Lottie. Her hat was crooked,
and there was a rouge spot on his cheek.

Q. said: "Here's a pass from the Sheriff." He handed
Politos a half-century.

Politos looked at it and said:

"O.K., boss. I know his writing." He winked.

Q. handed over another.

"And here's one for the lady."

Lottie said: "Thanks! You're kosher!" But she didn't get
into our car. "I've a roadster somewhere," she said. "What
did you do with it, Frazier?"

Frazier said it was just ahead, hidden in the trees. She
passed him a bill. Q. did the same.

"Take my advice," he said to him, "and ditch the blonde.
The red-head may not be good-looking, but she's a swell
cook."

Frazier said: "Yes, sir," and "Thank you, sir."

Lottie, Margot, and Pearl Dukes were in their car. Margot blew me a kiss, and Lottie called out to Q.:

"See you in Paris, *darling.*"

She drove off through the gate and turned south, toward the city.

We turned north, toward the flying field. I said:

"Like hell you'll see her in Paris! "

Q. told me: "A lot you know about women! When I kiss 'em they come back for more. She'll be waiting in Paris, all right."

"How you going to get there—swim?" I asked him. "All we got out of this job was a chance at the hot seat, and you've just blown the last of our dough."

"We've still got the Blade." He reached for his leather coat and felt inside. His face went funny. He felt around again, then he turned it wrong side out.

"When you kiss 'em they sure come back for more!" I said, and turned in the gate of the flying field. "Did you give it to her for an engagement present?"

Q. said: "The little devil!"

We were up to the hangar. The plane was there with Bill Mowbrick, ready to fly it.

"You sure know a lot about women," I said as we got out of the car.

Q. didn't say anything. He just grinned and turned back the front of his suit coat. Inside, where most guys in his line of business carry a gat, something was pinned to the armhole of his vest. It was the hot-water bottle.

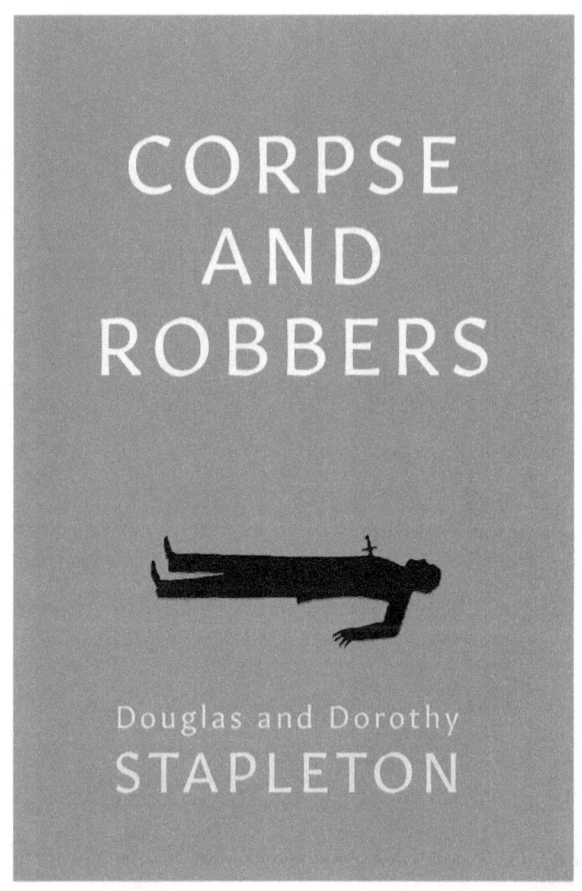

CORPSE
AND
ROBBERS

Douglas and Dorothy
STAPLETON

Details at
CoachwhipBooks.com

Available from your favorite online retailers

THE SERGEANT HARTY MYSTERIES
JOEL Y. DANE

MURDER CUM LAUDE
1
THE CABANA MURDERS

Details at
CoachwhipBooks.com

Available from your favorite online retailers

SULTAN'S HAREM MYSTERY

Drink the Green Water
The Milkmaid's Millions

HUGH AUSTIN

Details at
CoachwhipBooks.com

Available from your favorite online retailers

MURDER OF
THE HONEST BROKER

WILLOUGHBY SHARP

Details at
CoachwhipBooks.com

THERE IS
NO RETURN
THE ADELAIDE ADAMS MYSTERIES
ANITA BLACKMON

Details at
CoachwhipBooks.com

Available from your favorite online retailers

FULL CRASH DIVE

ALLAN R. BOSWORTH

Details at
CoachwhipBooks.com

Available from your favorite online retailers

THE
SARA ELIZABETH
MASON
MYSTERIES

MURDER RENTS A ROOM

THE CRIMSON FEATHER

Details at
CoachwhipBooks.com

Available from your favorite online retailers

Details at
CoachwhipBooks.com